Ophelia

Ophelia

LISA KLEIN

BLOOMSBURY

LONDON BERLIN NEW YORK

Published by Bloomsbury Publishing Plc in New York, London and Berlin

First published in Great Britain in 2006 by Bloomsbury Publishing Plc,
36 Soho Square, London, W1D 3QY

A CIP catalogue record of this book is available from the British Library

ISBN 978 0 7475 8733 0

Book design by Donna Mark

Printed and bound in Great Britain by Clays Ltd, St Ives Plc

10 9 8 7 6 5 4 3

FSC
Mixed Sources
Product group from well-managed
forests and other controlled sources
Cert no. SGS-COC-2061
www.fsc.org
© 1996 Forest Stewardship Council

The paper this book is printed on is certified independently in accordance with the rules of the FSC.
It is ancient-forest friendly. The printer holds chain of custody.

To my parents,
Jerry and Mary Klein

Prologue

St Emilion, France
November 1601

My lady:
I pray this letter finds you in a place of safety. I write in brief,
for few words are best when they can bring only pain.

The royal court of Denmark is in ruins. The final fruits of
evil have spilled their deadly seeds. At last, King Claudius is
dead, justly served his own poison. Hamlet slew him with a
sword envenomed by the king himself. Queen Gertrude lies
cold, poisoned by a cup the king intended for Hamlet. It was
the sight of his dying mother that spurred Hamlet's revenge
at last.

But the greatest grief is this: your brother, Laertes, and
Prince Hamlet have slain each other with poisoned swords. I
have failed in the task you set me. Now Fortinbras of Norway
rules in our conquered land.

Forgive Hamlet, I beg you. With his dying words he charged
me to clear his wounded name. Believe me, before the lust for
revenge seized his mind, he loved you deeply.

Also forgive, but do not forget,
Your faithful friend and seeker,
Horatio

The letter leaves me stunned, dazed with fresh pain so that I cannot even rise from my bed.

I dream of Elsinore Castle, a vast stone labyrinth. At its centre, the great banquet hall, warmed by leaping fires, where courtiers passed like lifeblood through a heart, where King Hamlet and Queen Gertrude reigned, the mind and soul that held the whole body together. Now all fire and all flesh are but cold ashes.

I dream of my beloved, the witty, dark-haired Prince Hamlet, before he was taken from me by madness and death.

In my mind's eye the green orchards of Elsinore appear, ripe with sweet pears and apples that bent the branches and offered themselves to our hands. The garden where we first kissed, fragrant then with sharp rosemary and soothing lavender, now lies blasted and all withered.

Through my dream gurgles the fateful brook where I swam as a child and where the willow boughs skimmed the water's surface. There I met my watery end and began life anew.

I see myself and Hamlet on the mist-shrouded battlements, where an unseen ghost witnessed our embracing, then turned Hamlet's mind from love to vengeance. I see the fearsome face of Claudius, Hamlet's uncle, who murdered his father and married his mother, my dear queen Gertrude, whom he poisoned.

Alas, my Hamlet is dead! And with him all of Elsinore ruined, like Eden after man's fall.

I, Ophelia, played a part in this tragedy. I served the queen. I sought to steer the prince's course. I discovered dangerous secrets and fell foul of the tyrant Claudius. But how did it come to this end, the death of all my world? Guilt consumes me, that I should live while all are lost. That I could not divert the fated course.

I cannot rest while this history remains untold. There is no peace for me while this pain presses upon my soul. Though I have lived only sixteen years, I have known a lifetime of sorrow. Like the pale moon, I wane, weary of seeing the world's grief, and I wax again, burdened with life. But like the sun, I will dispel the darkness about me and cast a light upon the truth. So I take up my pen and write.

Here is my story.

Part One

Elsinore, Denmark
1585-1601

Chapter 1

I have always been a motherless girl. The lady Frowendel died giving birth to me, depriving also my brother, Laertes, and my father, Polonius, of her care. I had not so much as a scrap of lace or a remembered scent of her. Nothing. Yet by the miniature framed portrait my father carried, I saw that I was the living image of my mother.

I was often sad, thinking I had caused her to die and therefore my father could not love me. I tried not to vex or trouble him further, but he never gave me the attention I desired. Nor did he dote on Laertes, his only son. He cast his gaze everywhere but on our faces, for he was ambitious to be the king's most valued and secret informant.

We lived in the village of Elsinore in a fine house, timber-framed with mullioned windows. Laertes and I played in the garden my mother had kept, the beds growing wild after her death. I often hid among tall rosemary bushes, and all day I would carry the pungent scent about me. On hot days we swam in Elsinore's river where it meandered through a nearby wood, and we captured frogs and salamanders on its grassy banks. When we were hungry we stole apples and plums from the marketplace and darted away like rabbits when the vendors shouted after us. At night we slept in a loft beneath the eaves, where on cold nights the smoke from the kitchen fires rose and hovered beneath the rafters, warming us.

On the first floor of our house was a shop where ladies and gentlemen of the court sent their servants to buy feathers, ribbons and lace. My father disdained shopkeepers as unworthy and low, but he consorted with them and curried favour with the customers, hoping to overhear court gossip. Then, wearing a doublet and hose in high fashion, he would hasten down the broad way to join the throng of men seeking positions in King Hamlet's court. Sometimes we would not see him for days and we worried that he had abandoned us, but he always returned. Then he would carry on excitedly about some opportunity certain to befall him, or he would be silent and moody. Laertes and I would peek through the broken panel of his chamber door and see him bent over a small pile of money and papers, shaking his head. We were certain that we would be ruined, and we wondered, lying awake in our loft, what would happen to us. Would we become like the orphan child we often saw in the village streets, begging for bread and eating scraps of meat like a wild animal?

My father's anxious office-seeking consumed our family's fortunes, the remains of my mother's dowry. But he did manage to hire a tutor for Laertes, a bookish, black-capped man.

"A girl should not be idle, for then the devil may do his work in you," my father said to me. "Therefore study with Laertes and take what benefit you may from it."

So from the time I could babble and my brother could reason, we spent hours in daily study. We read the Psalms and other verses from the Bible. I marvelled at the Book of John, with its terrible revelations of angels and beasts loosed at the end of time. I loved to read about Ancient Rome, and I was quicker than my brother to find the lessons in the fables of Aesop. Soon I could cipher as well as he. I also learned to bargain with Laertes, who disliked all study.

"I will translate these Latin letters for you, if you will first give me your cake," I would offer, and he would gladly consent. Our father praised Laertes' schoolwork, but when I showed him my neat rows of numbers, he only patted my head as if I were his dog.

Laertes was my constant companion and my only protector. After our lessons, we joined the children playing barley-break in the dusty streets and on the village green. Being small, I was easily captured and made to stand in the circle that was called hell, until I could catch someone else and be freed or until Laertes took pity on me. Once Laertes saved me from a dog that seized my leg in its teeth and raked my back with its claws. He beat the dog senseless and wiped the blood from me with his shirt while I clung to him in terror. My wounds healed and my father told me to be comforted, for the scars would not be seen until after I had taken a husband. But for years, even the sight of a lapdog in a lady's arms made me quiver with fear.

Surely I must have had nurses who tended to me, though I remember none of their names or faces. They were careless of me, leaving me to roam freely like a pet goat. I had no one to mend my torn clothes or to lengthen my skirts as I grew. I remember no tender words or scented kisses. My father sometimes made me

kneel while he put his hand on my head when he rattled off a blessing, but his was a heavy hand, not the gentle touch I desired. We were a family living without a heart, a mother, to unite us.

My father found employment before we became destitute. He chanced to discover some intelligence relating to Denmark's enemy, King Fortinbras of Norway. For this he was honoured with the position of minister to King Hamlet. From the way my father spoke of his reward, it seemed he would be placed at the right hand of God himself, and we would henceforth live a glorious life.

I was but a child of eight and Laertes was twelve when we moved from the village to Elsinore Castle. For the occasion I received a new set of clothing and a blue cap woven with beads for my unruly hair. Laertes and I skipped alongside the cart that carried our goods. I was full of excited chatter.

"Will the castle look like heaven, such as Saint John saw? Will it have towers sparkling with gold and bright gems?" I asked, but my father only laughed and Laertes called me stupid.

Soon the stark battlements of Elsinore rose against the blue sky. As we drew nearer, the castle appeared more vast than the entire village, and the sun itself was not able to brighten its grey stone walls. Nothing shone or sparkled. The countless dark windows serried close together like ranks of soldiers. As we passed beneath the shadow of the gates into the courtyard, my disappointment deepened into a fearful dread. I shivered. Reaching for my father's hand, I grasped no more than the edge of his cloak, its folds fluid as water.

Chapter 2

Two small rooms at ground level near the gatehouse served as our new quarters. Compared to our airy house that rose above the village streets, the castle rooms felt close, dark and damp. The only furnishings were an oak chair, three stools and a cupboard. To this my father added our few possessions that were fine enough for our mean castle lodgings: some embroidered cushions, goose-feather bedding and pieces of silver plate. Our windows overlooked the stables, not the busy courtyard with its many diversions. But my father rubbed his hands in delight, for even these lowly quarters proved his good fortune.

"I will rise in the king's favour and wear a fur-lined cape, and the king will tell me his most private business," he said with certainty.

At the first banquet we attended at court, I was too excited to eat. Everything was new and amazing. King Hamlet seemed like a giant to me with his vast chest and great beard. His voice was like the crack of thunder. Prince Hamlet, who was then about fourteen, sprang about the hall with much silliness and some grace, his dark hair flying wildly about his head. I was so delighted that

I, too, began to dance. Queen Gertrude came up to me and, laughing, chucked me under the chin. I smiled back at her.

Then I saw a clown in bright fantastical garb cavorting about the room. He wore a peaked cap with jingling bells and a suit of motley. It seemed that he and Hamlet were imitating each other's antics. Overcome with sudden shyness, I retreated to my father's side.

"That's my pretty girl," my father said. "The queen noted you. Go, dance some more." But I would not move.

I watched the clown, who reminded me of a firework sizzling and sparking. Though I could not hear his jokes, I heard the king roar with laughter and cough until his face grew purple and he began to choke. He half rose from his seat, and a guard pounded the king's back until ale spewed from his mouth. Then the jester seized his own throat and fell to the ground, his limbs twitching in a pantomime of death. Prince Hamlet joined the charade, tugging upon the jester until he rebounded like a tennis ball and jumped upon the king's table, where he commenced singing.

"Who is he? Why does he act so strangely?" I asked my father.

"His name is Yorick, and he is the king's own jester. Like an idiot or a madman, he can mock the king without fear of punishment. His antics are nothing," he said with an idle wave of his hand.

I watched as Yorick helped Hamlet turn a somersault before the queen, who clapped to see him tumble head over heels.

"The young prince is the apple of his mother's eye," murmured my father to himself.

"Why? Does she want to eat him?" I asked innocently.

"No, foolish girl; it means she dotes on the boy!" he replied.

For a moment I was envious of Hamlet. But I, too, felt my

eyes drawn to him, and after that night, I watched for the prince everywhere at Elsinore. I knew that with his lively ways, he would make a fine playfellow. Laertes thought so, too. When one of his companions announced Hamlet's coming, my brother hastened to the courtyard and I followed upon his heels. Indeed, Hamlet drew the youngsters of the court like a magnet draws pieces of iron, and he was kind enough not to disdain our admiration. I watched as he demonstrated tricks and sleights of hand he learned from Yorick, but I never dared to speak to him.

Hamlet had a companion, a fellow with reddish locks and lanky limbs, who accompanied him everywhere. Horatio was as still as Hamlet was active, as silent as Hamlet was talkative. While Hamlet rousted with the younger boys, with Horatio he would converse seriously. Horatio would smile when Hamlet smiled and nod his head when Hamlet nodded. Like a shadow, he always hovered near the prince.

I was ten years old when I first spoke to Prince Hamlet. It was his birthday, and Hamlet, together with the king and queen, was parading through the countryside and village. With my father and Laertes I stood among the crowd inside the courtyard of Elsinore, awaiting Hamlet's return. I hopped from foot to foot with excitement. In one hand I clutched a bouquet of pansies tied with a white ribbon. Their purple-hooded yellow faces began to droop in the sun, so I shielded them with my other hand. Then the cry went up, "The prince comes!"

"Arrogant young pups!" muttered my father through clenched teeth as two youths pushed in front of us. "Always taking the place of their betters."

"He cannot see us now!" I cried. "Please, Father, lift me up."

With much grunting and groaning he complied, elbowing the youths away as he lifted me to his shoulder. Now I could see all the way to the gates of Elsinore.

Musicians and attendants led the way as Hamlet passed through the gates on a grey mount with a black braided mane. Courtiers and well-wishers waved and cheered, throwing flowers and offering gifts to the young prince as he passed. Proud of its burden, the horse tossed its head and capered, while Hamlet acknowledged the crowd with grand gestures. The king and queen rode in a more stately manner behind him, alternately frowning and smiling at his antics. I leaned forward eagerly. My father gripped my legs to keep his balance.

"Huzzah, huzzah!" shouted Laertes. The red-haired Horatio was beside him, slapping his thighs to add to the din as Hamlet drew near.

I waved my hand with its bouquet of flowers and cried, "Pansies for the prince!"

"Louder, child," said my father as he stepped closer to the passing procession. At that moment Hamlet drew up on his horse and reached out to grip Horatio's hand and salute Laertes. I cried out in French this time, trying to draw his attention to me.

"Pensée pour le prince."

Perhaps it was my pathetic look and pleading voice that stirred the queen's mercy, for she called to Hamlet.

"Attend the little one!"

I was indignant at being regarded as "little". Had the queen looked more closely, she would have seen that I was in fact too big to ride on my father's shoulders. But I was desperate to be seen.

Obedient to his mother, Hamlet looked about. I thrust out

my bouquet. The frail blooms trembled on their thin stalks. He saw me, and when our eyes met I gave him my most engaging smile.

"Thoughts for the prince. Pansies for you, my lord. Think of me," I said, my small voice striving to rise above the noise. I had chosen the words myself, wanting to show off my French, hoping to please my father by bringing attention to us. And I wanted to touch the hand of a prince.

But I was disappointed. Hamlet reached out and took the flowers, not touching my fingers nor marking my words. As he went on, I saw the pansies spill from his gloved hand and fall to the ground, where they were trodden by the feet of many horses and men. I must have sobbed aloud.

"Do not waste your tears, little girl," said Horatio. "We boys are ever careless of flowers."

"Yes, give us swords or sticks instead," laughed Laertes, pretending to spar with Horatio. Still I pouted.

"Look," Horatio said kindly, taking my hand. "Yours are not the only gifts Prince Hamlet neglects. He cannot carry so much at once."

Indeed I saw the ground strewn with dusty ribbons and crushed flowers wilting in his heedless wake.

Chapter 3

I had been disappointed in my attempt to gain Hamlet's attention on his birthday. But soon thereafter, when I least wished for it, his notice fell upon me, causing me great embarrassment.

It was a busy market day in the village. Laertes and I were bickering. His companion, a dull-witted older boy by the name of Edmund, had thumbed his nose at me, putting me more out of temper. Suddenly a cart laden with bleating lambs rolled past, and one of the smallest creatures wiggled through the wooden bars of its cage and tumbled to the street. Finding itself suddenly free, the lamb trotted off. Laertes saw the chance for some sport and gave chase. A fast runner, he easily caught the lamb and pounced on it. Then Edmund ran up and began to poke it with a stick. The lamb's weak bleating roused my pity.

"Stop, Edmund!" I cried, but the stupid boy only laughed at me. In a rage, I threw myself at Laertes, sending him sprawling in the dust.

"Get off me, you she-devil!" My brother, choking on dirt, cursed me, but still he held fast to the animal.

"Let it go, you mongrel cur! It's only a tiny, innocent lamb," I cried, pummelling his back. "I hate you!"

"What's that? Who's there!" exclaimed a voice in surprise.

I looked up from where I sat astride my brother. There stood Prince Hamlet and Horatio. Edmund had run away.

"*Je le pensais.* I thought so!" said Hamlet.

Later I remembered that he spoke in French, and I wondered if he meant to show me that he had noticed my gift of the pansies. But at the time I blushed furiously to be seen by Hamlet while entangled in a fight with my brother.

"Why, 'tis the rowdy girl and her brother." He said to Horatio, "They are kin, you see, but not so kind to each other."

As it was too late to regain my dignity, I resolved yet to free the lamb. I pinched Laertes' elbows and with a little cry, he released his hold on it. The creature struggled a bit, then dashed away, unharmed. I dismounted from my brother's back and stood with my fists on my hips, pretending defiance though my legs felt weak.

Laertes scowled at me. Indeed his shame was greater than mine, to be mastered by a mere girl. I pitied him a little; still I savoured my triumph.

"Look here. I'll show you how to bag the little shrew," said Hamlet, winking at my chastened brother.

He seized me about the waist and lifted me above his head. I was too surprised to utter a sound. The pit of my stomach flipped with excitement. I grasped Hamlet's forearms to steady myself, and he whirled me around until I screamed with a desperate delight. Then he swung me down on to a pile of hay, where I sprawled, breathless and dizzy. Horatio reached out his hand, pulling me to my feet again.

"You will make the girl ill," he said, holding my arm while I wavered unsteadily.

"Oh, no! Do it again, my lord, please!" I begged, but Hamlet had already turned to my brother.

"Come on, boy, let's wrestle," he said to Laertes.

I watched my brother and the prince grapple, saw Laertes' fiery speed meet Hamlet's calm agility. The lamb was forgotten. A crowd of boys had gathered, and they clapped and cheered while Horatio stood by with an amused look. Now and then I shivered at the memory of the spinning and the thought that the prince had held me with his hands tight about my middle.

Laertes emerged from the match dusty, breathless and, it seemed to me, defeated. But he was proud, his humiliation forgotten.

That night, my brother boasted for our father's benefit, "Did you see, Ophelia, how I pinned his arms most firmly until I let him go?"

Having no desire to renew our conflict, I merely nodded. Father was pleased, for he had high hopes that Laertes would become, like Horatio, a trusted courtier and confidant of Hamlet.

"Serve the prince well and one day you will serve the king," my father instructed. "Serve him poorly, and our days are numbered!" He drew his finger across his throat. It was a simple fact known even to children that to anger a king, even one so good as King Hamlet, could mean death.

To please our father, Laertes took every chance to engage in fierce competition with Prince Hamlet. He knew that to advance at court, he had to master all manner of sports and combat. In time, he became skilled and could sometimes defeat Hamlet in an archery contest.

One day I watched them practising their swordplay with sapling branches. I noticed that my brother, though younger in years, was growing near in height to the prince. Wielding their harmless foils, Hamlet and Laertes thrust and feinted with a mortal seriousness. I held my hand to my mouth to suppress a laugh.

Horatio, who stood nearby as always, bowed to me and surprised me by speaking.

"I'll put my wager on the prince. And you, my lady?"

My skirt was torn and my hair unkempt. In truth, I was more tomboy than lady, despite being past my tenth year. But I do not think Horatio mocked me, for his smile was kind.

"Why, naturally I bet upon my brother," I replied shyly.

I was not being entirely truthful, for I could not say whom I favoured. Laertes was more agile, but Hamlet was more skilled. I watched the prince. His bright eyes focused on the battle, and the muscles of his legs and arms were taut with his strength. He allowed my brother to gain an advantage, then reversed their positions by parrying his thrusts. After a time, they called a truce, sweating and showing the welts and scratches from their makeshift weapons.

"A fine swordsman you will be, and a worthy opponent —" began Hamlet. I saw Laertes thrust his shoulders back and swell with pride.

"— in ten years' time!" finished Hamlet, laughing. I noticed his voice was that of a man now.

Thus life at Elsinore, even for children, was full of competition. We were also used to roughness and cruelty. The blows of the cook's wooden spoon, the harsh words of the schoolmaster, and my father's neglect were evidence of the world's indifference

to my feelings and well-being. Yet it did not occur to me that someone might intend to cause me serious harm. So I was unprepared when Edmund, whom I considered a common bully, began to present a more menacing aspect to me alone. One day he caught my arm and spoke lewd words to me. I did not know what he meant by them until I saw the motions of his hands. Then I simply turned away in disgust. Another day he pulled me behind a tree and offered me a coin if I would lift my skirts for him. Without a word, I ran from him like a startled deer.

"If you are going to tell your brother, I will say to him that you thrust yourself on me like a harlot!" he shouted after me.

More out of shame than fear of Edmund's threat, I did not go to Laertes. So when Edmund found me next, in a corridor of Elsinore, he boldly pushed himself against me and tried to kiss me.

"You will like this, and if you do not, then you are worth nothing," he said with a note of contempt in his voice.

This time I was afraid, though I did not know exactly what he meant to do as he fumbled to reach inside my skirt. I pushed at him, but to little avail, for he was stronger than Laertes. Then by chance my knee found a tender spot between his legs and he doubled over, cursing me as I fled.

I did not see Edmund for several weeks, and thinking I had finally deterred him, I resumed my usual habits. I was used to swimming alone, imagining myself a great sleek fish such as I had seen pictured in an ancient book. With slow, silent strokes I would glide until I reached the bend where the brook curved away from the castle. There the current, after running over rocks where village women scrubbed their clothes, widened into a calm pool. One day I floated there on my back, my eyes closed, listening

to the rattling cries of a bird, a kingfisher that skimmed the water's edge and crossed from shore to shore. I heard a small splashing but imagined it to be the kingfisher diving for its prey. Then I felt a hand grip my ankle and drag me under the water. I thought it was Laertes teasing me, but he would have let me go at once. I kicked and thrashed, but the hand did not loosen its grip. Another hand bore down on my shoulder. I grew desperate to take a breath. I must not lose my wits. Letting my body go limp, I hoped my opponent would think he had subdued me. Indeed I felt his hold on me loosen, so I twisted my body in a swift movement and slipped away. I broke the surface of the water and gulped air greedily. It was Edmund who swam away from me with fast, wild strokes.

"You foul, creeping snake! You toad, you wart!" I cried after him. He did not turn or look back.

As I choked on the water I had swallowed, strong arms grasped me from behind. Again I struggled, until I saw that it was Prince Hamlet who pulled me on to the grassy bank. My thin smock clung to me, and my arms and legs trembled weakly.

"What great monster of the deep do you strive against, little Ophelia?"

"That wicked boy. I hate him! But he is no match for me," I said with a feigned bravado. "There goes the toad."

I pointed to the stream's far bank, where Edmund sneaked away among the tall grass. Hamlet scowled.

"That knave is the son of my father's treasurer, a deceitful man. Proof that the apple does not fall far from the tree," he said. Seeing that I shivered, he took the short cloak that he carried and dropped it over my shoulders. "You should not be in his company."

"Do you think I sought him out?" I cried. "No, he assaulted me!"

"You should carry a dagger. I cannot be always at hand to rescue you from harm." This time he smiled, and his blue eyes were suddenly merry.

"I do not need to be rescued," I said, though I shuddered to think of the harm Edmund would have done me had Hamlet's appearance not frightened him off. "I can swim like the trout that live in this brook," I boasted, to cover my fear.

"One needs only to tickle a trout and it will jump into one's hand." Hamlet winked at me and wiggled his fingers.

Supposing that he meant to tickle me, I shrugged off his cloak, slipped into the water, and pushed off from the bank.

"You cannot lure me like a fish," I said, for I disliked his teasing.

"No indeed, for you are the proverbial eel, always slipping away from me," he called.

I swam upstream, feeling the current against me. Hamlet followed along the bank, mimicking my swimming motions.

" 'Tis a mermaid indeed! See, a woman above, with the tail of a fish."

I had none of a mermaid's curves, for my body was as slim as a boy's. Why did he taunt me? I turned on my back and kicked, trying to splash his fine clothes and force him to retreat. But he only laughed, pinching his tunic to show me that it was already water-soaked.

When I came to the place where the willows arched over a deep pool in the swift-running brook, I paused to tread water. I was growing breathless. My bodice and skirt lay draped over a branch of the tree on the bank, at a distance I would not cross under Hamlet's gaze.

"Good day, Lord Hamlet," I said, inviting him to be gone.

He smiled, bowed and turned away. Up he climbed through the meadow that swayed with golden-eyed daisies.

"I come anon, good Horatio! I have just caught a mermaid. I never thought to find such sport away from the sea!" he called out, laughing all the while.

I saw his friend at the crest of the hill, a witness to our encounter. Behind Horatio, the stark parapets of Elsinore were barely visible.

When they had gone, I crept from the water and in the shelter of the willow boughs put on my sun-warmed clothes. My heart beat fast with excitement.

Chapter 4

Someone must have spoken to my father about my unruly ways. Soon after the incident at the brook, he gave me a new satin dress and horn combs for my hair. With fingers unused to such tasks, he untangled my hair and brushed it until my head ached. Then he instructed me to follow him while he attended the king and to curtsy and nod in the presence of Queen Gertrude, but never to speak.

"Do not gaze at the sun, lest you go blind, but stand in its light and let it warm you," he instructed me. This was one of the many sayings he made me commit to memory.

Indeed Gertrude was so grand and beautiful that I was afraid to look at her, even when she touched my curls and asked my name.

"She is Ophelia, my daughter and my treasure, the exact copy and very picture of her departed and lamented mother," said my father grandly, before I could open my mouth.

Gertrude lifted my chin and I looked up into eyes that were deep and grey and full of mystery.

"She is sweet of countenance, a most fair child," she murmured. "And a lively one, I daresay," she added with a smile.

Feeling a vague longing come over me, I lowered my eyes and made a deep curtsy.

With Queen Gertrude's words of approval my fortunes changed, and I became a member of her household. A servant was sent that very day to fetch my small trunk. My father smiled to himself and hummed, pleased for his own sake.

I, however, was unwilling to go. Though I felt no great love for my father, his company was familiar to me. Nor did I wish to change my ways.

"I do not want to leave you and Laertes," I said in a pleading voice.

"But I cannot care for you. I have no idea how to raise a young lady. That is a task best suited for women." He spoke as if this were a truth evident to anyone with a speck of reason.

I planted my heels firmly and resisted the pull of his arm.

"Come now, no more dallying," he said, though more gently. "Attending the queen is a great honour."

"But what shall I do if she is not satisfied or grows harsh with me?"

"Obey her. That is all! Go now, girl, and do not prove a fool," my father said, impatient again. Then he pressed something into my palm. It was the tiny portrait of my mother in its gold frame. I felt a small flame of courage begin to flicker within me.

It seemed a long journey from my father's quarters at the outskirts of the castle to Gertrude's rooms at the heart of Elsinore. We turned many times, until I felt myself to be lost. I followed the servant past the lodgings of courtiers and ministers greater than

my father. I followed him through the guardroom, where men slept, talked idly, or played at dice. They gave us barely a glance as we entered the hall leading to the queen's dwelling. My steps slowed as I marvelled at the long gallery that overlooked the great hall below. It was lined with lifelike tapestries depicting gods and goddesses, soldiers and hunters, ladies and a unicorn. I began to think it might be exciting to spend my days amid such splendour.

When we came to a room near the queen's bedchamber, the servant left me, and I was alone. Narrow but drenched with sun, the room contained a bed, a stool, a crooked table and a rush mat. There was a grate where I might build a small fire for warmth. A window faced south, and I looked out to see the garden and a labyrinth far below. Not knowing what would befall me next, I clutched my mother's image, feeling all at once abandoned and chosen, despairing and hopeful.

Heavy wheezing and a shuffled step heralded the arrival of someone at my door. A woman of advancing years came into my room. Stout and short of breath, she dabbed constantly at her moist forehead and neck. From under her cap sprang white curls like sprigs of pale moss. This was Elnora, Lady Valdemar. It had fallen to her, like some undeserved misfortune, to teach me courtly behaviour and guide my education. She let me know at once that the task was an impossible one.

"I hear that you are wont to throw off your skirts and swim! That you run about the castle grounds rousting with boys!" Her voice rose with disbelief at the end of each phrase. "That will cease now, for nothing could be more unbecoming a lady of Queen Gertrude's court." Her curls jiggled as she shook her head in disapproval.

I felt it was unjust of her to scold me, but I only said, "I desire to do what is pleasing." My father would have been proud of this reply.

"Of course you do. Else you will be sent back to that cave from whence you came. What is your age now? Eleven years? You have been without rule all that time! Pah! No horse will take the bridle and bit after so long."

I did not like being compared to a horse.

"I can rule myself with study," I said. "I can sit for hours without moving if I am reading Ptolemy or Herodotus." I longed to show her that I had some virtue and no lack of education.

"There will be no more study of philosophy or the ancients," she said firmly. "No man wants a wife more learned than he is, for fear that she will prove a shrew and make him wear the skirts."

"I would not become a shrew!" I said, thinking of how I had often bested Laertes. But I held my tongue after this retort. Would I always be so contentious? "Please teach me how I should behave, then," I said mildly.

"What you must learn of proper decorum would fill volumes," she said with a weary sigh. "In those of noble birth, virtuous behaviour resides within. Others can practise and learn it, but the difficulty is very great."

I began to despair, but reminding myself of my skill in learning, I vowed to master this new subject.

Then Elnora made me remove my clothing, and she examined all my limbs and fingered the heartbeat in my wrist.

"A good, sound body. Strong of limb and well-proportioned," she said, the tone of approval giving me some hope. She lingered

over the smooth scars on my back and leg, and I told her how the dog had bitten me.

"Well, do not be ashamed. Many a young lady has had all her beauty dimmed by smallpox. You are fortunate."

She took the measure of my height and spanned my middle with a tape, noting the numbers. She said I must have a wardrobe of linens and simple gowns suitable for my new position. I was excited by the prospect of new clothing to replace the worn and plain attire that I had long outgrown. I even began to hope that Elnora would be kind, if I did not trouble her much.

But in the following days I was often sad, as if I had moved across the ocean, not merely across the courtyard of Elsinore. I missed my studies and the delights of following Laertes and his companions. Though I had joined the world of women, I still felt like a child, ignored and lost in this new realm. The court ladies, with their bright plumage and twittering voices, were like so many birds in a gilded cage. I was the plain robin among them, longing for freedom and unable to sing for the bars around me.

Elnora told me that I must not be sulky and discontented. Daily she repeated this rule for me: "A lady must always aim to please — first, the queen she serves, and second, the man she will marry." Then she would add, "It is only the child who may please itself. And you, Ophelia, are no longer a child." Her scolding made me more unhappy, as if being a child were a fault I had committed and must atone for.

Becoming a lady, I learned, was not easy. I was inept at my new lessons, especially with the needle. Gertrude's ladies took pride in their needlework, but to me the thin, sharp steel was an instrument

of torture. I pricked my clumsy fingers until they all bled and ruined yards of silk before I could master the simplest stitch. I would have been glad to sit for hours reading or writing, but I fidgeted all the while I sewed and sometimes wept with boredom.

Still, I worked hard, glad for any faint scrap of praise from Elnora. I believed her goodwill would in turn lead to the queen's favour. In this I tried to think like my father. I wished to be a dutiful daughter and not disgrace him by failing my lessons. So I laboured with diligence at my music, in which a court lady must be accomplished. I had some success with the strings of the lute, but my fingers fumbled on the keys of the virginal. I found that singing came naturally to me, and Elnora praised my voice. So to cheer myself I would often make up ditties. Sometimes these brought a smile that wrinkled Elnora's wide, round face.

I also wanted to please the other ladies, particularly Cristiana, for she was close to my age and I wished for a friend. Cristiana was of high birth, for her father was the queen's cousin. With her uncommon green eyes, she was almost a beauty, though her nose was overlong. Unlike me, she could be content stitching for hours, and she was proud of her needlework. Attached to her bodice and pressed against her bosom she wore a stomacher she had embroidered all over with ivy and butterflies. Even the queen had admired it. Cristiana could also limn with skill, painting lifelike birds and flowers and faces I could recognise as those of Gertrude and her ladies.

"Would you paint my likeness?" I asked her one day. She looked down her nose at me, appraising me coolly.

"I do not think so. There is nothing remarkable about your features," she said, and went back to her work.

Was I really so plain, I wondered. Another day I praised her needlework, thinking that flattery would soften her.

"Please, will you guide my hand with this new stitch?" I asked, holding out my sampler. "Your work is so precise."

"Why, you will never master this work, for your fingers are fat and clumsy," she said, waving my hand away.

Another time I was learning a dance, a lively bransle, for all Gertrude's ladies were expected to be graceful dancers. I practised with vigour, relishing the fast thumping of my heart. It was almost like running and swimming, sports that I longed for.

"Look at her!" Cristiana pointed me out to the others. "She leaps about like a goat. How unseemly! It would be better to put bells on her feet and have her dance at a country festival." They laughed among themselves and agreed that I should be more restrained. That night, Elnora found me in tears.

"What ails you now? Come, do not sulk. The bad humours will make you ill."

"Why does Cristiana so disdain me?" I cried. "How have I offended her?"

Elnora sighed and lowered her large form on to a wide bench. She patted the seat next to her and I sat down, daring to lean lightly against her. She did not push me away.

"Now that you are among us, Cristiana is no longer the lowliest, and with her little authority, she must torment you," Elnora explained with a weary patience. "Have you seen hens in the yard peck at each other, each hen choosing the one that is just weaker than she is? So it is whenever a new lady-in-waiting joins the court. I have seen it more times than I can count in my twenty-five years with the queen."

I drew in my breath. "Twenty-five years!" I said. "More than twice the length of my own life." I leaned a little more into her. "What else have you seen?"

Elnora hesitated, considering whether to indulge me or send me on some fresh business. To sway her mind, I slipped a cushion behind her back, and gratefully, she settled into it.

"Now I am old and tired," she said, shaking her head. "But I was not always so. Once I was robust and pretty, though not so fair as the queen. That she chose me to wait upon her was an honour beyond my deserving. I remember how I wept with joy to see her married to King Hamlet. Then she was a mere slip of a girl, nobly born and a very paragon of virtue. She was not raised in the court, but in the finest convent in Denmark. The king said that he had married an angel, for purity and beauty were so perfectly joined in her. For his part, he was a man of the world and a warrior. He has been a wise king, and a good judge of men. He chose my most deserving husband, Lord Valdemar, from the ranks of all his nobles to be one of his privy counsellors," she said proudly.

"And how did Lord Valdemar choose you?" I asked. Elnora smiled at the long-ago memory.

"His father and my father were in battle together against Norway many years ago, and they pledged us to each other when my lord was still a stripling and I was at my mother's breast," she said.

I longed to ask if she had been a mother, but I dared not. She, however, seemed to read my thoughts.

"We were not blessed with babes, alas, and that is to my regret," she said with a sigh. "But God's will be done, whether I will or no," she added briskly. "Instead I was blessed in tending to the

queen through her confinements. More than one ended in grief, with babes born too soon. It is a perilous nine-month journey, you know, for both the mother and her child."

"I do know," I whispered.

"Then came Prince Hamlet, wailing and thrashing from the moment he first drew breath. Though he was as strong as a young oak tree, his mother feared an accident or sudden illness would befall him. She scarcely let him out of her sight. But while the queen rested, I would take the prince and let him tumble about in the meadow to roughen him up. Sometimes I pretended he was my own son, so easily did he make others love him. Now the boy gives no thought to old Elnora." She sniffed and dabbed at her eyes. Then she looked at me as if surprised by my presence. "I should not be telling you these things!" she said, scolding herself. "Sit straight, not like a slug. No, get up. Go, and dress your hair more neatly."

"I promise I can be discreet," I said. I took her hand, with its puffed flesh and gnarled bones, between my own small hands, which were not, as Cristiana claimed, fat and clumsy. Then I got up and did as she bid me.

I learned how to please Elnora so that she would treat me kindly. I did not tire her by chattering, as young ladies often do, but listened while she rambled around in her large memory. She told me about the dark times when Denmark warred with Norway and a long drought brought starvation to the village and hunger to the castle. She told me how a strange plague once broke out, afflicting hundreds, Gertrude among them, and how she nursed the queen from the very brink of death to complete health again.

I was surprised to discover Elnora's deep knowledge of medicines and herbs. Courtiers and ladies came to her for love potions made of heartsease, another name for my beloved pansy flower. Those with rheumy lungs favoured her simple but pungent mustard plaster. Because Elnora's eyes were weak and her knees crippled, I helped her by digging roots and measuring tiny pinches of dried plants. I shadowed her like a familiar, doing her bidding and anticipating her wants.

With Elnora I made my first visit to Mechtild, the wise woman whose skill in medicine was legendary at Elsinore. She was a mysterious and reclusive figure whom few had ever seen. She dwelt beyond the far side of the village, where I had never ventured. From time to time Elnora would visit her to purchase herbs that did not grow at Elsinore and medicines that only Mechtild knew how to make. I begged Elnora for permission to go along. Not only did I wish to meet this strange woman, but it had been months since I had left Elsinore and I longed to be in the woods again. One day she relented, and we set forth from the castle in a litter enclosed by curtains and borne by servants. Through the village we travelled, stopping at the edge of the woods. We would walk the final way to Mechtild's cottage, for Elnora was secretive about her task. She leaned on my arm for support. I guided her around the rocks on the path and moved aside the brambles and branches that would snag her skirts.

"Did I tell you about the time that Mechtild was charged with witchcraft?" Elnora asked, pausing to rest against a large rock. "Her accuser recanted after he was struck with mysterious boils. Some said these proved his charges, while others said they were God's punishment for his wicked lies."

My eyes grew wide with wonder. "Is she a witch?" I asked. "I have read about those who practise the black arts."

"She is powerful, but not in the service of evil. Yet I would not deceive or cross her," she said.

Mechtild's small house with its thatched roof huddled at the edge of the woods. In a clearing spread a vast garden teeming with familiar and exotic plants, the ingredients of all the varied medicines and liniments favoured at court. The wise woman came forth with slow steps to meet us. She looked more feeble than powerful, and hardly dangerous. At her side trotted a little black dog as wiry and wizened as she. I shrank from it until the little creature licked my hand in a friendly greeting, and I could not help but smile at it.

"Do not fear, he will not harm you," Mechtild said. Though bent almost double, she stared up at me with black eyes that seemed to know my past, while Elnora stated her business.

"The queen has been troubled with sleepless nights of late. She wakens and cannot return to sleep, and her pulse beats fast. The barley water with crushed poppy no longer brings her ease."

Mechtild nodded wisely and beckoned for us to follow her into the garden. Its lush wildness embraced us, and strange scents greeted my nose. A black-stalked plant towered over us, its dark green leaves, broader than a man's hand, sheltering purple bell-shaped flowers. Mechtild fingered these thoughtfully.

"Nightshade, perhaps. A few berries only. Leaves, moistened in wine, applied to the temple." The old woman murmured to herself, but my ears caught her words and fed them to my memory. "Not the mandrake, much too strong. Perhaps infused with a drop of henbane instead." Having made her decision, she plucked some leaves and berries.

"For you, my child," Mechtild said, turning her sharp eyes on me, "I recommend the water of distilled strawberry, for it not only smooths the skin, it guards against the passions of the heart."

"I am a green girl. I know nothing of love," I murmured, looking down at the dog.

"Ah, but you soon will. No one who is at court can remain innocent in the ways of love. See that you mind your passions," she said, holding up a bent forefinger to underscore her advice.

I thought of the knavish Edmund and his dark desires. I remembered how I quivered when Hamlet pulled me from the brook and gazed on me. As Mechtild seemed able to pierce my mind, I wished to change the topic.

"Have you something for Elnora?" I said. "Though she will not complain, I know that a pain in her side often troubles her, making her breathing difficult."

"Ophelia! That is not our purpose today," Elnora said sharply, but her rebuke was a mild one.

"Hmmm, a thoughtful girl. Cumin is what I advise. Rare and odorous. Not in your queen's herb bed, I am sure. A poultice applied to the side. I will prepare it now." She led us towards the cottage.

Inside the small house, a large cupboard dominated the single room. Curious, I watched while Mechtild unlocked the doors to reveal all the tools of an apothecary. She drew out a mortar and pestle and began to grind seeds while Elnora tested the scale.

Meanwhile my gaze was drawn to the topmost shelf of the cupboard. I stared at a row of dark vials, sealed in red wax, the labels bearing the symbol of a death's head. I drew in my breath with an audible gasp that made Mechtild look up from her work.

"Tincture of belladonna. Grains of opium. Henbane distilled. If ill-used, these bring death," she explained soberly.

"Tush, Ophelia, turn away your gaze lest you tempt evil," said Elnora, crossing herself and pushing me away.

Mechtild closed the cupboard door and turned the key. Removing it, she thrust it deep into her pocket, where the curve of her old body surely protected many secrets.

Chapter 5

Not long after our visit to Mechtild, I discovered a book that Elnora had laid aside, for her weak eyes no longer allowed her to read. As heavy as a small coffer of coins, it was entitled *The Herball or General History of Plants*. It was a treasure more valuable than gold to me. When I tired of my needlework, which was often, I pored over this book with ever growing fascination. I studied its precise drawings and stored in my memory the virtues and uses of all plants. I learned that peony taken with wine can relieve nightmares or melancholy dreams. When a mother delivers her babe, parsley seeds aid in bringing away the afterbirth cleanly. Rhubarb purges madness and frenzy. Fennel sharpens the sight and is an antidote to some poisons. All this and more I committed to memory. Soon Elnora began to rely on me to create new mixtures and tonics. I copied Mechtild's cumin poultice and Elnora found relief from the pain in her side. She chided me less for my laziness and melancholy, and she allowed me more time to study and write.

Since Elnora allowed me to study this book that so entranced me, I tried to please her by attending chapel services with her. She prodded me to attention when the preacher railed against pride and vanity. I also read the conduct books she prescribed to teach me morals, though I found them most tiresome. They all said that I must be silent, chaste and obedient, or else the world would be turned topsy-turvy from my wickedness. I scoffed at this, suspecting the writer had no knowledge of women and even less liking for them. Another manual advised me to be silent, but not always so, that I might cultivate the art of witty but modest conversation that was the mark of a court lady. I preferred this book.

However I had no occasion for witty discourse, except with myself. Sometimes as I worked, I imagined both parts of a conversation between a beautiful woman and her noble suitor. Or I contended in my mind against the ignorant writers who condemned women as frail and lacking in virtue. These exercises distracted my mind from the menial tasks that fell to me as the lowest of Gertrude's ladies. I had to empty the queen's closet stool, which before had been Cristiana's task. I also had to fetch large pitchers of water for Gertrude's bath and empty the tub afterwards, until my feet were swollen from running to the well and the latrines, and my arms ached.

It was dismaying to be chosen like a new bauble and then forgotten, a mere passing fancy. Gertrude rarely spoke to me, but I gazed on her, my eyes drinking in her beauty. Her hair shone like oiled oakwood, and her grey eyes seemed to hide her soul. She was still shapely and her face was unlined. Her ladies evermore praised her beauty, and she loved to be told that she was too young to be the mother of a grown prince. Like her, I dressed my hair in a long braid, which I sometimes tucked under a coif that I embroidered, rather crudely, with pansies. I longed to know if she approved of my dress and manner. It hurt me to think that she took no notice of my attempts to please her.

Humility was a hard virtue for me to learn, for I did not like to be always meek, with downcast eyes. Though looking down one day, I made a startling discovery: New curves had appeared in my body. Small breasts rounded out my silk bodice. They began to ache and throb. One day my flowers commenced with a stream of bright blood and a sharp pain in my gut. I ran to Elnora.

"I have hurt myself. I know not how," I cried in a panic.

She calmed me and wiped my tears. She brought me clean rags and explained how generation occurs. It amazed me that now my body was able to create a child, and it frightened me to think of the pain that lay in my future. It was like a sudden turn of fortune, to be thrust one day into womanhood.

Now that I was a young woman, I determined to take more pride in my gowns and ornaments, even though they had been worn by other ladies first. I thought that my lace cuffs set off my white hands. The stiff ruff that was then in fashion framed my face to good effect, though the first time I wore it, Cristiana insulted me.

"Your neck is so short, you resemble a bulldog!" she said mockingly.

"And you have spots on your face you have neglected to paint over," I countered, which made her fume silently. I had no need of paint, for my cheeks and lips were naturally bright, my skin softened by Mechtild's strawberry water. This pleased me, and I became a little proud, but I believed that a measure of vanity was required of me as a woman of the court.

I was now thirteen years old, an age at which many young women commenced courtships and some were already betrothed. Curious, I watched how men and women acted in each other's presence. I practised turning my head and shoulders in the manner I had seen one of the queen's ladies use while conversing with a young lord. I wondered if Hamlet would find such a movement appealing. Seeing my reflection in a bowl of water or a looking glass, I thought how amazed Hamlet would be to see me transformed from a wild girl into a lady. But we had not met since the long-ago day by the brook. Hamlet had left for Germany to study at the university in Wittenberg. Surely his mind was too full for thoughts of me, and I had only a few idle minutes each day to think on him.

Moreover, I was reminded daily that my favour at the court of Elsinore was unlikely and precarious.

"Your father is a nobody, and you are nothing, Ophelia," Cristiana taunted me. "I cannot fathom what the queen sees in you. Ha!" She laughed lightly.

I said nothing in my defence. I was still angry that my father seemed careless of me, and I was ashamed of our family's poor estate. Why indeed should Gertrude keep me?

The answer soon came to me. When the queen learned that I had been schooled in Latin and French, she bade me read aloud as she and her ladies worked on their embroidery. One of Gertrude's favourite books was *The Mirror of the Sinful Soul*, which, she told us, was written by Margaret, the queen of Navarre in France. Reading aloud and translating as I read, I was glad to exercise my mind and tongue again. Though I still performed my lowly duties, I dared to hope that my status at court was improving.

Gertrude knew that her other ladies disliked these pious exercises. They would frown at me for reading prayers and meditations when they preferred to gossip. But when Gertrude recited the devotions, they bowed and crossed themselves and seemed to pay close heed.

"We shall observe our likenesses in this mirror and reflect on our sins," she said, touching the book lightly. "I would be remiss in my duty, I fear, if I did not look after your spiritual welfare." Her words and tone almost conveyed apology.

I soon discovered that Gertrude's piety hid a secret pleasure. One evening she called me to her chamber. Her hair was loose, and its ripples shone in the candlelight. She wore a nightgown clasped at the bodice with jewelled buttons. Kneeling as if for prayer, she dismissed Cristiana, who set down the basin of scented water she carried.

"My tired eyes hinder my devotions," she said. "Ophelia shall read the scripture to me."

Cristiana glared at me like the proverbial green-eyed monster. I was struck at that moment with the unbelievable thought that she was jealous. I had no time to dwell on the discovery, however, for the queen was demanding my attention. Cristiana slipped out, closing the door, and I stood by, waiting. Gertrude rose to fetch a small book from a high shelf and returned to a cushioned settee, motioning for me to sit at her feet. I sat, as noiseless as a cat. The book she handed me resembled her other devotional books. It was called the *Heptameron*, and I saw that it was also written by the pious queen Margaret.

I opened the book to where a ribbon lay between the pages. I began to read aloud and found to my shame that this was no

book of prayer. I blushed and my voice was barely above a murmur as I read the tale of a noble woman seduced from her foolish husband by a handsome knave. Elnora would punish me for reading such a book! She would forbid me even to touch its binding! But night after night, Gertrude and I spent an hour or more in such devotions, reading tales of love and desire. Then the queen would return the book to its place and wish me goodnight. I would go to my room heavy with guilt yet consumed by curiosity.

One night when I had finished reading, Gertrude gave me some trinkets — a pearled comb for my hair and a small looking glass with a crack. I knelt and thanked her. Then, made bold by her show of kindness, I dared to ask a question.

"My lady, you are the queen. Why do you read this book in secret?"

Gertrude sighed.

"Good Ophelia," she said, "the king is a godly and proper man." She fingered a miniature painting of him she wore on a ribbon about her neck. "He would be grieved to know that I read such tales, which men say are not fit for a lady's ear."

"And because I am no lady, they will not harm me?" I said.

Gertrude laughed, a musical sound, like chimes.

"You are both wise and witty, Ophelia. Your words are saved and spent in good measure. Moreover, you are honest. I know you can be trusted not to gossip about my taste for romance."

"I, too, have developed a liking for these stories," I confessed, "for it pleases me to read of clever women who find love."

"You have the spirit of a lady, Ophelia. Though you were not born to high estate, you will rise to greatness," said Gertrude, kissing my forehead lightly.

42

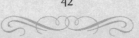

I almost wept at her touch, which lingered like a memory. Were my mother's lips this soft?

"Why am I so favoured?" I whispered.

"Because Elnora is a puritan and Cristiana is vain and foolish," she said, misunderstanding me. It was the kiss, more than the reading, that I treasured. "You, Ophelia, are sensible, but unschooled in matters of love and passion. It is necessary to learn the ways of the world and the wiles of men, so that you may resist them. So read freely, my dear."

I was surprised that Gertrude, who had not seemed to notice me at all, in truth understood me well. So at her bidding I read much, though in secret, and the stories completed my courtly education. While I learned the importance of virtue from Elnora's conduct books, Gertrude's romances held out the delights of love and the means to achieve them. I imagined and longed for the time when I would be old enough to enjoy such pleasures.

At times, however, I doubted the use of some story or another. One night I read to Gertrude about a jealous official who killed his wife with poisoned salad greens because she had taken a young lover. The tale made Gertrude merry, but I did not share her mirth.

"What, are you a puritan who will not laugh?" she chided.

"No, but it disturbs me to read that the woman's wrongdoing led her husband to kill her. She was more weak than wicked," I said.

"This is fiction, Ophelia, not a true history. Often we love to read of deeds and desires we would not dare to perform ourselves. That is the pleasure of a tale like this."

"But I cannot believe that men and women would do such wicked things in the name of love," I said.

"Oh, but they do, and they will," she replied in a knowing way, and that ended our conversation.

With my eyes opened by Gertrude's wisdom, my ears attended more closely to the gossip of Cristiana and the other ladies. I found it to be true that life at Elsinore was much like the stories Gertrude and I shared. Men and women alike sought ample delights with fewest sorrows. But while ladies desired to satisfy themselves in love, it was the lure of power that most tempted men.

My father, I realized, was among those men. It was knowledge he wanted, some secret intelligence that he could use for his gain. I began to be wary of him when he would visit me in company, wearing the mask of a loving father. For when he took me aside, his questions were pointed.

"My girl, what news from the queen's inner chamber?"

"None, my lord," I said, discretion guarding my tongue.

"Is Lord Valdemar preferred before me? Speak!" he demanded.

"I cannot tell, my lord." Truly, I knew little of Elnora's husband.

"You cannot tell?" he said mockingly. "Rather, you must tell me all you know. It is your duty as my daughter."

I was silent. I dared not remind him of his duty as a father to love and protect me. But I could not hide my resentment.

"I begin to see that you put me in the queen's service not for my own benefit," I said, "but to be your spy."

"Ungrateful girl!" he sputtered, and I thought for a moment he would strike me. "From where you are placed, you can see far and wide. And if you are clever," he said, tapping his head with a fingertip, "even greater advancement is yours. Now cease your

foolishness and answer me. How does the queen spend her private hours?"

I decided to risk his wrath. I did not tell him about the stories we read, but turned and walked away.

"Ophelia, come back!" he demanded, and I heard the fury in his voice. But I did not obey or even look back. I realised that I loved Gertrude and would keep her secrets forever.

Chapter 6

After four years in the queen's household, I had learned the art of being a lady. By the time I was fifteen, my shape was that of a woman. I almost matched my mistress Queen Gertrude's height, and I imitated her carriage, even the tilt of her head.

"Nature produced you, but nurture has perfected you," Gertrude often said with pride, as though I were her creation, carved from an unlikely piece of wood. Her words tempered somewhat the sting of Cristiana's criticism and the coolness of the other ladies. Unlike them, I was not the daughter of an earl or a duke or the cousin of a European prince. I knew they considered me unworthy of my place. I had no true friend at court, except Elnora.

I did take some of my father's advice to heart, for he was not stupid. I was careful and observant, and my reputation for honesty and secrecy began to advance me in the queen's favour. When the king came to Gertrude's chamber to dine, I was given the honour of attending them. At first I was terrified to be so near the king, but soon I realised he was mortal like any man. I filled his cup and heard him belch and removed his plate with the meat half gnawed from the bones.

Gertrude behaved lovingly towards her husband. She would stroke his hoary hair and tease him that it was no longer black like his son's. The king in turn spoke sweetly to Gertrude, calling her his turtledove and gazing on her in a way that made me ache. When their talk touched on matters of state, it was in low tones, for the king never failed in his discretion. However, one night I overheard an argument concerning Claudius, the king's younger brother. His lustfulness was the subject of court gossip, along with reports of his drunken carousing in the great hall. The king was angry at some recent transgression of his, the nature of which I could not discern.

"He defies me on purpose and drives me to madness," complained the king, while Gertrude sought to soothe his choler.

"Pity your brother, for he is a man of great desires and disappointments."

"Pah! You are too soft. He needs only two things: a wife to rein him in and his own bloody kingdom to rule," the king growled in reply. It was the only time I had heard the king and queen disagree.

When they were ready to retire, I would bring sweet wine and clean linens, trim the candlewicks, and withdraw, locking the doors behind me. In the morning the king would be gone and I would assist Gertrude as she washed and dressed. Curious, I looked for signs that love had changed her in some way, but she seemed to me only heavy-eyed and tired. Her inward self was veiled from me.

I believed that King Hamlet and Queen Gertrude loved each

other and were true. Also I believed that the king's ministers were loyal and the queen's ladies honest. But over time I realised that the court of Elsinore was a lovely garden where serpents hid in the grass. Many who seemed true were false. The fever of ambition drove men and women alike to seek advancement, even by deceit and betrayal. They swiftly rose on Fortune's turning wheel, and then as swiftly fell to their ruin. One of Gertrude's ladies lost her position when she was found to be with child by the king's chief minister. She fled to a cousin's house in the country, disgraced, while the minister kept his post and was deemed a generous man for acknowledging his son. Even I could see that the lady was very unjustly treated.

Favour was like a rose, glorious in bloom but fleeting, and hiding the thorn below its flower. The wicked often found favour, not the virtuous and humble. Elnora might be an exception, but Cristiana proved the rule, as did her suitors Rosencrantz and Guildenstern. These men had been dismissed with disgrace from the army of the Norwegian king Fortinbras for some unknown betrayal. Now employed by King Hamlet, they flaunted their rich clothes and gay manners, the fruits of their treason. They were alike as twins in their desire for favour with the king and with the ladies. Wooed by both men, Cristiana favored Rosencrantz, I think, but each was greeted with the same coy laugh and the same broad view of her bosom straining beneath its artfully loosened bodice.

I wondered how much Cristiana knew of the passions of love. All about me I watched amours unfold as in the bawdy French tales I read with Gertrude. In the great hall ladies and gentlemen drank until their talk grew ribald. Passing a darkened stairway,

I might stumble upon lovers grasping hands, touching lips, or more. I begged their pardon, but they only laughed at my embarrassment. Loudly, Elnora lamented the decline of honour in men and virtue in women.

"There is too much singing and dancing, such lightness as loosens the restraints of virtue," she complained, her white curls quivering. "When I was young we held to the courtly ways, but nowadays the world is running all to ruin."

I understood why Gertrude called Elnora a puritan. Though I doubted much that lovers' behaviour had changed so much in forty years, I did not contradict Elnora.

"Be moderate in your desires, Ophelia. Bridle your tongue, and lock up your chaste treasure," Elnora warned. She peered at me as if searching for faults. "I trust you will give no one cause to gossip about you. You are an honourable girl."

Despite Elnora's praise, I felt more cautious than virtuous. I spoke little, not because I found silence to be a superior virtue, but because I satisfied my curiosity by listening, observing and reading. Sometimes I wished I had been born a man, so I could have been a scholar. At least Gertrude approved of my habit of studying and allowed me to read whatever I wished. Once I had devoured the vast *Herball*, I hungered for more than the knowledge of common things that grew beneath me. I read about the distant countries of the Indies and fantastic creatures discovered by voyagers on land and in the sea. Laertes was now studying in France, and I pored over maps of Europe, marking the cities described in the letters he sometimes wrote to me. My envious fingers traced the routes my brother and Hamlet travelled in France, Germany and the Netherlands.

I longed for distant and unknown places, but even more I longed to know about love. I kept certain books hidden in my locked trunk, reading them late at night by the flame of a candle. In secret I devoured *The Art of Love*, for all the moralists condemned it as a dangerous book. I imagined visiting the wicked country of Italy, where the men are taught to overcome virgins and the women know many freedoms. Reading the poet Ovid, I learned that no one can resist love, for water wears the sharpest stone smooth, and even the hardest ground at last crumbles before the plough.

From the books I read, my knowledge of love was vast, but my experience of it was naught. I pondered this paradox as I lay at night upon my narrow, solitary bed. When would I find love?

Chapter 7

While I read books about love in the confines of Elsinore Castle, the wide world was Hamlet's school. He studied at the great German university and sailed to England and France with Horatio. He was away from Denmark for many months at a time, and Gertrude was always melancholy in his absence. Only a letter bearing news of his return would gladden her, and she would celebrate his homecoming with all the ceremony of a holiday or saint's festival. Great stores of provisions were delivered for feasting, musicians were summoned, and new livery brightened the guards and soldiers. At the prince's coming, excitement stirred Elsinore to its darkest corners.

When Hamlet arrived one summer, dark-skinned from some adventure upon the seas, Gertrude embraced him and petted him as if he were still a boy. At her bidding, I brought them wine and delicacies in her chamber. So absorbed was she in her son that she did not even look my way. Hamlet did not greet me, nor did our eyes meet. I was disappointed yet relieved, for I would have blushed and stammered had he spoken to me. Perhaps, I thought, he did not recognise me. I had changed much in four years. Hamlet, now twenty-two, was no taller, though more sinewy, and he seemed more intense than before. Experience had carved new expressions in his features and given him a worldly manner.

Gertrude was jealous of her son's company and spent many hours with him, laughing at his clever stories and hearing tales of his journeys. Sometimes the king joined them, and I saw Hamlet's father grow dark with disapproval at their lightness. But in the presence of their subjects, King Hamlet and Queen Gertrude were yoked to each other in rule and in love, bestowing all their pride on their son. Prince Hamlet shone with his own glory, and courtiers arranged themselves around him like the smaller lights in the heavens around their sun. I sighed and wished for his light to fall on me.

Soon my desire was rewarded. One day I lounged idly in the long gallery that led to Gertrude's privy chambers. Cristiana sat plying her needle in the sun that streamed through high windows and slanted across the floor, then spilled through the arches and into the great hall below. On the walls between the arches hung tapestries woven with scenes from Ovid's *Metamorphoses*, tales of gods and humans transformed by love.

I mused on the portrayal of Diana the huntress. Her bow rested on the ground while she bathed, half hidden in the pool. I recalled the day so long ago when I was swimming in the brook, free as a fish, and Hamlet came upon me. I studied the goddess in the tapestry. Her eyes were downcast, and her hair, woven in gold thread, covered her breasts, but her round hip and thigh were naked. Spying on Diana from the bushes was the hunter Actaeon, unaware of the grim fate awaiting him.

Cristiana picked up my needlework, some linen garment I cared nothing for.

"Your stitches are too long. You are simply lazy," she said, and tossed it aside.

I met her criticism with my own harsh words.

"My stitches would be finer if my needle were half as sharp as your nose," I said.

Elnora slept in a chair, her own needlework in her lap. Our voices did not even cause her to stir. Like an old cat, she slept more and more, some days awakening only to move into a new patch of sun and fall asleep again. I got up to fetch my *Herball*, for I had meant to try a new mixture of herbs for her latest pains. As usual Cristiana seized the opportunity to mock my habit of study.

"You will never get a man in your lap while you are making love to that big dusty book," she said with a tone of contempt.

"Tend to your own business, lest you are pricked unawares," I said coolly, as she stabbed the needle at her cloth and glared at me. I enjoyed seeing her fury.

The sudden entrance of Hamlet and Horatio put a stop to our argument. They were deep in conversation but halted their steps upon seeing us.

"I seek my mother, but I find younger game," said Hamlet. "What do you say to some sport with the ladies?"

Without waiting for Horatio's reply, Hamlet bent over and brought Cristiana's hand to his lips. She began to flutter like a moth and a honeyed laugh spilled from her.

"How does my lady Ophelia?" said Horatio, bowing.

"Well, I thank you."

I noticed that Horatio was now taller than the prince. His hair, still the colour of afternoon sunlight on ripe wheat, fell to his shoulders, revealing a high and wide brow over his frank brown eyes. He had none of Hamlet's noble beauty, but a woman might find him somewhat fair of countenance.

Hamlet then turned to greet me, though he did not try to take my hand.

"The wild doe has become a gentle deer," he said, showing that he recognised my transformation. I dared to look up at him.

"Indeed, my lord, this collar and chain do hold me fast," I said, touching my ruff and the links of the chatelaine at my waist, where my needlework tools were suspended. "I fear I have been forcibly tamed."

"She scored a hit, a palpable hit!" Hamlet cried, and staggered as if pierced by a sword. "Sharp as a rapier is this lady's wit."

I laughed at this playful outburst, seeing in Hamlet the lively boy he once was. Cristiana looked from me to Hamlet, suspicion flickering in her eyes.

"Let us ask the ladies to join our debate," said Horatio, seating himself on a stool so that his long legs stuck out to the sides. "Should beauty of the body or beauty of the mind be more prized by true lovers?"

I pondered Horatio's question in earnest, for this was a chance to talk of love like the noble ladies in Castiglione's *Book of the Courtier*.

"I maintain," said Horatio, "that a woman's beauty leads her lover's soul to higher goodness."

While I considered how to reply to this lofty idea, Hamlet answered Horatio.

"My friend, you know that beauty enchants men's souls and makes them lust for pleasure. Why, look upon Diana, whose many beauties distracted Actaeon from his hunting." He gestured towards the woven arras.

Frowning, Cristiana looked from Hamlet to Horatio, seemingly confused.

My hands trembled and I clasped them tightly together, for I was about to contradict the prince.

"My lord, Actaeon trespassed in gazing at the goddess. Being turned into a stag and devoured by his own dogs was a fitting punishment," I said.

"Indeed, though she was naked, the virtuous Diana did no wrong," Horatio agreed.

"Yes, and now you will tell me that desire turns men into beasts," said Hamlet with scorn. "I deny it."

"To return to Horatio's question," I said with a reasoned tone, "I believe that a virtuous mind outlasts the fleeting beauty of youth and thus is more desirable."

"Well spoken," said Horatio with a nod to me.

"If we were not beautiful, who would love us?" complained Cristiana, pleased that she had made a point. Then she pressed her shoulders back so that her breasts swelled forth, and looking from Hamlet to Horatio, she sighed at length.

Lady Elnora snorted and stirred in her sleep, and her cap slipped over her eyes.

"A blind man might love an ill-favoured woman," said Horatio, glancing towards Elnora. Cristiana laughed. Frowning, I reached over and straightened Elnora's cap so that she did not look so silly.

"Then the blind man is deceived, and the woman is an enchantress!" said Hamlet, slapping his thighs for emphasis. "And there you have it again: women are *wantons*, for they make men to *want them*."

Hamlet laughed at his own joke, but Horatio had the grace to look uncomfortable. I found Hamlet's conclusion unjust, and forgoing my modest manner, I spoke boldly.

"Lord Hamlet, it seems you see all women as deceivers, be they beautiful or ugly. Perhaps the fault lies in the man who trusts only his sight and is a slave to his base desire!"

My words were greeted with silence. Hamlet's eyebrows lifted in surprise. My heart pounded as if it would be heard. After a moment Hamlet spoke.

"I yield the combat. Horatio, this lady's mind is a fair match for mine, and her beauty grows with the wisdom she speaks."

Hamlet's eyes, blue as the sky at nightfall, met mine. I felt like a seafarer who has located the northern star and set his course from that shining point. Not until he rose and bowed did our eyes unlock.

Once Hamlet and Horatio had taken their leave, Cristiana turned on me.

"What nonsense is this about fair minds and pretty faces? And who is this lady, Diana?" she asked, as if we had spoken of someone at Elsinore.

"How can you be so ignorant?" I said, amazed. "Have you really never heard of Ovid's myth?"

"How can you be so shameless before the prince?" she shot back.

"It is no shame to speak reason, but it is to flaunt your bosom like a serving wench in an alehouse," I said, my temper rising.

Malice flashed in Cristiana's green eyes.

"You think that being witty will make the Prince of Denmark — or any man — want to marry you?"

"Ha! I have no designs upon Hamlet!" I cried. Perhaps I protested too loudly. "It is you who are baiting a trap with those two beauties you are so proud of."

"You are unkind," she said like a petulant child. "And you have stepped out of your place. Gertrude shall hear of it," she threatened.

I laughed carelessly, discounting her spite. I should have held my tongue, heeding Elnora. But humility was far from my mind, filled as it was with Hamlet's praises. My only thought was that I must find a way to see him again.

Chapter 8

I had not long to wait. That evening Gertrude sent me to gather fresh herbs in the garden. I was glad to escape Cristiana's carping and her threats. I ran down the tower stairs that turned in a spiral, emerging dizzy into the darkness. Above me, faint lights flickered in Gertrude's chambers. Though a fog had settled over the garden, I knew by heart the location of each bed and bower and could find my way in the dark. I walked secure and unafraid, knowing that the far reaches of the garden were bounded by walls. I picked sprigs of rosemary, feeling its sticky resin coat my hands. I would distill it, then steep it in cloves and other spices, making a concoction to sweeten the breath.

Detecting the scent of lavender, I knelt and let the sweet aroma tickle my nose and throat. As I crouched in the cool grass, I saw a dim and soundless shape approach. It puzzled rather than startled me as the figure emerged from the mist and took the form of Hamlet.

"How now, Ophelia," he said softly, standing before me.

I did not reply at first, for my tongue was bound by surprise. Hamlet reached for my hand and I stood up.

"Good evening, my lord," I then managed to say. "How did you see me in the dark?"

"You shine with virtue, and the light drew me like a moth to flame," he replied. A smile played around his mouth and, as if it were contagious, spread to my lips, too.

"You flatter me with a poet's praises," I said, looking sideways at him in order to hide my face. "But the simile does not suit us, for you are no moth, and I am not a fire."

"What should I say? I think you will suspect all my words," he chided gently.

"Say that you wished to see me again and watched for me, if that is the truth," I said in a rush. Startling myself with my bold speech, I withdrew my hand from his and clasped it with my other hand, thus restraining myself.

"It is true." He paused, and a long moment passed before he spoke again. "You have changed so much, Ophelia. You are not as I remembered you."

I thrilled to hear that he had thought of me while he was away.

"I feared the crows and jays who wait on my mother would have long ago pitched you from their nest, but you are safely fledged, I see," he said teasingly.

"Still I am beating my wings against the walls of my cage," I said ruefully, "for Elsinore sometimes seems a prison to me." Instantly I regretted my words, for I did not wish to seem ungrateful. "I only wish that I could freely come and go —"

I broke off, for Hamlet surprised me by brushing my cheek

lightly with the back of his hand.

"Will the bird be still if I come into her cage? Will she be content to stay?" he asked. His voice held a tender note that made my throat tighten.

What could I say to such a request? Unable to speak, I simply nodded. Hamlet took my hand again and put it to his lips. I could not help but look up into his face. When his eyes met mine again, I felt the truth of what the philosophers say, that love enters through the eyes and strikes the soul. Cupid's dart had struck me, kindling a flame in my heart and all my parts.

"I wished for you to come here," I whispered.

"I wanted to see you," he confessed.

Suddenly I was afraid of the fire as it burned within me, building a heat that spread to my face.

"This is too dangerous," I said, even as I swayed nearer to him. "You know that nothing goes unseen. Do I hear footsteps? I must go now." The words fell fast from my lips.

"No, stay," he pleaded as I began to pull away. "There is nothing to fear." I relented and let him take my arm, finding pleasure in the pressure of his hand.

"Come into the moonlight, for I wish only to behold your beauty and your wit, which you possess in such abundance, it stops my heart."

"Again you jest!" I laughed. "Your heart is not stopped, or you would be dead."

"Ophelia, you are a natural philosopher! If I admit that my heart still beats, will you allow me to admire your beauty?"

"I know your thoughts on beauty. I must look to my honour," I said. Yet I spoke lightly, and I let him keep my hand in his.

"Ophelia, you do not know me yet. Do not think that I argued my true beliefs today. To the world I wear a mask that hides my truer self, which you now see."

I scanned his face longingly but could not understand his meaning.

"I see nothing in this darkness. Alas, Lord Hamlet, I hardly know you, nor do I know myself. Goodnight." I turned and walked quickly away from him, startling a rabbit that fled before me like my own leaping heart.

I did not sleep that night, but lay awake rebuking myself for running away in fear. I rehearsed every word that had passed between us for its true meaning, but found no certainty. Had I seen Hamlet's real self or did he wear a mask? Did he truly think me beautiful?

In the morning I arose from my bed intent on revisiting the scene of our meeting. All day I was useless and distracted. So I offered to fetch fresh lavender to strew in Gertrude's bedchamber, and that night I knelt again on the ground, gathering the silvery, purple-tipped fronds of lavender into my arms. I breathed their scent to calm my roiled thoughts, even while I prayed for Hamlet to appear. And so he did, the insubstantial presence in the fog once again becoming the solid figure of Hamlet.

"We meet again, Ophelia," he said, touching my hand.

"I wished for you to come," I replied.

"And thinking made it so. Here I am."

As he spoke, he led me to the shelter of the tall hedges bordering the garden labyrinth I had often seen from my window. It was a secret place I had never dared to enter, fearing I might get lost. Now a sudden impulse seized me.

"Follow me, if you can!" I whispered, then turned and disappeared into the maze. I felt my way, dropping the lavender as I ran. I turned left, then right, again and again. I found myself at the centre of the maze, with nowhere else to run. Gasping for breath, I listened to the rushing of blood in my ears. When Hamlet appeared, carrying the herbs I had dropped, I uttered a small cry, like a child delighted to be found.

"Why did you run from me again?" he asked.

"I don't know. I used to run for the joy of it, when I was little."

Hamlet nodded as if he remembered. He rubbed a stalk of lavender between his fingers, releasing its sweet aroma, and traced the outline of my forehead and nose with it. I smiled in response.

"You amaze me, Ophelia," he said.

"I did lead you into this maze, that is true. And now I am lost here."

I could just see the edges of Hamlet's hair, lit by the moon. His teeth shone in a smile, though the rest of his face was dark.

"No, I am lost, and you are found. For at the centre of this twisting path, I have discovered . . . you." He began to fumble for his words. "You, Ophelia, whom I would love. If you . . . could love me."

Because they did not roll from his tongue like they had been practised, I believed Hamlet's words. I wanted them to be true. And my own reply was spoken in utter truth.

"I have never loved before," I confessed. "I fear to lose what little I possess."

He understood that I meant my virtue, my only wealth, for he replied, "Ophelia, I know you are most honest and virtuous. I

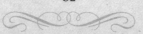

pledge to serve you truly and with honour."

I lifted my chin to better see his face, and his lips met mine. It was a brief kiss, but his mouth, though mild, seemed to draw up all my strength and leave me weak. His arms about my waist held me up. A second kiss he offered me, and I took a third one from him. Still I wanted more, for the touch of his lips on mine was pure delight. But I would not seem greedy or immodest, so I turned aside my face. Then Hamlet kissed my ear, and his breath tickled me to the very base of my spine.

"I must be gone now," I whispered. "Though I would stay."

Himself reluctant, Hamlet loosened his hold and led me to where the maze opened on to the garden. Then he took something wrapped in paper from his pocket and pressed it into my hand. After granting him one final kiss, I dashed through the dewy grass back to the castle. I had completely forgotten the lavender I had picked for Gertrude.

Alone in my chamber, I fairly trembled with excitement. How could it be that I, who had never been kissed before, had kissed the Prince of Denmark himself, not once but many times? Did he really speak to me of love? It was beyond belief that I, humble Ophelia, should be wooed by Prince Hamlet. Surely I had imagined it. Then I remembered Hamlet's gift, which I had thrust into my pocket as I ran. I took it out, unwrapped it, and found a framed miniature suspended on a chain. The painting depicted the god Janus with two faces, one masked like a comic player, the other wearing a tragic look. I puzzled over its meaning. Did the masks signify the disguises Hamlet spoke of wearing? Did the gift promise a new beginning of love, as the month of January heralds the beginning of a new year?

Sleep eluded me as my brain turned over these questions. Finally I arose in the darkest hours of the night intending to mix a draught of barley water and poppy seeds to calm my whirling thoughts. To my surprise, Cristiana was still skulking about. She sidled past and I smelled lavender. She fingered a fresh bouquet at her waist.

"You have disappointed the queen by not returning with the herbs, and now she has me to thank for the fragrance in her chamber." By the light of the moon that slanted into the dark corridor, I saw her eyes narrow. "Lavender makes a soft bed for love to lie on, does it not?"

I snatched at her skirt and saw that the hem was soiled and damp.

"Whose spy are you?" I whispered, scorn barely masking my fear. Had she followed me into the garden like a sly serpent? Did she only guess that I had met someone there, or had she seen us, despite the dark?

Chapter 9

Hamlet and I conducted our furtive courtship as if we guarded some secret business of the state. In the company of others, we exchanged only formal courtesies, arranging private meetings with our looks and with letters passed between us. We preferred to meet in the open air, for the dark recesses of Elsinore could hide spies as well as lovers. The willow tree overhanging the brook shielded us from all eyes, and the maze kept our secrets. No one but Horatio knew of our meetings. He was both our messenger and our guard. His watchfulness saved us from discovery many times.

One day, however, even Horatio's vigilance was not enough to shield us. Hamlet and I were walking in the king's orchard, where he often strolled with his advisers. We believed its paths to be deserted, for the king was absent on a journey. As we were passing by a gnarled, knotty tree, Hamlet plucked an apple and showed me the fruit streaked with red and gold like a sunset.

"How is it that a misshapen tree can yield such a perfect fruit?

This is seldom seen in human nature," he mused. Then he handed me the apple.

"Wait," I said, holding up my hand in refusal. I was learning to tease Hamlet and enjoying it. "Should not I offer the fruit to you, and you reject it? Then I would tell you about the fabled serpent who said it would make us wise, and you, longing to be wise, would eagerly bite it."

"No, for unlike our father, Adam, I would challenge you and say, 'Show me the serpent,' and you would not be able to produce him." Hamlet spread his arms wide. "See, no serpent, no Satan creeps in this Eden."

At that moment we heard Horatio's whistle, warning us that we were no longer alone. I knew that Cristiana would not be out of doors, for she had taken to her bed with a sore throat. But someone on a horse was approaching, singing loudly. There was no place to conceal ourselves, and so I pulled the hood of my cloak until it shadowed my face and turned away.

"It is Claudius, my uncle!" Hamlet hissed. "Pretend that you gather apples in your cloak. I will put him off." I bowed to my work and did not see, but only heard, their encounter.

"What ho, Hamlet! Come with me for some sport. Your father will not miss a doe or two."

"No, Uncle."

"What's this? Ah, you are already engaged. Let me see the wench. Oh, she hides herself, does she? I'll find out who she is."

"Uncle, you are drunk. Be gone."

"Some advice for you, boy. Give her a pinch and a paddling, too. The lusty ones love it, I can vouch for that. Heh, heh!"

Claudius's laugh sounded both sly and hearty. Burning with

undeserved shame, I wanted to strike at him with my words. In my agitation, the hood slipped from my head just as Claudius spurred his horse and seized the mane to keep his slack body from falling off. I looked at Hamlet, whose body was tense with anger.

"He insults me, calls me 'boy'. The drunken sot, unworthy to be my father's brother!" he said.

"And you said there was no serpent in this garden?" I said bitterly. The orchard's pleasures now seemed blighted by the intrusion of Claudius.

Horatio, full of remorse, then joined us.

"I am sorry I could not stop Claudius, for he came from the direction of the deer park."

"Where he poaches my father's game in his absence, the thief," interjected Hamlet. "But he is drunk as usual and most likely will not remember seeing us."

Hamlet forgave his friend, and henceforth we vowed to be more careful. It was my idea that we disguise ourselves as a rustic and a shepherdess, for the lovers in Gertrude's romances often did so. So I wore a linen smock and petticoat and, over them, a sleeveless bodice that laced below my breasts. It was plain and comfortable, unlike my stiff and fashionable courtly dress, and it gave me an ease of movement that I relished. Hamlet found some loose breeches and a homespun tunic and covered his curls with a leather cap. I liked him all the better for his plain attire and the easy manner he put on with it. When we wore our simple disguises, few people gave us a second look. Holding hands, we strolled openly through the streets of the town. Then like country folk without any cares, we lay in the meadow, surrounded by tall

grass, and wove garlands of white daisies and purple columbines to crown each other.

"Let us make up a song together," I said one day. "For I have read that shepherds like to engage in singing contests."

"Ophelia, you read much nonsense. What dung-covered lad can tell his ABCs, let alone rhyme a sonnet and count all its feet?" Hamlet said. "He whistles for his sheep, or rings a bell, or shouts 'hey'. I have heard none of them sing."

"Then we will be the first, and set the pattern for all herders of sheep in these hills."

So Hamlet thought for a moment, then sang:

> *"Where the bee lights, there dip I*
> > *my tongue;*
> *I'll taste the flowers until I die*
> > *so young!"*

Though his song was lusty, he kissed me very courteously. In turn, I sang:

> *"Here by the greenwood tree, fa la,*
> *Come, love, and lie with me, fa la."*

Taking my song as an invitation, Hamlet put his head in my lap, and I gently pushed him away.

"You are too eager, my lord," I said, and he withdrew at once.

"I did not mean to offend you, Ophelia," he said, taking my hand instead.

I got up to pick fresh flowers to replace wilted ones. Passing

through the meadow, I came upon a small brown bird that had fallen from its nest on a branch overhead. I picked it up and held it in my palm. Its heart, visible beneath skin more fine than the thinnest sheet of vellum, was no longer beating. When Hamlet came upon me, I was weeping, and this embarrassed me more than his head on my lap.

"I am sorry. I am not practised in love. When will you forgive me?" he pleaded.

"It is not that," I said, touched by his humility. "You have not offended me." I showed him the bird. "It is this that makes me weep, though I do not know why."

"Perhaps because this creature had a spirit, but now it is flown?" Hamlet offered. His brow was furrowed, as if my sadness confused and worried him.

"Where is its mother?" I whispered. "Why could she not save it?" I looked around to see dozens of birds flitting and singing, careless of the dead one in my hand.

"Nowhere. Nature is beautiful, but she can be cruel. Just like a woman," Hamlet mused. "Though not you, of course. Cruel, I mean. That is, you are beautiful, but not cruel."

Now Hamlet blushed and stammered, and I could not help but smile.

"Does it not say in the Bible that there is providence even in the fall of a sparrow?" I asked.

"Yes, and it says that every hair on our heads is numbered, for we are more precious than any sparrow. Therefore do not fret," said Hamlet, and with a kiss, I let myself be comforted.

Another day, as the sun fled across the sky, we roamed the woods between Elsinore and the village as Horatio followed us in

silence. At dusk, we came upon a deserted cottage of crumbling stones, which it looked like a hermit's dwelling. In the hearth we kindled a small fire against the chill. Horatio declined to join us as we ate our bread and cheese.

"Why is Horatio so unsmiling today?" I asked.

"He is not," denied Hamlet. "Like himself, he is ever the same. Give it no further thought." He shared his flask of ale with me, then drank of it himself. But I persisted, uneasy.

"Does he disapprove of our courtship?"

Hamlet spewed liquid from his mouth, and bitter words with it.

"The whole world would disapprove of our courtship, Ophelia!" he exclaimed, waving the flask in a broad arc. "Horatio fears I do but trifle with you. He is wrong, mind you. And your father! Your family's honour would demand that your brother challenge me to a duel."

"They do not know that we meet, nor can they prevent it," I said, with more certainty than I felt. For months my father had been away on the king's business, and Laertes was studying in France. I did not want to think about the consequences of being discovered by them.

"You know, I am the heir of Denmark —" began Hamlet, as if I had forgotten.

"Yes, and I am no one," I whispered.

"No, you are my love. But my father the king has alliances to secure by marrying me to a princess of France or Germany. He will prevent us." Hamlet's tone was matter-of-fact. He fell silent and fed sticks to the small fire.

I stood up awkwardly and stumbled to the cottage door.

Beyond its battered frame the black-barked trees grew straight to the heavens, disdaining the forest floor, where tangled heather and brush hid the path leading from this lonely spot.

How foolish I had been to think I was as free as any peasant girl and as worthy as any king's daughter! I gazed out into the forest.

"This courtship is ill-fated. No good can come of it for you or me," I said bitterly.

I heard Hamlet sigh. Or was he blowing air on the stuttering fire? I felt him come up behind me and touch my shoulder.

"When we come to these woods in our humble clothes, I am no prince, but a man who may have my will," he said, his words full and rounded with yearning. "Here I am simply 'Jack', and I choose you as my 'Jill'."

He turned me around to face him and kissed me warmly.

The touch of his lips somewhat banished my fears. I realised that Elsinore was for Hamlet, as it was for me, a gilded cage.

"In these woods and cottages there are no envious eyes, no carping tongues, no gossip or lies," I said. "So let us remain in this place always and speak only simple truth to each other." I rested my cheek against the rough homespun of his jacket, knowing that my wish was a vain one.

As soon as I returned to Elsinore, I felt constrained to lie, to deceive the queen herself.

"What ails thee, Ophelia? You are wan and distracted today."

"I studied late last night," I said. "And then I did not sleep soundly." In truth, I was tired, for I had been stealing many hours from my rest to spend with Hamlet. My absences were beginning to displease Gertrude and she grew testy with me.

"I do not like it when I call and you cannot be found."

"I was in the garden getting herbs for Elnora," I lied again.

Soon Gertrude suspected that I had a lover. Summoning me, she tried to catch me off my guard.

"Fetch me some lavender water, Ophelia. And tell me, what is his name?"

"I do not know what you mean, my lady."

"It is as plain as the daylight that you are in love." She held up a trinket, dangling it before me. "Wouldn't you like to wear this beaded comb?"

"No, it becomes you better," I said, fastening the comb in her hair and avoiding her gaze.

"Does he love you back? Perhaps a word from me will help smooth the path of true love."

So Gertrude probed, while I denied that I loved anyone. How could I tell the queen that it was her son I desired? That we talked and laughed for hours together? That we pretended to be rustics not ruled by custom but free to choose our love?

I wanted to confide in Elnora but was certain that her loyalty to Gertrude would prevail over our friendship. There was no one else I trusted. And though I said nothing, everyone suspected that I had a suitor. Did my looks, though guarded, betray me? Did I murmur to myself? Surely not, but the ladies still gave me sly glances and attempted to guess the aim of my desire. It was wicked of me, but I let them believe I fancied Horatio, for his good reputation put him above all reproach.

Gertrude knew that I was deceiving her, and she in turn began to hold me at a distance. I was no longer asked to wait upon her or to read to her. While I was out of favour, Cristiana slipped into my place and worked her malice on the queen's mind.

When Gertrude spoke to me again, her tone was cold.

"I am told that you spend your days in the country with a common boy, that you dress like some farmer's daughter."

Her misunderstanding would have been comic had we read of it in a romantic fable. She and I could have laughed at the mother's blindness and pitied the plight of the unequal lovers. But this was no fiction. I merely hung my head as she poured out her disappointment on me.

"Do you thus repay my kindness by disgracing yourself?" she demanded. "Surely there is some gentleman at court whom you could favour."

I was dismayed to be so fallen from Gertrude's esteem.

"My heart is in such turmoil," I cried, unable to suppress my tears. "You are right; I love unworthily." That at least was true. "I will strive against it," I promised, a fresh lie.

"I hope that you will return to your senses, Ophelia. This madness does not become you."

I was sure that it was Cristiana who spied on me and told the queen what she saw. One day not long after the queen's lecture, I caught Christiana in my chamber. I worried that she had searched my trunk, where my tokens and letters from Hamlet were hidden. But I saw with relief that it was still locked. I grabbed my homespun costume from beneath my mattress and thrust it at her.

"Here. Is this the proof you seek?"

"Why would you so disgrace yourself in these rags?" she said, fingering the dress in disbelief before dropping it. "Then again, I don't know why I am surprised that you love basely."

It was a wonder that Cristiana had not discovered that it was Hamlet I loved. I should have been thankful for her ignorance.

Instead I loathed her pride, her lies, and her disdain of me when I should have despised myself for lying to Gertrude. But I was blinded and had no use for reason, desiring only to take revenge on Cristiana for her cruelties to me.

Chapter 10

The idea for my plot began with a ribald tale of mistaken love I had once read to Gertrude. I saw how, by imitating it, I could trick Cristiana and sow discord to the confusion of all.

I told Hamlet my plan, disguising its motive, for I did not want him to think me too unkind.

"An excellent device, worthy of a playwright." His praise was like honey to a bee, and I sucked it up.

"By this means I will test the mettle of Cristiana and her two suitors," I said.

"May it prove them false, like bad coins," Hamlet replied. While I aimed at Cristiana's pride, Hamlet relished the opportunity to trick Rosencrantz and Guildenstern. "This will pierce their puffed-up ambitions," he exulted.

"But we must hide our authorship of this work," I cautioned, and Hamlet agreed.

Our plot was to unfold at the banquet celebrating the twentieth year of King Hamlet's rule. The evening would be filled with masking, dancing and feasting. In preparation, men and women borrowed each other's finery and planned fanciful disguises. An excited Cristiana collected feathers of every colour and stitched them to a mask, for she had found this note in her pocket:

By your cloak of red and feathered face
You give me proof that I have won the race.
My prize I'll take, 'tis earned but free
Beneath the spreading boughs of the willow tree.

The verse was signed Rosencrantz, the name perfectly executed by Hamlet. Meanwhile I had copied Cristiana's hand to write the note Hamlet delivered to Rosencrantz's rival. This note read:

I can no longer hide my longing for you, gentle Guildenstern. Tonight the red bird perches in the willow tree. She awaits the hooded black crow. Catch me and I am yours.

On the night of the banquet, firelight flashed on the walls of the great hall and rush torches sent up their oily smoke. Spiced wine poured from spigots, overflowed pitchers and goblets, and was consumed like water. Tables groaned under joints of venison and pork, smoked fish and meat pies. I drank a little wine, though not enough to make me tipsy, and sat with the ladies, sucking on plums and sweet figs. A juggler made his way through the crowd, keeping several oranges aloft at once. Dancers wearing bells stepped high, clapping to the beat of tabors and the whistle of pipes.

From his throne, King Hamlet beheld the scene, his queen beside him. In deference to the glad occasion, his foot kept the rhythm of the dance and his usually stern mien was softened. Old

Yorick had died, and a younger fool now made King Hamlet laugh, though not so heartily as he used to.

By contrast, Claudius took his pleasures fiercely, carousing with his cup in hand. His mask was lifted, the better to feed himself. Drops of wine, ruby red, splashed his tunic and the floor. He pinched the curves of many women, careless of the spilled wine that stained their costumes. Before the king he made an exaggerated bow, nearly toppling to his knees. He began a speech, but the king cut off his slurred words. So Claudius seized Gertrude's hand, urging her to join the revelry. With a show of reluctance, she left her husband's side to appease Claudius by dancing. King Hamlet's look grew dark.

This drama was but one of the night's shows. My own plot was of greater interest to me then. In my dark blue cloak and plain mask I moved about the hall, watching my actors. Guildenstern arrived in a black cloak and a mask with a beak. Cristiana flitted about in a crimson gown and long cape. The musicians started to play, and the dancers paired for a stately pavane. I found myself facing Hamlet, who wore a mask emblazoned with two faces.

"Good evening, Lord Janus," I said, thinking again of the strange token he had given me in the garden.

"Will you dance with me, hidden here in plain sight?"

"It is a contradiction I delight in," I said. Taking his hand, I could sense an expectation of pleasure that matched my own. Then in the whirl of dancers, I heard Cristiana's tinkling laugh.

"Will the red bird yield herself to the crow?" I wondered aloud to Hamlet. The masks made it possible for us to speak without drawing the attention of others.

"If she does, it will devour her, I know." Hamlet spoke in my ear, sending a shiver down my back.

Then we switched partners, and I was thrust into a high-stepping bransle with the nervous Guildenstern, who nearly stumbled over his long cloak.

"I see you eyeing the red bird," I said to him.

"Methinks she preens her feathers just for me," Guildenstern boasted. He affected an accent that almost made me laugh.

"Who could she be?" I was teasing him, for I thought no disguise was sufficient to hide Cristiana's manner. But Guildenstern seemed mystified.

"Some fine lady, a newcomer to the court," he said, following the red-clad Cristiana with his eyes. She danced with many men, no doubt seeking Rosencrantz under each disguise. But Rosencrantz was not at the ball, for he had been sent by Hamlet on a fool's errand.

I was dancing with a fleshy but nimble-footed gentleman when I saw Cristiana leave the hall, the folds of her red cape billowing behind her. Hamlet signalled that Guildenstern had followed her. Pleading my weary legs, I left my partner and slipped out of the steamy, smoky hall. With light steps I made my way through the outer courtyard and the gates, descended through the meadow, and crouched amid the rushes by the brook.

Hamlet, silent as fog, was soon beside me. The night was damp and chilly. Clouds hid the moon, and the willow tree was shrouded in darkness. But Cristiana was visible, her red cloak enfolding another in a close embrace.

"See how the fish first nibbles, then swallows the bait!" Hamlet whispered with glee.

"Yes, both are sorely hooked," I admitted.

I had imagined that Cristiana and Guildenstern would soon discover the game. I expected them to recognise each other and part with embarrassed laughter. But as we watched, the cloaked figures sank to the ground without breaking their grasp. I was overcome by shame.

"We are not meant to see this private passion," I whispered.

"Then let us close the curtain on this scene," said Hamlet.

We withdrew ourselves and returned to Elsinore in silence. I turned aside from Hamlet's lips after one chaste kiss, and we parted for the night.

Instead of returning to the dance, I went to my chamber, undressed and prepared to retire. I listened to the distant sounds of revelry while the night deepened. Though I still hated Cristiana, I took no delight in my trick. I tossed on my bed, unable to sleep. Hours later, when I heard light footsteps, I went to my door in time to see Cristiana pass by, her feathers bent and her cloak dirty. Her cheek was deeply flushed and her hair disarranged.

The next day, while I sat among the ladies in the queen's gallery, Rosencrantz paid court to Cristiana. She was breathless and coy and blushed to excess. Rosencrantz was confused, and when he left, Cristiana complained that men were so unaffected by love. Soon thereafter Guildenstern called, bringing a love token and speaking honeyed words. Cristiana was cold to him, but Guildenstern took this for discretion and left in good cheer.

I wondered greatly about what I had seen. Cristiana behaved as if it were Rosencrantz who had made love to her the night before. Yet it seemed impossible that she could have mistaken

Guildenstern for Rosencrantz, even in the dark. Had Cristiana recognised Guildenstern and taken her pleasure nonetheless? Did her conscience prick her for being unfaithful? Was she willingly untrue, or had she been truly deceived? Finally I gave up my speculations and concluded that in life, as in stories, foolish lovers will go to great lengths, deceiving themselves for the sake of pleasure.

Later Hamlet told me that as he shared drink with the two courtiers, Guildenstern boasted of his lovemaking to Cristiana. He and Rosencrantz came to blows, and Hamlet leaped up to part them.

"I said the lady was a light one, undeserving of their love. They both agreed, shook hands and were friends again." Hamlet laughed, rubbing his palms together with satisfaction.

But I grew angry at the thought of the three men disdaining Cristiana. I had not intended for Rosencrantz and Guildenstern to triumph from my trick and be so satisfied with their stolen favours.

"Though Cristiana is a fool, she does not deserve their scorn! They are not men of honour," I said.

Hamlet looked at me in surprise.

"What? Do you now pity your former enemy?" he asked. "How like a fickle woman," he teased.

"I have no appetite for your jesting," I said. "But when you men wrong one of my sex, I cannot be silent."

"We have not wronged the ignorant girl, but helped her to be rid of false loves," he said in a gentle voice. Then his face darkened and resembled his father's stern features. "She would surely have come to further grief, for Rosencrantz and Guildenstern are

deceivers both. They are vile traitors, loyal only to themselves."

Cristiana was for a time chastened. Spurned by both her lovers, she silently bore the gossip about her reputation. I did not fear her revenge, for I did not think her clever enough to suspect that I had contrived the events of that night. And loyal confederates, Hamlet and I never revealed that we were authors of this tragicomedy.

Chapter 11

Within a week of the celebration of King Hamlet's rule, Prince Hamlet returned to Wittenberg. We said farewell in the foyer near his chambers as the dusky shadows consumed the day's light. Our parting was hasty, the moments stolen from his hours with his mother and the king. He promised to write often, but I longed for dearer words from him.

"Do you love me?" I dared to ask at last.

"Do you doubt that I do?" he replied, parrying my question.

"I will not doubt, if you say so."

"I believe I have not heard you declare your love," he said, his brow furrowed in thought.

"Then you have not been listening to me," I replied lightly.

"Ah, let us end this vain discourse and let silence speak instead," Hamlet said, kissing me one last time.

After Hamlet was gone, I searched my memory of all our meetings. It was true. I had never said to him "I love you". Indeed, I did not know if what I felt could be called love. I only knew that Hamlet's absence left me bereft and confused.

Gertrude, too, grew moody and mournful without her son nearby. I attended her with renewed humility until she admitted me to her favour again. I knew she had forgiven me when she asked me to read to her a volume of love sonnets, which were said to be the latest fashion in England. As I read aloud it seemed that the poet, longing for his absent love, exactly summed up my own sorrows.

"He is gone, while I alone lay lingering here." This could be my heart's refrain. I read another poem. *"Hope art thou true, or dost thou flatter me?"* Did Hamlet only flatter me with his attentions? I thought of my lowly birth. How did I dare to hope for Hamlet's love? There was little comfort for me in this poetry.

It was the sonnets that praised a lady's fair lips and eyes that made Gertrude wistful. She gazed in her mirror, lamenting her increasing age and her declining beauty. I tried to lighten her mood.

"What woman would wish for coral lips and eyes like stars?" I asked. "Coral is hard and pitted, and stars are only faint specks on the dome of heaven."

"Tush, Ophelia, you lack a poet's sensibility," Gertrude chided. She picked up the book and read aloud as I brushed her hair.

"These amber locks, the nets that captured my heart." She looked up and sighed. "Once I had such locks. Now my glass shows white hairs like wires growing from my head," she said.

"They gleam as silver threads amid the gold," I replied, twining the masses of hair into a single thick braid.

"Now you speak like a poet," she said. "And poets are all liars."

Gertrude would not be pleased, so I was silent.

"Fair is my love, and cruel as she is fair," Gertrude read. "Why is

it, think you, that the mistress always disdains the poet who worships her?"

"Maybe she does not love him," I suggested. Gertrude was silent. Sometimes she posed such questions to teach me of love. "But what think you, my lady?"

"I think that she must be cruel if she wants to be loved," Gertrude explained. "For once a lady succumbs to the man's desire, he rejects her as unworthy of it."

Hearing this I grew concerned. Because I showed my love to Hamlet, would his ardour diminish? Was love like a hunger, easily satisfied by feeding? Or did it grow by what it fed on? Should I have withheld my kisses and thus increased his appetite for them?

But to Gertrude I only said, "Perhaps the lady waits for the poet to marry her before granting him anything."

"No, they will never marry! It is the nature of love not to be satisfied so easily," she said bitterly.

"Then the poet does not lie, for thwarted love is the subject of all these sonnets," I said lightly.

"I concede the argument, Ophelia," Gertrude said with a weary wave of her hand. "Now rub my temples with this oil and let me sleep."

Alas, Gertrude's discontent could not be eased by my attentions. She and the king argued in her chamber, their voices audible but not their words. I sometimes saw her eyes swollen with tears. I wondered if it was Claudius who sowed a bad seed between them. While the king grew grey and serious with the burdens of government, Claudius, with his brown beard, was still vigorous and lusty. His red lips were moist and his black eyes bold and piercing. Ladies seemed flattered by his attention, but the mere thought of being touched by his fleshy hands made me shudder. Fortunately he left me alone, as game too small for his ambitious appetites. But he often made Gertrude laugh and blush. Perhaps in his presence she imagined herself young and beautiful again, the sonnet lady desired by a man who could not have her.

I hoped to read of Hamlet's longing for me in his letters, but they were nothing like sonnets of love. One May afternoon, I sat near a window at the west end of the queen's gallery, trying to decipher the tortured wit of his latest letter.

My love, inflame me no more, lest you consume all my wit and betray my will. Let men not censure my name that I call your love, that for which I rise and fall.

These words I read over and over, but could make little sense of them. Was this the true passion of a lover in defiance of men or the complaint of a scholar plagued by false passion? Hamlet, absent from me, grew a mystery to me, a masked god with two faces, both of which hid yet another self.

How should I reply to this strange sentiment? An idea came to me as I looked out over the king's orchard. Not five months ago, Hamlet and I had admired the gold-red apples there. Now the trees were thick with blossoms. I would write a sonnet describing the petals, white and rose-coloured, that fluttered to the ground, borne upon the warming breeze. Not knowing the intent of Hamlet's letter, I would take care not to express my longing for him.

As I wrote and blotted many phrases, lamenting my dull wits, Gertrude appeared at the door of her chamber, looking fretful.

"Ophelia! It grows late. Has the king summoned me yet?" she asked.

"No, my lady, I have received no word," I replied, rising. "Perhaps he is especially weary this day." It was the king's habit, after dining at midday, to rest in his orchard.

"Mark the time!" Her tone was urgent but her voice quivered. "Attend here," she ordered, hastening away. I waited, as bid, wondering at her agitation. Cristiana resumed her needlework as if nothing were amiss. Elnora, whose eyes were too weak to see her stitches, merely sat with some unsewn pillow covers in her lap and closed her eyes.

I returned to composing my poem. Was it possible to rhyme *blossom* with *bosom*? Would Hamlet consider the verse clever or merely forced? Perhaps, I thought, I should forego the nonsense of rhyme.

While I was entertaining these trivial thoughts, a momentous and terrible event was unfolding close by. Sudden screams pierced the quiet and startled me so that I dropped my pen, blotting my words with smeared ink. The screaming echoed from the walls as if a horde of demons shrieked from the stones. I rose from my seat but could not move further, feeling my feet rooted to the stones beneath them.

Elnora jerked to her senses.

"Oh, what a frightful dream I have had! Beyond all imagining!" Her breath came in short, quick bursts. "I must be bled of these black humours!"

Having relented a moment, the screams resumed. And the words that came to my ears amid the cries made my blood stop in my veins.

"Help! The king is dead! Help, oh!"

Cristiana began to tremble and mew like a cat. Elnora fainted.

I tried to revive her by tapping her cheeks, then eased her bulky form on to its side and left her to recover.

"The king is dead?" I whispered, the words making no sense to my mind. "How can such a thing be true?" I flung open the window and leaned upon the ledge to see guards running helter-skelter in the orchard, their pikes and swords in hand. They shouted and beat the trees, looking for the thief who stole the king's life, but no murderer was found there. Petals fell from the branches like a late, wet snowfall.

That night it was reported that a serpent had stung King Hamlet and its venom had instantly paralysed his heart. I was doubtful of this official word. I had never heard of poisoned snakes around Elsinore, nor had I read of any such creatures in Denmark. Then a rumour arose that those who had seen the body in the orchard noticed a loathsome crust like a leprosy covering the skin. It was whispered that the king had been murdered as he slept and the false traitor had fled to Norway. Another suspicion grew, too terrible to be spoken aloud, that the unknown murderer was still in Denmark, even at Elsinore among us.

That night I dreamed of the king's pale and bloodless corpse sprinkled with innocent white and pink blossoms. A black and mighty whirlwind arose, scattering the flowers and cracking the trees, carrying screams upon its currents and making the very stones of the castle shudder. I knew in my heart that goodness had been murdered and that a reign of evil had begun at Elsinore.

Part Two

Elsinore, Denmark
May–November 1601

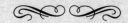

Chapter 12

When the earth quakes, mountains fall and rivers alter their courses. With King Hamlet's death, the state of Denmark was in a like manner shaken to its foundations and chaos took the place of order. Greed, suspicion and fear ruled all hearts. Edmund's father seized the king's treasury, and the lords contended for control. Labourers refused to work, merchants cheated their customers, and brigands ran at large. No one knew his place in this disordered and kingless country.

Gertrude also left her queenly seat, making two thrones vacant. Overcome with grief, she closeted herself like a nun and received no one for weeks. She lay in the dark of her bedchamber or knelt in her oratory, praying until her knees were stiff. Elnora and I ministered to her with the juice of bitter roots and crushed flowers to purge her foul humours and ease the pains in her head. But the queen remained as dull as a stone. One day, hearing a crash from her chamber, I entered to find her in a frenzy. A pile of books lay on the floor, and one by one she flung them from the open window as she wept with hysteria. I was horrified at the sight and ran to close the window.

"Please, my lady, stop!" I pleaded.

"Alas, it is over and done with! Love is nothing but folly," she cried.

I seized her hands in mine and led her to her bed.

"Oh, do not say such things. I know how you loved the king," I murmured, trying to soothe her.

"You are but a child! You know nothing of a queen's desires," she said bitterly, thrusting me away.

I did not take offence, considering her grief, but stayed by Gertrude's side until her raving ceased and she fell asleep. Then I removed the remaining volumes to my own chamber. In the garden the next day, I found the book of sonnets, torn in half, its damp pages scattered among the herb beds.

Meanwhile, Denmark was like a ship without a rudder. Lords and councillors met in secret in the king's state rooms until late at night and argued openly in the great hall. Foremost was the question of who should succeed King Hamlet. In many countries the king's son inherited the crown, but this was not the law in Denmark. Some called for Prince Hamlet to be elected, despite his youthfulness. Others argued that Denmark needed a more warlike king to challenge Norway, which stood poised to strike our leaderless state. Gertrude, all queenliness drained from her veins, cared nothing for these matters. She refused all appeals and, like a black-veiled prophetess, declared Denmark cursed. But Claudius was everywhere at once, serious with seeming grief for his brother. His eyes, not clouded with drink but clear of purpose, were fixed on the captaincy of this reeling ship. At last the lords agreed, though with much ill will, to elect Claudius as king.

King Hamlet's body was interred beneath the floor of

Elsinore's chapel, near his father's bones and those of his father's father. At the funeral, Gertrude, wrapped in black veils, followed her husband's coffin. She walked alone, with no man to guide her steps. Elnora cried loudly. I felt some sadness for the king's passing, but even greater pity for Gertrude, bowed by the weight of her loss. What would it be like to lose a husband of so many years, I wondered.

Neither the election nor the funeral could be delayed for Hamlet's return. Weeks were lost in bringing him to Elsinore, for the messenger who had been dispatched found him not in Wittenberg but travelling in the direction of Italy. He did not arrive until after midsummer, when hard young fruits hung on the boughs that had shed their blossoms at the king's death.

Only with Hamlet's return did Gertrude uncover her face. She was thinner, with pallid skin to match her grey eyes, and her hair had turned more silver than gold. She clung to Hamlet like a vine to an oak tree. The prince wore a suit of black as a statement of sadness. His usually sensitive face was unreadable, as if he wore a mask.

I longed to see Hamlet, but feared to approach him. I hoped for him to seek me out, but he did not. So I went to the great hall, looking for Horatio. It was bare, stripped of King Hamlet's liveries and banners. Garbage was strewn about and dogs scavenged for meaty bones. Courtiers seeking an office waited to meet with Claudius. Among them I recognised Edmund, the bully of my youth, now fat and losing his hair. He played at dice with some rough-looking companions. I also saw my brother, who had come to Elsinore for Claudius's coronation. He was with Rosencrantz and Guildenstern, whom I still despised, so I did not approach

him. Instead I beckoned him to come and converse with me, but he only bowed as if I were a stranger and not his sister.

Then Claudius entered the hall. My father hurried after him with rolls of vellum documents spilling from his arms. He had wasted no time in currying favour with the new king. He saw me, shook his head, and continued on his way.

Overlooked by my family, forgotten by Hamlet, and ignored by the queen, I felt as lonely as a leper. Thus I was delighted at last to see Horatio. He was plainly dressed and looking ill at ease among the courtiers hoping to catch the king's eye with their finery.

"I did not think to see you among this eager crowd, Horatio. Do you also come to ask favours of the new king?" I said lightly.

"I do not," he said, with some indignation. "I have no desire for power, no taste for politics, and no skill in base flattery."

I saw that I had offended him, and I tried to remedy the hurt, but only stumbled further.

"A king needs men like you, Horatio, who are humble and true-speaking. But do not think I aim to flatter you. My purpose is to ask you how Lord Hamlet does. He looks most troubled."

"Indeed, sorrow for his father vexes his spirit, making him quite melancholy," said Horatio.

"Then the queen and her son are alike in their passions," I said, "for Gertrude's grief exceeds all bounds. I fear her health is in danger." It was a comfort to speak of my worries to Horatio.

"Truly I have never seen Hamlet in a blacker mood. His thoughts are dire, and it takes all my wit to reason with him."

"Is he angry at the lords' decision? For I have heard him speak of the time when he would be king," I said.

"He has no love for his uncle. You know that much. I cannot say more, for I must keep his counsel," said Horatio, who was always discreet.

"Tell him, please, I long to speak with him . . . Nay, tell him only that Ophelia grieves with him."

"He shuns the company of all and will see no one," Horatio said, giving me a regretful look.

"Save you," I said, correcting him. "For like a true friend, you are the buffer between Hamlet and the world's sharp blows."

Horatio bowed and took his leave of me, saying he would carry my greetings to Hamlet.

Soon I realised that I was greatly mistaken in believing Hamlet and his mother to be alike in their passions. It was only three weeks after King Hamlet's burial, and the flowers of summer were in their fullest bloom when the news blew through Elsinore like an icy wind. Those who heard it first were numb with disbelief. Some were certain it was a wicked rumour and were afraid to repeat it. Others declared openly that it was an insult to the prince and to King Hamlet's memory. But they vouched for the terrible truth of the news, for the new king himself boasted of it.

Gertrude would marry King Claudius.

Chapter 13

The news stunned me at first. How could this have happened? I thought back on the preceding weeks. When, since her husband's death, had Gertrude ever conversed privately with Claudius? Had grief for King Hamlet weakened her mind? Was her choice of Claudius free or compelled? The matter was beyond my understanding. I gently pried into Elnora's thoughts, looking for an explanation. But she seemed afflicted with the same malady that depressed Gertrude's spirits.

"I am not well, Ophelia; do not trouble me. As for the queen, I do not know her mind. She is worthy to be a king's wife; what else should she be?" Elnora closed her eyes and waved me away. Even when I offered to fetch a tonic, she only shook her head and would say no more.

Thinking that the worldly Cristiana might understand Gertrude's behaviour, I mused aloud to her as we sat stitching, "How could the queen marry the brother of her dead husband?"

Cristiana only laughed bitterly.

"How little you know of men, and of the queen, your mistress!"

she said, as if she were privy to some deeper knowledge. But she did not share it with me, and I doubted that she understood any more than I did.

I was still perplexed as I helped Gertrude prepare for her wedding. Elnora sniffed constantly as she fitted Gertrude's dress of grey satin. Whether it was sentiment or rheumy eyes that troubled the old woman, I could not tell. As I fixed pearls in her hair and brushed carmine on her pale cheeks, the queen was impassive and did not meet my eye. So distant was she, living in her country of sorrow, that I dared not question her.

The wedding feast was a pretence of celebration. Tables sagged under the weight of venison, roast pig, smoked fish, and every kind of vegetable and desirable fruit. An army of servants clad in bright blue livery for the new king bore jugs of posset and poured spiced wine in pewter goblets stamped with the seal of Claudius. Ladies and courtiers wore their finest silks and jewels, and musicians sounded their tabors, drums and lutes. Beneath the finery, however, many held themselves in restraint and hid their disapproval, though drunkenness made others loud and careless.

Gertrude smiled and danced with a reserved grace, but I could see that she veiled her pain behind her cool eyes. Towards her new husband she displayed a tame submission I had not seen before, while Claudius strutted like a proud and possessive cock.

Hamlet stood near the entrance to the hall, his arms crossed in defiance. He was alone. From his cap to his boots, his clothing was inky black, and his pale face seemed lined with cares. In both his dress and his manner, he disdained all festivity. I saw him frown darkly, and though he reminded me of a cloud about to burst, I decided to brave the storm and speak to him.

When I was sure my absence would not be noted, I slipped behind the pillars that girded the hall, keeping to the shadows until I stood beside Hamlet. He did not look at me, nor did he greet me, but he stirred, as if restless, and sighed profoundly. Claudius raised his cup to Gertrude and drank. Then with his wine-dark lips he kissed her on the curve of her breast just above the embroidered fabric of her bodice. She turned her head to the side, whether to permit him the gesture or to avoid seeing it I could not tell. Her face was now directed towards the dark corner where Hamlet and I stood, but her gaze was impassive and unseeing. I saw Hamlet's scowl deepen.

"There is disease in Denmark. My father is not two months dead, his flesh still clings to his bones, and yet my mother takes a new husband. Indeed it is the cold funeral meats that furnish today's wedding table," he said bitterly, speaking more to himself than to me.

I fumbled for words befitting the strange circumstance, for the wedding had followed with improper haste upon the king's funeral. "Truly, I am sorry for your father's death," I said with earnest feeling.

Hamlet did not acknowledge my speaking. Nor did he walk away or bid me leave, so I stayed.

"Claudius not only wears my father's crown, but he weds my father's wife!" he said in a tone of disbelief. "I always said he was a thief. And my mother! To forsake my father, who was like Hyperion, the sun god, and bind herself to this demon! Where is her judgement, where is her reason?" He appealed to me as if I had an answer. "They are gone!" He flung his hands wide apart.

"The queen is much changed," I murmured. "I do not understand it myself."

"Look now, Ophelia. You see how she hangs on him? It is un-natural. Is there no shame in her? No strength, only womanly frailty?"

Though I shared his confusion, I rose to Gertrude's defence.

"You are unjust, my lord," I said gently. "We women are not all frail. I for one am strong and true." I touched his cheek, turning his face. His eyes were wet and betrayed his anguish. "Test me, Hamlet! I would not fail you."

He reached up and pressed my hand against his cheek.

"Dearest Ophelia, I have so longed for you." He sighed deeply, with a shudder that stirred his whole body. "Let us leave this scene of shame and seek out a quieter place." He took my arm and, looking around to be sure we were not being watched, guided me out of the hall through its vast doors.

"Shall we go to our cottage in the woods?" I asked hopefully.

"No, it is too far. I cannot wait so long." Instead he led me up the stairs to the guardroom outside the king's chambers. No one was there. I followed Hamlet through a maze of corridors to a far tower in a wing of the castle where I had never been. We felt our way up the winding stairs of the dark tower until we emerged on to a deserted parapet overlooking the field and the river below.

It was near dusk. The warm air blew wisps of damp fog about us. The anger in Hamlet's face had melted away, leaving only sadness. I waited for him to speak.

"Now we are alone. What is it you would say to me?" I asked.

"Nothing, Ophelia. Words have no meaning. I would have only silence."

So without speaking, we gazed over the parapet to the fields and hills beyond Elsinore. The mist crept over them and they

99

grew cloudy and insubstantial. Soon we could not see the ground. Then Hamlet spoke.

"What is a man's life but a prelude to his death?" Hamlet's voice was flat, without feeling. The words, as they left his mouth, were scattered by the wet wind. "And what is death but a long sleep, a most welcome forgetfulness."

"You are weary with grief, my lord. Let me fix you a sleeping draught."

"After the sleep of death, we waken eternally," Hamlet continued as if I had not spoken. "But in what land?"

"Who can tell?" I said lightly. "For no one returns from there to tell us tales."

"Thus the fear of that future makes us pause in the present," he said, leaning on the stone ledge that was cold and slicked with damp. The stone face of Elsinore was sheer and high. Suddenly realising where his thoughts tended, I seized his hands in mine.

"My lord, do not dwell on such things! In time, all that lives must die. It was your father's time, but your time has not yet come." I went on desperately, trying to turn his mind from dire thoughts to loving ones. "In due season all that lives returns to dust, making the earth fecund with life. Smell how the air tonight is pregnant with the flowers' blooms and their bee-sought sweetness." I drew the night's thick air deep into my lungs.

"My senses are black and unfeeling; my mind is dull and stupid. My hopes of advancement are dashed," Hamlet said with bitterness.

"So you are not the King, but you are still the Prince of Denmark."

"I am nothing."

"You are my Jack, and I am your Jill. Do you remember?" I said to lighten his mood and curtsied, playing the shepherdess.

"That was child's play. Now my father is dead, and I am no longer young," he said despairingly.

I looked up at Hamlet's noble countenance, his wide, intelligent brow now furrowed with grief. "I wish I had a glass where you could see yourself. For you put me in mind of the psalm: '*You have made man a little lower than the angels, you have crowned him with glory and honor, you put all things under his feet*'."

"But the very ground has been taken from beneath me," Hamlet said.

My eyes were wet with tears. I fell to my knees before him.

"Hamlet, you are a piece of God's work, the glory of Denmark, and my beloved," I whispered.

He knelt, too, and his arms came around me. We clung to each other as if we would save ourselves from drowning.

"No, Ophelia. You are the marvellous work, so noble in your reason." His hands cupped my face. "The beauty of the world." His voice broke with emotion as his fingers traced the outline of my lips. "You, too, remind me of a divine song, for you are fearfully and wonderfully made, and most curiously wrought." His fingers on my side numbered my ribs. Beneath my skirts they found the scars on the backs of my legs. Gently he lowered me to the earth.

There, with the cold stone at my back and my arms about his neck, I tasted the salt of his tears and I consoled him with all the strength of my body. I understood that grief and love were close cousins, for from his loss Hamlet finally spoke the words I had longed to hear.

"I vow to love you most truly and for ever," he whispered in my ear.

"And I you. Hamlet, I am yours."

We then confirmed our vows with the deed of love itself.

Chapter 14

Within days of the wedding, the guests who had travelled to Elsinore departed and quiet returned, but little peace. My own thoughts were at war within me as I pondered what Hamlet and I had done. I had given him my most valuable gift, one that could never be taken back.

"*It is nothing, for 'tis common enough that a girl gives her maidenhead to a man,*" said a worldly voice in my head. It resembled Gertrude commenting upon a tale of love.

"*This is no common delight, but a true and lasting love,*" countered a voice from a book of courtly ideals.

"*You are ruined and undone by this sin!*" a puritan's voice rebuked. The face of Elnora came to my mind's eye, lamenting the waste of all her teaching.

"*No, you are made new by love. A maid no more, but born a woman,*" said a wiser, more generous voice.

"*What's done is done and cannot be undone,*" came a stern voice like my father's.

"Ah, but what am I to do next?" I wondered aloud.

"*Pray that this secret does not come to light*," counselled the worldly voice, and ruefully I agreed.

As I debated with myself, a summons came from my father. I wondered what it could mean, for he had ignored me for many months. When I reached his chambers, he was bustling to and fro securing boxes and bundles for my brother's return to France. From the way he tugged at his beard and hemmed in his throat, I knew he had other matters on his mind. I should have knelt before him, but I felt disinclined to show this respect. After all, he had neglected his duty to me. So I stood before the table, waiting for him to speak.

Across from me, my father leaned on the table and asked in a low voice, "What have you observed lately of the queen and Claudius?"

"Nothing, my lord." It was the truth.

"Don't act so innocent, child! Have I not taught you to look closely about you?" he asked, his voice sharp.

"Yes, Father, I keep my eyes guarded," I said, pretending humility. But he seized my chin and lifted it, forcing me to look in his eyes.

"Many think it strange that Claudius has wed his brother's widow with such haste. Tell me what is said in secret among you ladies," he demanded.

Now I was suspicious of my father. What knowledge did he seek and on whose behalf? In fact I knew nothing, for we ladies spoke with caution where our mistress was concerned. I judged it safest to defend Gertrude.

"Why may she not choose her husband? She is accustomed to being the wife of a king and would not be content with less," I

said, echoing what I had heard Elnora say before.

Mindful of deeper matters, my father did not mark the defiant tone of my words.

"Some say she was false to King Hamlet," he whispered, leaning closer.

The idea struck me with horror.

"I have seen nothing!" I said. Then I countered boldly, "Why? What do you know?"

My father started back in surprise and pursed his lips. Instead of speaking again, he shook his finger at me, turned and swept out of the room just as my brother entered it. Laertes fell against a pile of boxes to avoid colliding with him.

I stifled a laugh. But I was glad to see my brother and hoped he would speak kindly to me. He looked fine in a russet travelling cloak thrown over his embroidered doublet. His silk hose set off his strong legs. With his stride he gave the air of a man even more intense and combative than he had been as a boy.

I came out from behind the table and reached out in a tentative way, inviting an embrace. Laertes grasped my hands briefly, holding me away from him.

"Dear sister, before I take my leave I have advice you must heed." His tone spoke of business. I drew back, hurt.

"It regards Prince Hamlet. I have learned that you often meet him in secret, wearing a rustic disguise. I doubt your silly games are merely innocent," he said.

Speechless, I looked down to hide the sudden flush that came over my face. How had Laertes discovered our love?

"Hamlet's blood is hot, and you are fair. Perhaps he says he loves you now, but do not believe him. He cannot choose you, for

he is subject to his birth. Nor is your will your own."

I did not wish to hear this irksome lecture.

"Why may I not choose my love? Who will prevent me?" I asked, thrusting my chin out, as I used to do when we argued as children.

"You know that is a foolish question. Our father will decide whom you will marry and when. Or I will, when he grows infirm."

I did not dare to argue with Laertes further, lest he trap me into admitting my love for Hamlet. But I would not grant his point.

"You cannot control me," I said, crossing my arms and determining to stay silent.

Then my brother changed his manner and began to plead with me.

"Dear Ophelia, my reputation is also at stake in this matter. Consider the loss to your honour — and to our family's name — if you believe Hamlet's songs of love and open your chaste treasure to him."

Were spirits and spies the witnesses while Hamlet and I made love on the battlement? No, for if we had been seen, Laertes would know his warning came too late. With my finger I prodded his chest.

"You, dear brother, take this advice of me. Tend to your own honour, and I will tend to mine. Do not show me the steep and thorny way to virtue, while you take the primrose path of ease."

He laughed in derision. I wanted to throw myself at him and scratch his face. Why should men be allowed freedoms that were deemed sinful for women to take?

At that moment, our father stumbled into the room, waving his arms to hasten Laertes' departure. He flung out all his

favoured maxims as if strewing flowers after my brother.

"This above all, be true to yourself, and then you cannot be false to any man," he cried to Laertes' departing back.

What empty words these were coming from my father, a man so used to fitting his form to the mould of power that he had no true shape of his own! I noticed for the first time how his back was becoming bent with age and the hair on his head was wispy. I saw him dab at his eyes and sigh like a fond father as Laertes finally disappeared. Had he ever shed any tears for me? Had he loved my mother and wept when she died? Would he have been different had she lived? I longed to ask him these questions, but I had not the courage.

"Ophelia, what did Laertes say to you?"

"Something touching on the Lord Hamlet," I said lightly. "It was nothing important."

"I hear that you have been most free and bounteous, giving your private time to him. What is between you?" His brows were pulled together in a single line, his eyes intent upon my face.

Did Laertes and my father conspire against me? What my brother knew, my father must also know. I would speak the truth and not provoke him further.

"Prince Hamlet has bestowed on me some signs of love," I said, choosing my words with care. I dared to hope that because he had loved my mother, perhaps he could be made to understand my love.

"What signs? Tell me now," he said, as if he were coaxing candy from my fist.

"Letters, tokens and true promises," I said, bringing my hands to my heart in the hope that my evident joy would move him.

"And you believe his tenders of affection?" he said with scorn. In his presence I felt small and insecure. Doubts began to prick me that Hamlet was sincere.

"I do not know, my lord, what I should believe," I said, my voice trembling from the effort to control it. I felt the familiar vexation at my father rise within me.

"Then listen to me. Set your price much higher. In short, tender yourself more dearly, or you'll tender me a fool!" He held his forearms in imitation of a mother cradling a baby.

I gasped, shocked by my father's rude mockery of my virtue.

"He has pledged his love to me in most honourable fashion," I said, drawing my dignity about me like a torn cloak. Tears began to sting my eyes.

"Do not believe his vows! They are traps to catch a woodcock!" he fairly shouted at me.

My effort at mildness failed utterly. I was unable to contain my anger and hurt, which spilled out uncontrollably.

"I trust Hamlet!" I cried. "Why do you not trust *me*? I am not a child, a green girl as you seem to think. Look at me!" I thrust myself upon him, tapping my breast violently, then turning my palms upward, demanding his attention. "I am almost of the age my mother was when she bore me. Do you see me? Do you remember her?" I was careless of my words, wanting to wound him, if he had any tender places left.

He took my wrists and stilled them. His grip was not hard, but his icy look hid from me any tender feelings he might have harboured.

"I would not have you give words or time to Lord Hamlet henceforward," he said in a hard, cold voice that forbade me to

defy him again.

I looked down to hide my sadness and my fury. I decided that from this moment on, I would no more be my father's daughter. Yet I would let him think that he still ruled me.

"I will know if you defy me, girl," he warned.

"I shall obey, my lord."

The lie I gave my father was in truth the vow I gave Hamlet. I had given everything to Hamlet. He, not my father, was now my lord.

Chapter 15

Through absence and neglect, the ties that bound me to my father and to Laertes had frayed since I had entered Gertrude's service. Now they had broken altogether, like a rotted rope. Unmoored, a boat upon the open waters, I would steer my own way through the waves. And I would see Hamlet again as often as I pleased.

These were my thoughts as I returned to my room after the confrontation with my father. There I found a message from Hamlet urging me to meet him that day. The hour was almost upon me, so in haste I donned my shepherdess costume. I wondered how Laertes had learned of my disguise and rued the change in my brother, who cared for me less than for his own reputation. I felt the injustice of my father's treatment, who fondly indulged Laertes while cruelly denying me. My lips trembled but I repressed my tears. Why should I care that my father's love was lost, when I had Hamlet's love? I rushed to meet him as if any delay would risk losing him.

Leaving the castle grounds by a roundabout way, I looked

back, expecting to see a spy set upon me by my father. But no one followed me. Despite the midday heat, I wore a cloak over my rustic dress as if it were the burden of all my thoughts. I longed yet feared to see Hamlet, remembering our loving words and our embracing on the battlement. Had that night changed everything between us? Would he greet me now as sweetly? Or did he summon me in order to end our love? Heaven forbid it! Yet here I come, like a servant at his beck and call! Perhaps I should speak first and cancel our vows, thereby saving some shreds of honour. So the diverse voices contended within me, and joining them were the scornful ones of Laertes and my father, until I began to believe that I was indeed a foolish girl who had squandered her virtue.

Filled with these doubts, I slowed my steps, reaching the shaded bower between the meadow and the wood. It was a deserted spot that Hamlet and I favoured for our meetings. There I unbound my hair and let it fall free, as it pleased Hamlet. The cool air calmed my heated heart. Butterflies darted among the daisies and teasing birds sang from their hidden nests. I spotted Hamlet and Horatio reclining in the shade of a great bush, while their horses grazed on sweet grass nearby. At the sight of me, Horatio rose and took his leave. As he galloped away, Hamlet cried after him, "Make haste in your errand, for remember, I will be shriven today."

I noted his words, for they fed my tortured thoughts. Of what sin would Hamlet repent? Was it the sin of loving me?

"My love, Ophelia, what ails you this fine day?" asked Hamlet, perceiving my troubled mood. I avoided his kiss while he took the cloak from my shoulders and spread it on the grass for me.

I sat down, holding myself stiff and straight. I regarded the smiling Hamlet, who sprawled on the ground with ease. His was not the manner of a lover intending to spurn me. But I chose my words with care from those that would pour from my mouth.

"I have quarrelled with my father and Laertes, who suspect our love and doubt your good intentions. They have been watching me. I feel like a deer beset by hounds!"

Hamlet held out his arms to me and sang, "*Come to me, my Rosalind, I am a hart that lacks a hind,*" but I drew away.

"I am not in the mood for merriment today, Hamlet. I only wish to be free, and wherever I am, someone is trying to bind me," I said, struggling to describe my fears without seeming to complain. "Your embrace is just the trap where my father would wish me to be caught."

"You do me wrong, Ophelia, for I would not yield you to him or his hounds," said Hamlet.

"Then they will tear me to pieces there! My honour sullied, I will be dismissed from court and packed off to a nunnery somewhere, never to marry!"

"That will not happen, for I will marry you."

"Hamlet, I warned you that I cannot bear your teasing today, is your lightness a ploy to put me off from you? Tell me in plain words that you regret our embracing!"

"I do not jest," he said with a wounded look. "I have pledged my love to you, and now I will marry you. Then we may touch each other most nearly without it being a sin, and no one else may touch us."

I hardly believed his words. It was true that being married to Hamlet would free me from my father's power. It was a tempting

thought. But how could I be certain that Hamlet spoke in earnest?

"You know you are not free to marry me. You have said so yourself."

Hamlet started up and spoke with sudden passion. "Not free to marry? Who will stop me? My father? He is dead. My mother, who married again almost before his body was cold? No! May Claudius command me in this? Never! He is not my father, nor is he justly my king."

"But my father would not permit me to marry whom I wished," I lamented.

"On the contrary, nothing would suit Polonius's ambitions better than for you to marry me," said Hamlet coolly.

"Fie on his ambitions! I do not want his permission; I will not please him!" I cried in confusion and frustration.

"Then marry me and thwart him for ever!" Hamlet replied swiftly, like one who delivers the winning thrust in a fencing match.

I scrambled from the bower and seized my cloak as if to flee. Hamlet followed me on his knees into the sun, which shone full on him. His tunic was open at the neck and his sleeves were rolled to the elbows. His black hair was tousled, his cap and rude leather shoes thrown on the ground close by. He smiled, his blue eyes sparkling, and I felt weak with love. I knew I would do anything he asked of me.

"Marry me, Ophelia," he said, reaching for my hands, which clutched my cloak.

I gasped, for he had read my very thoughts.

"I swear to you, my ambitions aim no higher than your heart,"

he said with feeling. The top of his head was level with my bosom, and I resisted the urge to bury my fingers in his hair. "If you were beside me, I would choose this grassy seat over Denmark's gilded throne."

My eyes grew wide to hear him renounce all desire for the throne unjustly seized by Claudius.

"In faith, I think you speak in earnest," I said slowly. "You will not wrong me, love?"

"I swear by heaven, though now I must be shriven for doing so! Therefore come, let us go and together lose our sins."

I let him take my arm. He led me to his horse and lifted me into the saddle. He mounted behind me, and the horse with its double burden carried us easily into the pathless wood as if it knew our destination. Leaves lightly brushed us as we passed, and birds flew before us, drawing us on with their calls. The trees grew straight, then arched overhead like the vaulted ribs of some great church, their stained-glass windows the green leaves dappled with golden sunlight. We did not speak, but breathed as one person.

We came to the tumbledown stone cottage where we had met before. There, a figure waited, dressed in a brown cloak with a hood. It was the village priest, brought there by Horatio to forgive, as he was told, a poor soul near death.

"I am he," said Hamlet, "who will die if this lady will not have me."

Then Hamlet instructed the priest, taking his Bible and showing him which passages to read.

"We will have the Song of Solomon, the praise of love," Hamlet said. Then aside to me he added, "I doubt the education of maids permits the reading of this scripture."

The priest took the Bible from Hamlet and considered the passage, stroking his bearded chin. Then he cleared his throat at great length before speaking. The thought came to me that he should be treated with a hot mustard plaster, but I chased it away as unfit for the solemn moment at hand.

"This book indeed is most fit for this occasion," the priest began, "for it expresses Christ's own espousal of his Church, who promises fidelity to her Lord."

Hamlet interrupted with an impatient wave of his hand.

"Save the preaching, good father. Make haste to marry us, and God will reward you." Horatio jingled the coins in his purse, and the priest nearly dropped his Bible in his eagerness to comply. He commenced to play his part with the zest of one who delighted in marrying secret lovers. If he suspected that it was Denmark's prince who stood before him, he did not reveal it.

"*The flowers appear on the earth; the time of singing has come, and the voice of the turtledove is heard in our land,*" he read. How aptly the verses suited the forest scene, I thought. "*My beloved is like a gazelle or a young stag. Behold, he comes leaping upon the mountains, skipping upon the hills!*" That would be Hamlet, my wild lover, I thought. The priest held the book in one hand while gesturing with the other towards the woods around us as if summoning this gazelle, which was no doubt some marvellous creature, a wonder suited to a tale of romance. My delight in the moment was so great that I had to close my eyes to hold back my joyful tears.

"*Let him kiss me with the kisses of his mouth, for his love is better than wine,*" the priest intoned, while Hamlet kissed me most tenderly. Though we stood in Denmark's woods, there floated as on a

breeze the imagined scents of the distant Bible lands: myrrh and aloe and henna and cinnamon. But Hamlet's touch told me that I did not dream.

"Yes, I will be married now," I whispered, consenting to myself before I would consent to Hamlet.

"*My beloved is mine and I am his. Set me as a seal on your heart, for love is as strong as death.*" With these words, a holy stamp was set on our desires. Hamlet had proved the truth of his love for me. He held my hand firmly to his breast, and my own heart beat with unaccustomed joy.

So Hamlet and I were married in our rustic attire, with woodland flowers to deck us. I said my vows believing that I would love Hamlet until my death. He also spoke his vows with evident faith, and Horatio was our witness.

That night at Elsinore no royal banquet celebrated the prince's marriage. But Hamlet and I feasted on each other's sight and touch, and we dared to sleep in his bed. As the clock struck the midnight hour, a loud knocking made me start up with fear. The door burst open, its lock giving way, and Horatio stumbled into the room.

"To the ramparts, Hamlet. It comes! It comes anon!"

Hamlet bolted from the bed without a word, seized his clothes, and disappeared with Horatio into the darkness.

Chapter 16

I lay like a still and silent effigy on a tomb in the blackness of Hamlet's chamber while questions coursed through my brain. What terrible thing would lead Horatio to disrupt our wedding night? Had our secret marriage been discovered? What was the meaning of his fearful look and his words, *It comes*? Was Elsinore being attacked? I listened but could detect no disturbance in the castle. Only my heart made a pounding sound I mistook for footsteps. No one stirred or shouted. Silence covered Elsinore like a heavy blanket.

I did not think it safe to stay in Hamlet's bed. So I dressed, and through the deep and unfamiliar dark, I crept back to my room and lay upon my maiden cot. I listened to the mournful calls of the doves in the stone crevices of the castle walls and envied the lowly birds who nestled freely and without fear.

When daylight broke, I arose and put on my yellow damask gown. I picked up some embroidery, but my fingers would not even hold a needle. I only gazed at the unfinished piece with its gillyflowers and pansies in blue and purple silk, while I whispered to myself, "I am Hamlet's wife." The words sounded strange and impossible. I began to doubt the prior day's events, as one would suspect a vision of the open heavens to be a figment of the mind. Had I merely dreamed our wedding?

I leaned on the window ledge and watched the morning sun contend with the fog. Its weak rays shone on the dewy grass and made the herbs in the garden glisten as if under a spell.

"Hamlet is my . . . husband?" I said to myself, the statement rising to a question as I recalled how suddenly he had abandoned our bed. Why had he leaped up and vanished, without a word of explanation, a kiss, or a promise to return? That was no good omen for our marriage.

Thus I plucked at my worried thoughts that stuck like burrs in my brain. When I heard a deep sigh, I looked up, startled to see Hamlet framed by the stone arch of the doorway. How long had he been standing there? Why did he not greet me?

"My dear, my love," I said, "I could not sleep for missing you." I spoke mildly, for I did not want to scold my husband on the morning after our wedding, though I thought his behaviour warranted it. "What was the matter —?"

I broke off when I noticed his unkempt appearance. His stockings were torn and dirty and his doublet unlaced. His face was pale and he shook as from the cold, though it was July.

"Why, my lord, you look as though you have been visited by a ghost!"

He started like a guilty man.

"Have you seen it, too?" he whispered.

"Seen it? What do you mean? Hamlet, you frighten me." I stood up to go to him.

"Come no nearer, Ophelia." He backed up and held me at arm's length.

"That is no proper way to greet your new wife," I complained.

"Shhh. No word of that now; be more secret."

"Why? Who will hear us in this room? My lord, you look so distracted. What troubles you?"

"I cannot tell."

"Trust me. I am your —"

"No! You should remain innocent of my deeds," he said with sudden feeling.

"What have you done?" I asked, my voice rising with fear. When he replied, his words were weighty and spoken with a grim resolve.

"Nothing yet. But what I am bound to do will drive a wedge between me and you."

"I do not understand, my lord. Pray explain your meaning," I begged. Did he mean to divorce me?

I leaned closer so that he could smell my rosemary-scented hair, and I put my hand to his cheek. He held it there for a moment. Then he thrust my hand away and shook his head once, twice, and then a third time.

"Do not push me away," I said, my voice choked with tears. "I am bound to share your fate, and you mine."

I could see him struggling with some inner force.

"Speak to me," I whispered.

"Swear that you will tell no living soul what I am about to reveal to you." His hands pressed on my shoulders.

"I will tell no one." Despite my confusion, I felt excitement, waiting for his revelation.

Then I listened in amazement as Hamlet related how he had gone with Horatio to the parapet last night, to the very place of our embracing. There the guards had lately seen a ghostly apparition. My skin prickled as Hamlet told how he, too, beheld the ghost of his dead father, armed from head to toe. How he followed the beckoning vision into the darkness despite Horatio's warning that it might tempt him to madness. How his very bones froze as the perturbed spirit revealed that he, King Hamlet, had been murdered.

"Murdered?" I echoed. "But how? And why?"

"Yes, murdered. Claudius was the serpent who stung my father," Hamlet said, agony in his voice and eyes. "The spirit told me how my uncle poured juice of henbane into his ears, curdling his blood and cutting off his life."

I remembered Mechtild's cabinet with its array of poisons, an easy means of evildoing for a villain with the heart of a fox. I thought of the bad blood between King Hamlet and his brother, the rumours that flew after the king's death, and my father questioning what I had seen.

"It is the crime of Cain, a brother's murder," I said.

"This Cain then stole his brother's wife and took her to his incestuous bed. And he stole his brother's crown — my father's crown and mine by right!" said Hamlet through clenched teeth.

"I thought you did not want the crown! Only yesterday, before we wed, you said you would forswear Denmark's throne." My protest seemed a feeble one now, and Hamlet ignored it.

"But beware, Claudius, for I have sworn by my father's sword to avenge his foul and most unnatural murder." Each deliberate word measured his firm intent.

I shuddered to hear Hamlet's vow. I struggled to understand the horror he described, a murder spurred by jealousy.

"This is the stuff of a strange fiction." I shook my head in disbelief. "How can you take the word of a ghost for truth?"

"I do not doubt the vision. Why do you doubt me?" Hamlet's words were sharp.

"Horatio may be right. The ghost may be a demon sent to plague your mind with grief," I said, trying to reason with Hamlet. "Can you be certain it does not deceive you?"

"It was the very image of my late father and spoke with his voice. Truly it was no demon!"

"But why must you be the one to seek justice? To kill a king! Do not think of it, but leave revenge to heaven!"

"I have taken a sacred vow, and vengeance is mine," he said, unyielding.

"Does the request of a ghost overrule the plea of a wife? How can your vow of vengeance usurp our marriage vows?" I demanded.

"You yourself have said, Ophelia, that we are bound to share each other's fate. This is now my fate."

Hamlet knelt before me in a parody of his marriage proposal.

"Swear to be silent and tell no one what you know."

"Why did you tell me this?" I cried, holding my hands over my ears. "I do not want the knowledge of this evil!"

Hamlet took my hands firmly in his own.

"Once you said to me, *Test me, I will not fail you.* I test you now. Do not fail me, my love."

I shook my head slowly, more in defeat than denial.

"Swear it!"

Feeling compelled, I swore, as he bade me, not to reveal his plan of revenge. My heart felt like a sack laden with stones and dropped into the deepest sea.

"With your help, I will not fail. Ophelia, promise me your aid!"

"What choice do I have?" I said, despairing. "I am vowed to you, and you are vowed to revenge." My tears began to fall, and Hamlet became again the very picture of a loving husband. He lifted his hands to wipe my cheeks and kissed my brow.

"Once this vow to my father is fulfilled," he said, "I will honour you. We will be known as husband and wife and you, Ophelia, will be my queen."

I should have been glad to hear those words and to think of myself as a queen. But alas, I would have bartered my high estate to be plain Jill to Hamlet's Jack.

"I will do as you bid me, my lord," I said, but my heart was deeply unwilling.

"Meet me at dusk tonight in the chapel," he said. Then he was gone, his feet soundless on the stones beneath them.

Chapter 17

All that day I was sorely troubled by what had passed between us. Was Hamlet mad, I wondered, with his talk of ghosts and murder? How had it come to pass that I consented to aid his revenge? Why had I taken a husband so little known to me? I needed the wisdom of someone who had long been married, such as Elnora. So I sought her out and, concealing my situation and my tormented thoughts, offered her a drink of cooling mint and fanned her while she sipped it.

"I have been reading a tale of a good wife severely tested by her lord, and it caused me to wonder about marriage. Did Lord Valdemar ever perplex you with his behaviour and seem a stranger to you?"

Elnora regarded me with surprise and, I thought, some suspicion.

"Why, what a peculiar question, Ophelia."

"I only seek some wisdom for when I shall be married," I said, affecting carelessness.

"Every wife wakes up one day and wonders if she has made a mistake by marrying," said Elnora. "So do husbands, I suspect. By then it is too late, for they are yoked to each other like oxen for the long haul."

I tried another question that might yield better advice.

"Was it difficult to bend yourself to the will of Lord Valdemar when you were first married?"

"A young bride will easily bend to her husband's desire. Ha, ha!" Elnora nudged me with her elbow. "But truly, Lord Valdemar was no different from any man. He thought to rule me, as will your husband one day. *I am the head,* he will say. So grant him that," she said with a shrug and leaned closer. "But remember this: the husband may be the head, but the wife is the neck, and it is the neck that turns the head which way she pleases."

"I hope my years will make me as wise as you are," I said with a sigh. I was sure that few husbands behaved as strangely as Hamlet was behaving. Moreover, I had little confidence that I could lead my new husband as Elnora had learned to control Lord Valdemar.

When evening drew near, I went to the chapel to wait for Hamlet. I sat on a bench in the arcade beneath the windows and further pondered Elnora's words. Since King Hamlet's burial, the chapel had been little used and dust motes drifted in the light beams. No ghostlike shapes appeared; the peace was undisturbed. I watched as the sun dropped towards the horizon and the glass of the sanctuary windows cast beams of blood red and royal blue across the dim nave.

I saw Hamlet enter, a large book in his hand. He had changed

his tattered clothes and was again dressed in his customary suit of black. His manner was calm, but he was deep in thought. He looked up as if seeking answers in the ceiling bosses where the arches met over the nave. My heart leaped to see the outline of his noble face, its beloved features unmarred by the morning's frenzy. I prayed that he had put aside his dire thoughts.

Then Hamlet looked down to find that he stood before the newly placed stone, beneath which his father was buried. He shook his head and the deep sigh that escaped him echoed like a wind in the empty chapel.

"Here I am, my lord," I whispered, beckoning from the darkened arcade. Hamlet whirled around to his right, then to his left, before he saw me and drew near.

"I did not mean to frighten you," I said, taking his hand between my palms and holding it gently to my cheek. But Hamlet was in no mood for such a mild touch. He grasped my head in both hands and kissed my lips with a passion, letting his book tumble to the floor with a great noise.

His hands and lips were warm and full of life, but at my back I felt a chill. I withdrew from his embrace and looked about. A stone effigy of some long-dead king stared at us with stern rebuke. In a painting dark with smoky grime, a naked Adam and Eve turned from the avenging angel. I felt their woeful eyes on me and shivered with unease.

"A cloud of long-dead witnesses marks our embracing," I said. "There is no privacy in this holy place."

"How is this chapel holy if no one prays here any longer?" Hamlet said. "We will sanctify it anew to the god of love."

"Though it is unused and empty, some holiness still clings to this place, and I would not dishonour it. So let us make love later in a better suited spot."

Hamlet did not contend with me but loosened his embrace, and his ardour cooled like an ember when the wind ceases to blow. His attention returned to his book, which he retrieved from the floor. He held up the large calf-bound folio, and I saw by its gilt lettering that it was a book of anatomy by Vesalius.

"I have been studying the question, Ophelia, of where evil resides in men."

His quick fingers turned the pages until they came upon an engraving of a man's body, its skin flayed open to reveal bones, the human heart, and a maze of conduits and sinews. I was both curious and appalled but did not hesitate to fill my gaze. Hamlet's voice grew animated.

"When I heard of my father's death, I was travelling to the university in Padua, where thousands come to study with the masters of medicine, to dissect every part of man and discover his secrets."

"Is this not a heresy?" I said with a gasp. "An offence against God's creation, to cut open a human body?"

"Those who say so are the enemies of reason and learning," Hamlet scoffed.

"Tell me what this signifies," I whispered eagerly, my finger tracing the intricate drawings.

"The vital spirit originates here, in the heart, and is perfected by the lungs, which inspire the blood with air," Hamlet explained. "In a wicked person, the vital spirit is corrupted, either by a disease of the heart or some disturbance of the organs or humours. And it leaves its mark within — a canker on the liver or a blackened spleen." Hamlet paused before coming to his point. "I wish to discover whether a surgeon, by cutting out the cankered spot, could restore the vital spirit to perfection."

"But does not evil, like an invisible worm, work inside the fruit, even while the fruit seems fair?" I asked. "One cannot remove the worm without destroying the apple."

"Yes, and as the apple's fair outside finally shows its inner ruin, so evil thoughts in time corrupt a man's features."

I thought of Claudius. Though I did not like his looks, I could not say his face appeared corrupted. I decided I would gently dispute with Hamlet, using my reason to stir doubt within him. Thus I might act as the neck that turned my husband's head away from his revenge, I thought, remembering Elnora's advice.

"If what you say were true, then the murder of your father would be written on Claudius's brow," I said. "But it is not. Perhaps he is innocent?"

The very mention of his uncle caused Hamlet to leap to his feet.

"Claudius! I could send his soul to hell!" He paced to and fro with growing agitation. "But why is it, I ask you, that in some men, thoughts of action never move from the head to the hand?" He regarded his own hand as if it were unknown to him.

"You are not such a one, Hamlet, for think with what haste you wedded me yesterday. I hesitated, and you spurred me to action," I said, hoping to divert him to thoughts of love. But Hamlet would not be moved.

"You mistake my meaning," he said.

"I do not," I said firmly. "I know you speak of crimes and evil deeds. But I believe that such dire thoughts are unfitting for the Prince of Denmark and my husband."

Hamlet did not acknowledge my opinion, but went on in his former vein.

"You must help me understand, Ophelia. Tell me, how does it happen that in some men, dark thoughts become deeds whose consequences shake whole nations?" he asked, pressing his forehead as though to force an answer from his brain.

I saw that Hamlet's mind was stuck on the idea of revenge, like a wheel lodged in a ditch. If I could force it back to the smooth highway of common sense, then Hamlet would be himself again.

"Answer me!" he demanded. "If there is already crime in the thought of killing, why does the deed of killing not follow with ease?"

"I do not know," I said. "Perhaps the hand of heaven stays your hand. Or perhaps reason is your master. It is only those who are ruled by passion who allow their thoughts of violence to become violent acts." I was determined to make Hamlet, by reasoned thinking, doubt his bloody course of action. And Hamlet, as if he followed me, picked up the thread of my thoughts.

"Such deeds of violence," he said, nodding slowly, "corrupt the body and soul of the man who commits them. But what if the act, though it seems evil, is the will of heaven? Then the supposed evildoer must be God's agent!"

"No! For the deed of killing defies justice, both human and divine," I argued with a fervour that matched his own. "Surely there can be no further debate about this truth."

"I will consider your words, Ophelia, for they are weighted with wisdom," said Hamlet, closing the anatomy book and ending our discussion.

My own mind was spinning from the ideas we had bandied back and forth so rapidly. Had I succeeded in dissuading Hamlet from revenge? I was hopeful, for I knew how great a store he set by reason.

"Meanwhile," Hamlet said, "we must find a way to divert the king and your father so that none may suspect our secret deed. Our marriage, I mean."

"I wish we did not need to hide it," I said wistfully, though I knew that it was wisest not to provoke my father and the king by the revelation. And I had grown accustomed to secrecy and the excitement of our plotting.

"In due time, Ophelia, it will come to light," said Hamlet, though he seemed not to be thinking of our love, for his face was grim.

"I have a plan, husband," I said brightly, touching his arm to regain his attention. "What better way to hide that we are married than to pretend a courtship? You shall pursue me, for my father believes that you do. I will deny you and seem the virtuous daughter, while we steal secret kisses from each other."

"Yes! We will feign love to hide love. This is a paradox I will act with pleasure," said Hamlet, leaning in to kiss my throat where my heartbeat was visible.

I held his head there and stroked it. I knew that I would break my unwilling promise to Hamlet. Like one who digs a tunnel beneath a fortress, I would undermine his revenge, not aid it. This game of love would distract him from his dire course.

Revenge was Hamlet's plan; this was mine.

Chapter 18

My simple device to deceive Polonius and the king grew, under Hamlet's hand, into a plot with ever more complex motives and uncertain ends.

"Remember, I will appear mad with love for you — or with a general madness — but I put on this disposition to divert and test them all," he said.

"Why do we test them?"

"To make a trial of their wits and an ordeal of their judgement," he said as if he relished confusion itself.

"Why must you put on madness?" I asked, not understanding his drift. It was late at night and we were in Hamlet's chambers. A single candle gave the flickering light by which we made our plans.

"Thwarted lovers are melancholy, and is not melancholy a form of madness? Let them doubt my mind to be sane," said Hamlet. He took a pen and paper and in a few minutes had penned a sonnet.

"Listen," he said, and began to read with a feigned accent.

His comically arched brows and broad gestures made me smile, and the injured look he then assumed caused me to laugh until I was weak.

> *"Doubt thou the stars are fire,*
> *Doubt that the sun doth move;*
> *Doubt truth to be a liar;*
> *But never doubt I love."*

"Not bad, but not at all good, either," I said. Indeed the hasty poem was lacking in music and halting in meter.

"*Never doubt I love* can also signify *Never suspect I love.* See?"

I nodded, though the meaning seemed obscure.

"It matters not, for I know you love me," I said with a coy tilt of my head.

But Hamlet was all business in his reply.

"This should serve my purpose well," he said.

"How, exactly?" I asked.

"If Claudius has done evil, his reason and judgement will be corrupted, and he will be deceived; that is, he will believe that what we act is true. If he is innocent, he will perceive the truth: that we only play at being lovers."

"You know it is not true that we are only lovers. We are married," I reminded him gently.

"Of course." He waved his hand. "It is the truth of our play to which I refer."

"And how should my father react?" I asked, doubting the soundness of Hamlet's reasoning.

"Polonius, not being evil but only foolish — I beg your pardon,

but he is a fool — will believe this nonsense is proof of my love," explained Hamlet. "Now, we will contrive for this poem to be made public and observe their response."

"It needs a letter showing that you intend the poem for me," I pointed out.

"Yes, of course. I did not think of that." Hamlet took up his pen again and wrote a letter hailing me as the *beautified Ophelia*. "You see, I should say '*beautiful* Ophelia', for with the mistaken phrase I suggest that your beauty is painted on."

I tried to smile, but I could not see how his purpose was served by writing of me this way. Hamlet sensed my hurt and looked up from his writing.

"I do love you, Ophelia, my own true wife."

"And I you, husband of my heart," I said, contented again.

"Remember, when we are in company I will play the languishing lover to your disdainful mistress; you will show me no pity, and yet I will fawn upon you. Let us see how they do greet this love."

"Yes, I will relish this sport," I said. "Like a pair of licensed fools, we will tweak the beards of our elders." I tucked the letter into my bodice and kissed him goodnight.

The next morning, I ran to my father, pretending distress, and told how Hamlet had come into my room while I sat sewing. I described his ungartered stockings, his unlaced doublet and his pale visage. Imitating Hamlet's astonished stare, I showed my father how he had gazed upon me. Seizing my father's hand and pressing it hard, I let him feel my desperation. I passed my other hand over my brow, as Hamlet had done. I nodded, sighed and backed away from my father, all without speaking.

"This was his manner exactly!" I declared. "He said nothing, but his movements spoke of some terrible suffering. It was most strange!"

My father reacted to my pantomime just as Hamlet had predicted he would.

"This is the very ecstasy of love!" He rubbed his hands with delight and pinched my cheek.

Thus encouraged, I played the false role of obedient daughter with even more zest. So well did I act my part that even my father, despite being schooled in deceit, did not perceive my mask.

"I have refused Hamlet's letters and avoided his presence, as you, dear Father, have commanded. Here, I yield you this, its seal unbroken."

He snatched the missive from me as if it were money. Upon reading the letter and the poem, he crowed with pleasure and, forgetting me, hastened to find the king. After a moment, I followed, half pitying my father for being so gullible. He darted this way and that, until he determined that Claudius was holding court in the great hall. While he descended there, fairly tripping in his haste, I took the tower stairs to the arcade, where I could look down and observe their encounter without being seen.

Seated on a dais, Claudius was speaking in low tones to Rosencrantz and Guildenstern. Gertrude leaned against him, seeming bored by their business. She held her crown in her lap and polished it idly on her skirt. I was surprised, for I had never seen her look so undignified. Then I was startled to see a guard in blue and white livery approach and stand at the king's side. His legs were spread and his arms crossed in a menacing way. One hand clutched a tall pike, the head of which bore a sharp point and a fearsome curved blade. I recognised the guard as Edmund. How fitting, I thought, that the villain had found a position as a mercenary soldier, paid to protect Claudius and fight his battles.

As the two courtiers prepared to leave, Gertrude leaned forward and called them back. I strained to overhear her speech. Her brow was creased with concern. She seemed to be begging Rosencrantz and Guildenstern for some favour. They bobbed their heads, eager to comply. I caught the words *friends of Hamlet* and *visit my much-changed son.*

A welcome visit that would be, I thought with scorn. Hamlet would pounce on these agents like a wolf on a pair of ducks.

My father rushed in, announcing the arrival of the ambassadors from Norway and promising, upon their departure, his own news of great importance concerning Hamlet's recent disposition. I had to smile at the means by which my father hastened his eventual reception. The ambassadors then swept in, wearing capes edged with fur and bearing maps and many papers. The chief ambassador proclaimed loudly that by his wise diplomacy, Prince Fortinbras's challenge to Denmark had been deferred. Fortinbras was no light threat, I knew, for his mission was to reclaim lands that his father had lost to King Hamlet in battle. But Claudius merely waved the men away and bade them join him in feasting that night. How poorly, I thought, the mantle of kingship rested on his careless shoulders.

Edmund escorted the ambassadors to the door, then returned to the king's side and stood, unmoving. My father stepped forward and began a speech as stuffed with words as an actor's coat is stuffed with bombast to make him fat. Finally Gertrude interrupted him and bade him come to his point.

"My liege and madam, I have found the cause of Hamlet's lunacy," he declared. "He is distempered in his brain — mad, that is, out of his mind, and the cause is this. I have a daughter, you know. Ophelia is her name. He, Hamlet, your son, is mad with love for — my daughter!"

Holding my breath, I observed Gertrude's response. She sat upright and her eyes grew wide with interest. I longed to read her thoughts. Would she be angry with me? Then she gave a little nod, as if she had known. Claudius, his face like a stone, revealed nothing.

"Have I ever been wrong in my advice, my lord? Have I ever said 'This is so' when it was not?" My father fairly cringed in his effort to convey an attitude of humble service. "Believe me, I have not."

Without replying, Claudius waved impatiently for my father to proceed. So with a flourish, he produced his proof, the letter. He read it aloud, pronouncing each phrase of the sonnet with elaborate gestures.

In my hiding place, I laughed, almost revealing myself. My father had seemingly swallowed the bait Hamlet had fashioned. Was the king deceived as well?

Claudius leaned forward and questioned my father in a low voice. I considered how canny my father was, despite being a fool. He did not show his delight that Hamlet was in love with me, for then Claudius might suspect his ambitions. Instead, I heard him assure the king that he had kept his virtuous but unworthy daughter away from the most noble prince.

"It is this denial," he announced, "that has plunged the prince deep into the melancholy of love. Fasting, brooding, sighing and disordered dress are its most infallible signs."

The king pressed his jewelled forefinger to his fleshy lips, contemplating his next move. My father waited with an expectant air. No doubt he hoped that Claudius would regard me as the cure to Hamlet's madness. Then he, the wise Polonius, would be advanced for his good counsel.

I, too, awaited the king's move, like his pawn on a chessboard. I wished and prayed to hear Claudius say, *Let him court her. There is no harm in it. I give my consent.*

What would Hamlet wish? Did he want to love me openly, or did he plan to use our love to cloak his darker purpose?

And what of Gertrude? She pressed her bosom against Claudius's arm and murmured in his ear. She smiled at my father, so it seemed she favoured us. But Claudius stood up, drawing away from Gertrude's touch.

"I will find where truth is hidden," he said darkly, tapping the letter.

My father was prepared. "I will produce a stronger proof. Let us set my daughter in Hamlet's way, and we will secretly observe their meeting."

Claudius, liking this plan, nodded in agreement.

Before their interview was fully ended, I was on my way to find Hamlet. I had to tell him of Claudius's doubt and warn him of their plan. I searched high and low until my breath grew laboured, but I found the castle strangely deserted.

Near the king's guardroom I nearly met my father head-on, but I hid myself in the shadows just in time. He scratched his head and muttered strangely as he passed.

"Still harping on my daughter! He calls me a fishmonger? He knows me not. Truly, he is mad."

His meaning was a mystery I had no time to consider.

A distant fanfare sounded, announcing an arrival at the castle. When I reached the gatehouse windows, I saw below a throng of lords, ladies and servants cheering and waving. A painted cart piled high with trunks rolled into the courtyard, pulled by a weary nag in bright trappings. A train of curious villagers followed. A young fellow somersaulted backwards from the cart to the sound of drumming, while a fat man wearing a red jerkin and bells on his trousers danced a jig, and another played the tabor.

The crowd parted to make way for Hamlet, who was accompanied by Rosencrantz and Guildenstern. How quickly they had followed the queen's instructions, finding Hamlet before I did! I silently cursed them, for I knew they would cling to him like leeches.

Hamlet greeted the young tumbler with an embrace and welcomed all the men, slapping their backs and shaking their hands.

A troupe of actors had come to Elsinore.

Chapter 19

The arrival of the actors put Hamlet into a merry mood. Indeed, everyone at court was cheered by the prospect of several nights of singing, juggling and playacting, for who did not wish to forget for a time King Hamlet's suspicious death and the strange marriage of Claudius and Gertrude? I also welcomed the chance to see the plays of this famed troupe, which had not visited Elsinore in several years.

Hamlet spent every hour in the players' company and I longed to join them. I imagined the lively scene, the actors and Hamlet devising a comedy to lighten the mood at Elsinore. Perhaps I would suggest something witty that would please them and be added to their play. Three times during the day I looked for a message from Hamlet, an invitation to join them, but I was disappointed. I spent the night alone and miserable in my room. Hamlet seemed to have forgotten me.

The next day I decided to linger near the place where the actors gathered and hope to gain Hamlet's attention. After some searching, I found them rehearsing in the castle foyer, Hamlet directing their actions. My father sat on a stool, observing Hamlet's behaviour while pretending to watch the actors. Seeing my father, I groaned inwardly. It would not suit our game for me to be seen looking for Hamlet. I fell back into the shadows to watch unseen.

"Suit the word to the action and the action to the word," Hamlet instructed his men, like a tutor before a class of students. "Do not overstep the bounds of nature."

The actors, poised in their places, paid close heed. They knew their fortune depended upon his pleasure.

"Come, give me a passionate speech," Hamlet directed, vaulting on to the trestle table that served as a prop. There he crouched and twisted his face into a fierce expression. "Give me the speech of Pyrrhus, who with arms black as his purpose, sought vengeance on old Priam!"

The first player, the one with the large belly, nodded with vigour and rubbed his hands, ready for action. He cleared his throat and spoke with a deep bass rumble as he stalked forward, his right hand raised and thrusting an imaginary sword.

"Well spoken," said my father, clapping. He fell silent as Hamlet glared at him.

"No, do not saw the air too much with your hand!" Hamlet ordered to the player. He was irritated and jumpy, like a firework throwing off sparks.

" 'Tis my sword, seeking its mark," the actor protested. Then Hamlet seized the player's invisible sword, broke it in half, and cast it to the ground. The players laughed nervously.

"You must temper your passion to suit the scene!" Hamlet said with an intensity that made the veins in his temples stand out. In a strange passion himself, he seemed desperate to control

the players, their every movement and word. "Begin again," he ordered, and this time, the player's sinister tone made my very skin prickle.

"Excellent, excellent," murmured Hamlet.

"This is too long," complained my father, wiping his brow with a cloth.

With a sudden wave of his hand, Hamlet ended the rehearsal. The players began to gather their props, but they were not quick enough for Hamlet. With growing vexation, he swore at them until they ran away like startled sheep, leaving their costumes behind. My father followed the actors, shaking his head.

Wary of approaching Hamlet, I hid myself beneath a nearby table covered with a long carpet. I was bewildered by the seeming madness that possessed him. Unlike our playful plot to deceive the king and my father, this device that Hamlet rehearsed had a dark and serious purpose I could not fathom.

Hamlet was now alone, or so he believed himself to be. He picked up Priam's breastplate and helmet from the heap of costumes left by the actors and contemplated them. This was my chance to come forward. I would behave as if I had happened upon him by accident. By his familiar smile, I would be assured of his love. Then I would warn him that Claudius and my father planned to spy upon our next meeting.

But I hesitated, and the opportunity was lost, for Hamlet threw the helmet to the ground with a curse. The clash of metal on stone echoed in the empty chamber.

"Oh, what a rogue and peasant slave am I!" he cried, seizing his forehead in his hands. His face was twisted with agony. Was he rehearsing the role he meant to play at that night's entertainment?

No, for he spoke to himself, not to an imagined audience. I held my breath and strained to hear his words. The speech of Pyrrhus had moved him greatly, and he lamented that the actor's passion was greater than his own. But I had never seen Hamlet speak and move with wilder emotion. He plucked at his chin and grabbed his throat. He called himself a coward and a dull rascal. He beat his fist against his palm and railed against a bloody, bawdy villain — Claudius, no doubt.

I was sweating and my own breath came in quick pants. With shame I realised that I was spying on my husband like some low, suspicious wife. But how else could I hope to understand this man who was so near to me and yet such a stranger? Moreover, I had trapped myself beneath the table and could neither approach Hamlet nor retreat without being seen. Nothing remained but to observe, in secret, his private and deep distress.

Hamlet's mood shifted, like a violent storm whose fury is spent. Now he appeared calm and deliberate, as if making a plan. I caught only the words *the play's the thing*, before he dashed from the room.

I crawled from under the table, bringing the carpet and the table down upon my head in my haste. By the time I freed myself and righted the table, Hamlet had disappeared and not even his footsteps echoed in the empty foyer.

Chapter 20

The following day the king performed his plot to test the cause of Hamlet's madness. I was an unwilling player but could not choose to quit the scene. Claudius led me to the stage, the broad foyer where Hamlet often passed and the very place where I had watched him instruct the players. My father directed me to return Hamlet's gifts and speak nothing that would encourage his attentions. Gertrude tended to my costume, smoothing my hair and tucking a sprig of fresh rosemary in my bodice.

"I do hope it is your many beauties that are the cause of Hamlet's wildness," she said, appraising my dress and figure with an approving smile. Her voice was low so that Claudius could not overhear.

"Thank you, my lady," was the only reply I could manage.

"I pray your virtues will restore him, that honour may come upon you both," she whispered. She pressed into my hand a Book of Hours with a tooled leather cover and gilded pages. "Keep this," she said before Claudius sent her away.

That honour may come upon you both. Did these words mean that she would approve our marriage? It occurred to me, with the force of a revelation, that since Hamlet was now my husband, Gertrude was already my mother. And, alas, I could acknowledge neither! When I raised my eyes from the book, the queen had disappeared.

Claudius and my father stood with their heads together, conversing in whispers.

Then my father turned to me and said with an impatient gesture, "Walk there, and read."

My reluctant steps took me to the centre of the wide foyer, where I waited, a hook baited to catch Hamlet unawares. At the sound of footsteps approaching on the stones, hope and dread battled within me. I saw Claudius and Polonius steal like silent ghosts behind an arras. Hamlet appeared at the far end of the foyer, conversing with himself in his new and strange fashion. I could not make out what he said. I bowed to my prayer book and read the words without comprehending them.

My thoughts were in turmoil. How would Hamlet treat me, coming upon this unexpected scene? Would he feign the role of a suffering lover, on the chance that we would be seen? Or would he be naturally affectionate, believing me alone? I saw him pause in his reflections, and as he approached me I tried to warn him with my eyes that we were being watched.

"The fair Ophelia," Hamlet said by way of greeting. "In your prayers, remember my sins." His black hair was wild and his eyes were darkly circled. I wanted to reach out and smooth his hair, but I restrained my hand and only returned his greeting.

"Good my lord, how does your honour?"

"Well, I thank you. Rosencrantz bade me come this way. I guessed I would find you here, though I was surprised at your choice of a messenger," he said.

"I did not send for you, my lord," I said evenly. Then I added, in a whisper, "It was Claudius." But I must have spoken too softly, for Hamlet did not seem to hear me. He turned and looked all about as if he sought something that were lost or hidden, then rested his gaze on me with an inquiring look.

With trembling fingers I lifted a bundle of letters from around my neck and held it out by its satin string. I felt the force of Claudius's secret gaze compelling me to speak the words I abhorred.

"Since you are here, I desire to return these remembrances to you."

He looked at me strangely. "I gave you nothing," he said lightly.

"You gave me yourself. Was that nothing?" I murmured, praying that Claudius and my father would not overhear.

"I did not. It was not," said Hamlet loudly and with an offended tone.

His words confused me and his eyes were veiled. Did he deny our marriage, or was he playing our game? What should I say now? The silence grew heavy. The stone walls seemed to press in on us. The arras that hid my father and Claudius barely stirred. Then, in the distance, a dove uttered a mournful note that resounded like the call of my own heart.

"My lord," I began, "you know you gave me these gifts, and

with them sweet and gentle words." How his denial pained me! "But take them back, for rich gifts wax poor when givers prove unkind." I thrust the letters upon him, that were such a treasure to me. He took them and threw them to the ground.

"Are you honest?" He shot the words at me like barbed arrows.

I flinched, wounded by the question. The last time we met, he called me his true and honest wife. How could he doubt my faithfulness? I gazed at him, bidding all my love to show forth in my eyes.

"Do I not seem honest to you?"

"Seem?" Finally he looked at me. Cold suspicion narrowed his eyes. "Indeed, you *seem* honest, but do you *act* so?"

"No, my lord — I mean yes," I said. "My actions are true." I felt confused and trapped by his tricky words.

"Ha!" he cried as if he had proved something to himself.

Why did Hamlet torment me without cause? I would bear it no more but vex him in return.

"I am not like your weak mother, who was false to your father, as you yourself have charged," I hissed in a low voice.

Hamlet's frown deepened and his dark eyes searched my face. "Are you fair?" he demanded.

What did he mean? He knew I did not paint my face, as other ladies did. I lifted my hands to my cheeks, inviting him to look upon what he had so often praised.

"I once loved you," he admitted, reaching towards me with his hand. Then he withdrew it and denied himself. "I loved you not."

The words fell, one by one, as lightly as leaves from a dead tree, and I was left, like winter's branches, bare and defenceless.

"Then I was deceived!" I cried, the words catching painfully in my throat. I began to doubt that this was my husband. Was the scene of our wedding in the woods a false dream? Was I mad?

"Get yourself to a nunnery. Go!" His face twisted in disdain as he retreated from me.

Stunned, I made no move to leave. It was Hamlet who was mad. The words he shouted at me made no sense. Why should he send me to a convent? This was surely some cruel joke of his.

Then Hamlet's tone shifted, and he spoke as if he summed up all the sorrows of life.

"Why would you be a breeder of sinners?" he wailed, rolling his words into a great wave of anguish.

"What sin have I bred?" I begged for an answer, riding my own wave of grief at his cruel rejection. "What have I borne besides this unjust abuse?"

My question was lost in Hamlet's fresh torrent. He raged against his birth. He said he loathed mankind, for men were all knaves and women deceivers.

Then, interrupting himself, he asked, "Where is your father?" He peered at me in suspicion.

"Somewhere. About. I don't know," I stuttered. It no longer mattered that he and Claudius were watching us. Yet perhaps Hamlet knew, and he was performing for their benefit. In this scene that I unwillingly played, I understood nothing of my role.

"To a nunnery!" he cried again, his voice echoing from the stone walls of the vast foyer. "Go! Or if you will marry, marry a fool, for wise men know what monsters you will make of them!"

"You have made yourself a monster!" My voice broke with tears I could not control. "Indeed, I hardly know you."

Hamlet did not reply. Instead he uttered a decree that came like a thunderclap out of the storm of his language.

"I say, we will have no more marriage!"

I sank to the floor, weak with disbelief.

"Would you disown me, your honest and true Ophelia?" I whispered.

"Those that are married already —" Hamlet paused, and I gazed up at him with a remnant of hope. He did not look at me, but with a loud voice, he cast his words wide about — "all but one shall live."

How reckless and foolish Hamlet was to make this threat, if he knew that Claudius listened! I saw that revenge was still at the front of his mind, overthrowing all thoughts of love. On my knees, I fiercely cried out, "No!" My cry echoed from the four walls before melting into silence. Hamlet slowly shook his head from side to side, and a look of great anguish twisted his features. I saw tears come into his eyes, then spill down the side of his nose, but he made no move to wipe them away. He stepped backwards, yet reached out his hand towards me. It seemed that he debated whether to hold me or to thrust me away.

"To a nunnery — go, and quickly, too. Farewell!" He spoke in a low and pleading tone. Then he spun on his heel and dashed away, leaving me alone.

Hysteria rose within me, and I cried out between sobs, "His noble mind is overthrown. Why, oh why did I grant him my love? I am undone!" My lament subsided into bitter tears that left me shaking as if all my limbs would come loose from my body.

Claudius approached with my father, who protested, "I still believe his grief sprang from neglected love."

"Quiet, Polonius!" Claudius thundered. "Love? His thoughts do not tend that way." His face flushed blood red. "No, this is a dangerous melancholy, and it bears close watching," he said as he turned his angry gaze upon me.

Chapter 21

Weeping, I leaned on my father and allowed him to lead me to my chamber, where I fell upon my bed. My tears did not stir his sympathies. He offered no words of pity, but rather poured the blame on me.

"It was your manner of giving back the gifts that caused Hamlet's temper to flare. Had you spoken more honeyed words, it would have awakened his ardour, not his anger," he scolded.

I would not let his criticism stir up my anger, nor would I be falsely meek.

"I am sorry, my lord," I said in a dull and sullen tone. Indeed, I was full of sorrow for myself.

"Perhaps his melancholy was due to some other cause than love," he said, frowning. "Could I have been mistaken in my judgement? Did you deceive me, girl?"

My injured pride rose up and made me defend myself.

"Hamlet did love me; he spoke and acted so. I did not lie."

Shaking his head in doubt and confusion, my father left me alone. Then the memory of Hamlet's words tormented me and my own tears wracked me until, exhausted, I fell into an uneasy slumber.

Later in the day, I awoke to find my father seated on my bed.

"Wake up, Ophelia, and hear me." He shook me, though not roughly, and clawed at his beard in evident distress. "I have been thinking, daughter. It was not wise of me to put you in Hamlet's path. My intent for your advancement, and my own, was foiled."

I sat up, astonished at his words, which were near to being an apology.

"Now the king's suspicions are aroused, and he is as dangerous as a baited bear. It is bad enough that Hamlet rages like a madman." He frowned and a dark look covered his features. "Keep within doors, Ophelia. I would not have you appear in public view," he ordered. Pressing dry lips to the top of my head, he departed again.

This time I was not inclined to disobey him. But despair, more than filial duty, made me compliant. I remained in my room for two nights and days, not caring that I missed the entertainments in the great hall. Elnora brought me a tonic of wild thyme and vinegar to ease my lethargy. I drank it meekly, but it curdled in my stomach. Nor could I eat anything without becoming ill. Elnora took my pulse, smoothed my brow, and in a wheedling tone tried to discover my woes.

"What have you done that your father bids me guard you closely?"

"Nothing. Truly, I am innocent," I said, but could speak no more without starting to weep.

"Virtuous though you may be, a reputation is a fragile thing, easily lost and often never regained," she said, searching my face as if looking for evidence there.

151

How her words touched my fearful soul! Was it true, that I was ruined?

"By heaven, I swear that I am honest. He lied to me when he swore he loved me!"

"Ah, a broken heart. It will mend," Elnora murmured. Her pity only made my tears spring anew, but my deeper secrets remained close within me.

On the second day, Gertrude summoned me. I went to her, though I was pale and weak.

"The king says my son is not in love with you," Gertrude said plainly. "I am sorry, but do not take it so much to heart. He is still young and merely plays at being a lover." Her words did not console me, for she spoke like a mother excusing the rudeness of her young child. But how could she know that Hamlet had been so cruel? She had not viewed the scene between us.

"Now go and rest, for you look most unwell," she said with a pitying look.

But my uneasy thoughts gave me no rest. Hourly I relived my encounter with Hamlet, and the memory brought fresh sorrow. Why did he despise me and mock my virtue? Rail against marriage? Deny he loved me?

We are knaves. Believe none of us.

Must I believe none of Hamlet's promises to me, neither his loving words nor his wedding vows? Did he also lie when he said *I loved you not*? I could not make sense of this Janus-faced husband who spoke false and true at once. Vexed and annoyed, I cried out to the absent Hamlet, "You are a knave indeed to abuse me so with your lies and promises! You are not worthy of my love!"

But as the scene replayed itself in my mind, my bitterness

relented. I imagined that I heard something beyond despair and anger in his words.

Go to a nunnery. Go! Farewell.

Was Hamlet somehow begging me to leave the court of Denmark? If so, why? Perhaps he did not want me to witness his revenge and its terrible outcome. Did he then command me to a convent for my safety, not to hide my shame? My questions found no answers, and my thoughts continued to torment me until I feared that madness was beginning to afflict my brain.

By the third night, I could no longer bear my solitude. I had to see Hamlet and speak to him. I donned my best gown and a high-necked bodice, not daring to appear immodest. I dressed my hair, tucking it beneath a silk coif embroidered with flowers. I joined Gertrude's ladies as they assembled in the arcade to make their way to the great hall for the evening's play. They laughed and prattled, anticipating the night's pleasures, while I stayed soberly quiet.

Cristiana was animated with excitement. Her cheeks glowed red and her bosom swelled over her tight bodice. A green jewel that just matched her eyes glittered at her throat. Despite her earlier disgrace, Rosencrantz had begun to court her again. Sometimes she favoured Guildenstern to make him jealous, and sometimes all three were fast friends.

"I hear that Lord Hamlet has created a most exciting entertainment this night," Cristiana said, speaking aside to me with her hand held to her mouth.

"I know nothing of it," I replied.

"But surely you do know what makes the prince so wild and mad lately. Some say it is his father's untimely death, while others blame his mother's hasty marriage."

"It is natural for grief to disorder the mind for a time," I said evenly. I would spend no more words on the matter, for I suspected she meant to bait me.

"Still others say . . ." She paused until I looked at her. Had she heard a rumour of our marriage? Then she loosed the arrow from her bow, a sharper one than I expected.

"They say that the prince is possessed with love for a woman who is unworthy of him."

My heart pounded, but I did not flinch.

"And I hear that she plays him false, which sends him into a frenzy," she said, searching my face for a sign that she had hit her mark.

Surely I betrayed my alarm, though I struggled to hide it. Because I had given Hamlet no cause to think me false, someone else must have planted the rumour that made him doubt me. I suspected it was his false friends Rosencrantz and Guildenstern, set on by my enemy Cristiana. I felt the blood drain from my face and feared blackness would overwhelm me.

"Why, Ophelia, you look pale as the moon," said Cristiana, now gripping my arm. "Sit down on this bench."

I pushed her away and she shrugged, sweeping ahead of me into the great hall. Now anger surged through me, restoring my strength. I hated Cristiana and her spying minions, and I was furious with Hamlet for believing their false gossip. This night I would confront him and demand to know with whom he thought I had been unfaithful, and when. I vowed, stepping into the great hall, that I would find out what had turned Hamlet's love to hate.

Chapter 22

Along the length of Elsinore's vast hall, torches flamed in their sconces. At the far end an area framed by curtains was prepared as a stage. Ladies in their finest gowns and courtiers with brimming cups of wine sought the best seats on benches, chairs and cushions. Some were already drunk, and the women's flushed bosoms drew their lovers' eager eyes and sometimes an unrestrained hand. In the centre of the room, a dais with carved chairs awaited Gertrude and Claudius. Some ministers of state stood by it, arguing and looking grim, but my father was not among them. Guards, motionless as statues, held their places while richly clad nobles and their ladies swirled around them. As I watched, one guard left his post to press a serving girl into the shadows. If she resisted, her cry went unheard.

The scene before me was a hollow pretence of grandeur and gaiety. It seemed that all love was nothing but lust, all seeming truth only a mask for lies. I thought of Hamlet's anatomy book that showed a skeleton laid bare beneath the skin, a grim reminder of waiting Death. I knew I would never again take delight in the painted glory of Elsinore. Yet what could I do now but play the game, pretend some pleasure? So I moved through the crowd, smiling coyly and nodding to my right and left. When I felt myself bump into an unyielding figure, I turned in some annoyance to beg his pardon. My hand flew to my throat and I stifled a cry of alarm when I found myself facing Edmund. He stood with his legs apart and his arms on his hips, making himself quite large. My eyes were drawn to his face, which bore a terrible, raw-looking scar that reached from his crown to his jaw. He reeked of sour wine, onions and sweat. I drew away as if from a scalding pot. But he had recognised me.

"Why, it is the prince's whore," he said in a low voice, sneering.

Even fear could not quench the rage his words provoked in me.

"You lie, you vile piece of carrion flesh!" I countered.

In reply he only threw back his head and laughed, making the scar flame on the side of his face.

I retreated from him in haste and, settling on a stool by the wall, tried to calm myself. Edmund's insult rang in my ears, still red with undeserved shame. Then I recalled that he had witnessed my father telling Claudius that Hamlet was mad for my love. The stupid man was only jealous, I decided. I would put him from my mind.

Then Cristiana's high, rippling laugh caught my ear. Turning towards the sound, I watched her greet Rosencrantz, who bowed as he doffed his hat, its feather brushing her cheek and making her smile. Seen from this distance, Cristiana seemed fair, even graceful. I weighed her spiteful words about Hamlet's love. What did she know of the prince's doings?

As if sensing that I watched her, Cristiana looked up and our

eyes met. She frowned and I looked away. I moved my stool into the shadows so that I could observe others without being seen by them. But Cristiana surprised me by appearing at my side in her stealthy way. She spoke in a low and urgent voice.

"Listen, Ophelia, if you value your life. Rosencrantz is in the king's particular favour now. He says that Claudius fears a plot against himself and suspects Hamlet. I would not for any price be a friend of the prince."

Before I could search her eyes, Cristiana had slipped away. I did not know whether to believe this intelligence, considering its source. Was she testing me, looking for a sign that I was in league with Hamlet? I had been, until Hamlet rejected me. *Go to a nunnery. Go!* His urgent bidding sounded again in my mind. Denmark had become a dangerous place, where lust led to murder and tyranny and bred new revenge. Perhaps Hamlet wanted me to leave this evil place, lest I be corrupted. But why commit me to a life of cold, forced chastity behind convent walls? I would not consent to that!

While I considered how poorly I would fill the role of a nun, Hamlet entered the hall. He wore black hose and a doublet of black velvet in the latest style, its breast and sleeves slashed to reveal a bright red fabric beneath. His hand gripped the shoulder of Horatio, who stooped slightly to him. He spoke intently to his friend, then laughed and clapped his back as they separated. Hamlet went to confer with the players, while Horatio approached me. I was not well hidden after all.

"How does my lady Ophelia? I — we — have missed you these two nights," he said, bowing. He spoke as if he knew nothing of my grief and mistreatment.

I blinked to stop my springing tears.

"I am the saddest of wives, Horatio, for my husband loves me not." I dared to speak honestly to the one person who knew of our secret marriage.

"What do you mean? I know he does love you," said Horatio, taken aback.

I glanced about me. Despite the press of people, no one heeded us. I spilled my sadness to Horatio, and it surged like waves against a stalwart dam.

"In the ten days since our marriage night was disrupted, my wedded joys are all turned to sorrow. Now Hamlet finds quarrel with my virtue, but there is no cause."

A blush spread across Horatio's face, for my speaking of the woes of marriage embarrassed him. But I was desperate to understand the reason for Hamlet's coldness, and Horatio seemed my only hope.

"I know there is no cause," he said.

And little comfort, I thought, from the modest Horatio.

"Horatio, you know his mind, if any man does. What of this ghost? Do you believe it?"

"I have seen it, but it did not speak to me. It was a harrowing sight."

"But was it real?" I persisted.

"It was not corporeal, to be touched like you or me," he said.

"Horatio, you speak like a philosopher who equivocates truth and falsehood," I said impatiently. "I tell you truly, I doubt this ghost. But the vision has made Hamlet mad. I do not know him any more."

Horatio paused, battling with his native discretion before

replying.

"Indeed, he does not govern himself, nor will he take my counsel," he said. "I fear for him."

A burst of applause made us look towards the stage. I held my breath to see one of the players juggle oranges while balancing on an overturned chair. Then a sudden fanfare of trumpets sounded and he jumped to the floor, bowing deeply as Gertrude and Claudius, arm in arm, descended the processional stairs into the great hall. We stood until the king and queen were seated on the dais. Faint clapping of hands and a few cheers sounded, but Claudius scowled and did not acknowledge them. He sat gripping the arms of his great chair. I considered that there could be truth in Cristiana's warning.

I saw Gertrude reach out to her son, beckoning him to sit beside her. He regarded her for a moment, then shook his head and turned away. Looking over his shoulder at his mother, with deliberate steps he crossed the room to my side. I saw her smile fade, and I drew in my breath at his unkindness.

When Hamlet reached my side, Horatio took his leave, saying, "In faith, Ophelia, I remain your servant." The kindness in his eyes consoled me briefly.

Now Hamlet knelt before me, like a spring coiled tight with energy. His eyes were bright with reflected light, his cheeks flushed. He grasped my hands, sending a spark through my body that made me feel weak with longing for him. But I was determined to remain aloof until I knew his feelings for me. Most of all, I wanted an apology for his cruelty.

"Lady, shall I lie in your lap?" He raised his eyebrows to highlight the question.

This rude request was no proper greeting.

"No, my lord, this is hardly the place," I replied, my voice sharp with rebuke.

"I mean, simply, may I rest my head upon your lap?" he asked, pretending boyish innocence. Did Hamlet now mean to play our game? How should I know his changing mind?

"Yes, my lord," I said, for this seemed to fit his role of pleading lover. I let him lean against me, certain that a gentle apology would follow. But instead he made a lewd joke about fair thoughts lying between a maid's legs. His eyes aimed at what he spoke of, and I pushed his head from my lap and turned away from him.

"I am fair, and I am honest. A maid no more, but your honourable wife," I said.

My indignant words found no response. Instead they were drowned in the applause that greeted the players as they stepped out from behind the curtains. Hamlet's play was about to begin. The torches were covered, save those near the stage, bringing darkness to the hall. I hoped the play would take my mind from his strange behaviour, but it offered nothing diverting or pleasant. The speeches were long and formal, and my attention wandered.

The play's the thing, Hamlet had said. So I struggled to attend to the tedious speeches. The player king lamented his impending death. His queen, acted by a boy speaking in a high voice, vowed never to remarry, while the king doubted her resolve. The action of the play closely resembled recent events at Elsinore, but I could not discern its purpose. Why would Hamlet stage scenes that rubbed the still-raw memory of his father's death and his mother's remarriage? I stole a look at the figures on the dais, but in the dim light I could not see the expressions of Claudius and

Gertrude.

Like a rude commoner watching performers on some village green, Hamlet commented loudly throughout the play.

"Your wit is keen," I assured him, raising my hand to silence him. In reply he took my hand and brought it to his lap.

"Then will you take off my edge?" he whispered.

I pulled my hand away. Offence and anger rose in me. Did he hold me as lightly as a whore that he could speak so crudely with me? A sudden thought struck like a blow to my belly, leaving me breathless.

Was Hamlet unfaithful to me?

Fearful doubts oppressed me. But boldness urged me harder. I could not let Hamlet cast upon me the burden of his sin. I would confront him with his own question, *Are you honest?* and observe his response.

Watching the play, I waited for an opportunity to speak. Hamlet's excitement mounted as the black-robed villain crept from the curtains, holding a vial and praising its rank and poisonous contents. I saw the villain pour the potion in the sleeping player king's ear and heard the gasps around me.

"Watch! Now you shall see how the murderer gets the love of the king's wife," Hamlet said bitterly.

I realised then that Hamlet believed it was a man's lot to be cheated by the woman he loves. I would make him see the injustice of such a thought, and I would discover whether I had been betrayed. I gripped his arm and when he looked at me questioningly I spoke with firm intent.

"Hamlet, my husband, this I ask you. Are you honest?"

At that instant, Claudius bolted from his chair and cried out

in a voice strangled with fear, "Give me some lights! Away!"

My question received no answer, for Hamlet threw off my hand and leaped to his feet. Guards drew their swords and surrounded the king. His attendants came running with flaming torches. Ladies and courtiers drew back as the king fled from the hall with Gertrude at his side. The players took refuge behind the curtains. They knew that a king's displeasure could mean their death.

I must have looked pale, too, for I found Horatio at my side, supporting my arm.

"Did you see, Horatio?" cried Hamlet with glee. "My uncle's guilt is now plain. The ghost is an honest one!"

"I noted it," said Horatio. "Be more discreet." He seized Hamlet's doublet, but Hamlet pulled away and clapped his hands, calling for music. The players scrambled for their instruments and struck up a wavering tune while Hamlet dashed among the crowd, trying in his manic way to restore their festive spirits.

"He has lost his reason and is possessed by his father's demon," I said in amazement.

"There is, he says, a reason in his madness," Horatio said, but with doubt in his voice.

"It was utter folly to have the players enact his father's murder in the presence of Claudius himself. How is this revenge?" I whispered, unable to hide my deep dismay.

"Violence goes against his nature, which is gentle and prone to thought," Horatio said, close by my ear. "He seeks revenge, and yet he shuns it."

While Horatio and I conversed as intimates, a new fear took hold of my mind. This night Hamlet had revealed, through the play, his knowledge of Claudius's crime. Cristiana had warned me of the

king's anger and suspicion. And Claudius had behaved like a man afraid for his life. He knew that I consorted with Hamlet. What if he began to suspect that Hamlet had revealed the king's crime to Horatio and me?

My eyes met Horatio's and I saw that his thoughts ran in the same course as my own. At once he withdrew from me, holding out his arm to prevent my speaking.

"Hamlet's play puts us in mortal danger," he said. "You should not seem my friend; nay, be a stranger. Therefore, go."

Chapter 23

After Hamlet's play broke off and the audience dispersed, worried and whispering, the night turned even more foul. Damp, foggy winds blew through the castle's every hall and chamber and whistled in the ramparts, sounding like faraway screams. Torches flickered and died until darkness reigned both within Elsinore and without.

For hours, sleep eluded me. Finally I rose from my bed to mix a calming draught. I made my way through the queen's gallery, where the tapestries with their wordless stories hung dark and silent. I passed the gallery and came upon the tower stairs that led down to the apothecary. An evil presence seemed afoot, and my skin prickled as if touched by invisible ghosts. At the top of the steps I froze. A dim figure cloaked in black approached. By his gait, I knew my father.

Fumbling with a key while trying to steady his candle, he unlocked the nearby door that led to the king's lodgings. It was used by Claudius and formerly by King Hamlet to come and go secretly from Gertrude's rooms. My father did not lock the door behind him, so I slipped in and followed him with silent steps through the retiring chamber and into the bedchamber. The vast bed of state, its curtains drawn back like the wings of a giant bird about to seize its prey, was empty. No doubt Claudius was ensconced in a secure room blazing with light and surrounded by his guards.

I longed to know my father's business here. He raised his candle, whose light threw shadows that trembled, for his hand shook. With another key he opened the door of a tall cabinet near the king's bed. I crept closer and concealed myself behind a bed curtain. My father appeared to be looking for something. The light played over the contents of the cabinet — a jumble of books and boxes, rocks, carvings and other curiosities. Then I saw in the corner of an upper shelf a small glass vial lying on its side. Its label bore a death's head, and broken red wax surrounded its unstoppered mouth. In its shape, size and smallest detail it was like the vials of poison I had seen in Mechtild's cabinet. Elnora's words on that occasion came to me: *Turn away, lest you tempt evil.* Should I turn away and forget the sight? Or should I go forward and satisfy my curiosity? *No, turn away from evil!*

I must have spoken, for my father whirled around and fell against the open cabinet. Books fell down with a thump and boxes crashed around him.

"What spirit is this? Who comes?" he asked in a tremulous voice.

Dropping the curtain and moving swiftly from the shadows into the candle's weak light, I reached for the vial. My fingertips touched it. Standing on my toes, I closed my hand around it. I confronted my father, whose face revealed his alarm and confusion.

"Is this what you seek?" I asked, opening my hand.

"Give me that, girl! It must be destroyed."

"No, I must give it to Hamlet, for it proves the ghost an honest one." I held the vial up to the flickering candlelight and saw that it was half empty.

"What nonsense do you speak?"

"No nonsense, but truth. Claudius is a murderer."

My father seized my wrist and the vial was dashed from my hand into the darkness.

"No!" I cried, falling to my knees and pawing the floor in vain for the lost bottle.

Then the far door of the chamber was flung open and one of the king's guards stepped into the room, a cup of ale in one hand and a sword at his side. Despite the dark, I recognised his shape, and when the light from a lamp behind him illuminated the hideous scar on the side of his face, I knew for certain that it was Edmund.

"Who's there? Declare yourself!" he called in a voice slurred with drink.

"Go, child, make haste to save yourself!" my father whispered, flinging his cloak around me.

"Is it Polonius? Who runs away? Halt!" growled Edmund, staggering forward.

I needed no urging from my father to run as fast as my feet and the darkness would permit. As I fled, I saw my father, his arms held wide to block Edmund while he declared in a torrent of words that he was doing the king's bidding.

I do not know if he spoke the truth. I never learned what became of the bottle, that evidence of Claudius's evil, and I never saw my father again.

Chapter 24

In the grey dawn of the following morning, a noisy and riotous dream disturbed my sleep. I opened my eyes to the sound of wailing and pounding outside my chamber door. Then Elnora burst in and seized me in her arms.

"No, no. Poor child, she must not hear it!" she murmered, covering my ears. I shook off sleep and Elnora's suffocating embrace.

"What has happened? Tell me!" I demanded, suppressing my rising fear that Hamlet was dead, slain by Claudius.

A dishevelled Gertrude appeared in the doorway, wringing her hands and weeping as Cristiana tried to comfort her. Seeing Gertrude, I was certain. "Something terrible has befallen Prince Hamlet!" I said in a rush, forgetting all discretion.

"I must speak to her myself. It was but a tragic accident!" Gertrude cried, pushing Cristiana away. "Hamlet stabbed at the arras in my room, thinking it hid a spy. Alas, it was your father, and now, oh! Now he lies dead."

Still lethargic from my sleep, I wondered if this was a game, a joke of Hamlet's.

"My father? Dead? Is this true?" I asked in dull confusion.

"Hamlet's intent was only to protect me. My dear son. Pity his madness! Poor Ophelia, forgive him and forgive me!"

With a loud wail, Gertrude fell to the floor before me. It was a dreadful scene, like something acted in a tragedy. Denmark's queen lay begging at my feet. Hamlet, my husband, had slain Polonius, my father. What mistaken revenge was this? Was all of nature's order turned topsy-turvy? I shrank into Elnora's arms, shaking from the awful news, unable even to speak. Weakened by the expense of her passion, Gertrude allowed Cristiana to lead her away.

I never saw my father's body. Claudius arranged a quick and secret burial, and I was not told of it. Nor was Laertes present, for he was abroad. I wept and raged against the king when I found my father was in the cold ground. Elnora tried to calm me by saying that Hamlet, not the king, was to blame, but I cried all the more. So she prepared draughts of barley water, lettuce juice and poppy seeds and poured them in me, promising they would bring sleep and forgetfulness. But nothing could make me forget the terrible truth that my father was dead at the hands of my husband. My dreams were frightful, full of ghostly figures that resembled my father. Sometimes the person of Death visited me, and I beat it with my fists and begged for it to depart, waking myself. I found Elnora's arms around me, and though I must have bruised her with my thrashing, she did not complain.

Though I had felt little love for my father, sadness like the constant tide swept over me, leaving me limp. Guilt mingled with my despair as I thought of how I had fled into the dark while he faced Claudius's guard, protecting me. I wondered if I had

misjudged his love. Then I would become angry that he had placed himself in danger. Why had he been in the queen's chamber, spying on her and Hamlet? Were his ambitions without any bounds? In death, as in life, my father remained a mystery to me.

I also despaired because Hamlet had not come to me. Fear and shame, I was sure, kept him away. I felt like one who dwelt alone in the farthest Antipodes of the earth, where the sun's heat and light could not dispel the cold and darkness.

One day I heard Cristiana and Elnora whispering outside my room and I crept to the door to listen.

"It is said that Hamlet cried out *I see a rat!* before running Polonius through with his sword," Elnora said. "The rats at Elsinore are not so big! The prince is surely mad."

"And then to hide the body while it was yet warm and bloody? He would not tell Rosencrantz and Guildenstern where it was, saying only that it was being eaten by worms," said Cristiana with a shudder in her voice. Was this gossip true? I did not want to believe that Hamlet could be so cold and remorseless in his actions. I returned to my bed, buried my head beneath my covers, and wept.

Finally I asked Elnora, "Do you think that Prince Hamlet regrets his rash deed? He should express some sorrow for my loss, at least."

"For what he has done, he ought to seek your pardon on his knees," she said with vehemence, then added, "I must not say such a thing, for he is still the son of my queen." She sat down beside me and took my hand. "The prince did try to see you the day after your father's death. But for your safety I would not let him pass," she said. "When he persisted, I said the door was locked

and the king alone held the key. Yes, that was a lie, but surely a pardonable one."

"Why did you prevent him? For I would have heard from his own lips why he killed my father!"

"Hear me out, Ophelia. When I told him to leave, the prince acted so desperate and mad, I said that I would call the guard or lay hands on him myself if he tried to touch you."

I sighed and buried my head in my hands. I could not blame Elnora for trying to protect me. Who could guess what Hamlet's intentions were? To beg my mercy, or to harm me? To declare his love, or to vent his hate? What did it matter now?

"Then he sent his man Horatio, who had a message for your hand alone. Suspecting his purpose, I gave him the same treatment."

"But Horatio is as harmless as a lamb, and a most honourable man," I wailed, full of regret. He would have brought truthful news of Hamlet, but now I would never hear it.

"So it is Hamlet's friend you favour! Perhaps he will try again to see you," Elnora said with a hopeful smile. But Horatio did not come again.

Nor did Gertrude visit me. Like her son, she remained silent and cold. With recent griefs of her own, she did not wish to share mine, I thought bitterly. Still, her abandonment added to my hurt. I even longed for my brother, despite his rudeness to me when we last parted.

Cristiana sometimes relieved Elnora, bringing me food for which I had no taste. A bowl of sweet figs, which I usually relished, gave off a sickly smell that turned my stomach, and I pushed them away. Indeed I had never felt so strangely before.

"They are not poisoned, if that is what you fear," said Cristiana, eating the figs herself.

I did not mind Cristiana's presence, for at least she held her tongue, perhaps out of respect for my loss. And I guarded my own, not wanting to give her matter for gossip. But one day she appeared in tears and needed no invitation to tell her woes.

"Gertrude is moody, for she and Claudius argue about the prince. So to cheer herself, she has taken on a new favourite, the niece of an ambassador. Now she will not let me wait on her."

Cristiana's worries seemed petty to me, but I had not the will to be sharp with her.

"To kings and queens we are like lutes," I said. "They play us for our flattering songs, and when we are out of tune or they are fretted, they cast us aside."

Cristiana fowned at me as if considering whether I had lost my reason.

"It is a manner of speaking, something a poet might write," I said wearily, waving my hand. The next day she came with the news that Rosencrantz and Guildenstern had left Elsinore.

"They are gone, their destination a mystery," she said in her usual manner of investing idle news with importance. "It is some secret errand for the king, which if they perform well—" she paused, waiting for me to look up. Her eyes were bright with pleasure — "Rosencrantz will be allowed to marry me!" She noted my surprise. "It is true. The king has promised, and the queen also gives her consent."

I had been about to say that Rosencrantz and Guildenstern were mere puppets, not men, but I thought better of it. I would let Cristiana have her happiness.

Then Elnora came to report that Hamlet had sailed to England.

"Wherefore?" I cried aloud, stunned by the thought that he had deserted me.

"It was the king's order. Most likely, for Hamlet's own safety." She looked at me carefully. "Lest Polonius's death be charged to him as murder."

"Murder! Who dares to call him a murderer?" I cried in horror. Elnora made shushing noises and reached out as if to soothe me. "Did Horatio go with him?" I asked, pretending calm.

"No; it was the king's pleasure to send Hamlet alone," she said.

Hamlet's sudden departure was strange and unwelcome news. My hope that we would be reconciled grew dim, and I was filled with new regrets. Perhaps Hamlet would have forgotten his hate, even taken me to England with him, had he learned of my new suspicion. Lately my breasts and belly ached, though my bleeding had failed to commence. My stomach was easily sickened. Perhaps this discomfort was due to grief. But might I be carrying Hamlet's child? Alas, now he would never know of it! Full of doubt and confusion, I decided to put this uncertain matter from my mind.

"Be thankful!" Elnora interrupted my thoughts. "Though his poor mother is distraught at his departure, you will have nothing more to fear from that madman." Thinking to reassure me, she frowned to see my tears start up.

I brooded continually over the timing of Hamlet's departure and its meaning. Had we but spoken after my father's death, he would know that I had seen evidence — the poison vial — that could convict Claudius, bringing a just revenge that would leave Hamlet's own hand unbloodied. I doubted that Claudius would send Hamlet away simply to protect him from justice in my father's death. Who besides the king could charge Hamlet with the crime? And Claudius would never dare to bring Gertrude's son to trial. He had a darker purpose in sending him away. Would he now take my husband's life?

Then I thought about my father's death, growing more certain that it involved foul play. I did not doubt that Hamlet's sword mistook its mark for Claudius. I supposed that Claudius had sent my father to spy upon Gertrude and her son in the bedchamber, knowing that the wild Hamlet would expect the king — and not my poor father — to be lurking there. How could loyal Polonius refuse the king's command? I thought of his distress after my scene with Hamlet in the foyer. He knew he had overstepped his ambitions in bringing Hamlet's madness to light, rousing Claudius's suspicions. He feared for himself and for me. Was my father, as he crouched behind the arras, yet another unwilling player in a drama contrived by Claudius? Did he even suspect his fate? Was Hamlet, too, an actor in Claudius's malevolent plot, forced into the role of villain on the stage of his mother's room?

I shook my head, unwilling to believe such machinations could be possible. Were my ideas as wild as Hamlet's ghost-driven revenge fantasies? Why should the king wish to kill my foolish and insignificant father?

The answer, I knew, lay in the discovery of the poison vial. The knowledge of it put my father in danger. Had he found the evil proof on his own, or was he sent by Claudius to destroy the evidence of the foul murder? Ruefully I considered that the truths I sought had died with him, and the only other person who could shed light on these questions, Hamlet, was himself a mystery. I wept to recall how he spurned me and abused my love, and I rebuked myself for trusting him. Bitterness rose in me at the thought of his rash deed, stabbing blindly at a curtain on the mere hope that it concealed the king. I beat my fists into my bed in helpless fury that I could not comprehend Hamlet's behaviour.

When this rage was spent, I considered my changed position at court. Fortune, which had favoured me, even to the height of marrying a prince, now turned her wheel to grind me down. I did not have a father's protection. Gertrude no longer favoured me. Laertes was away, seemingly unaware of our father's death. And my husband had abandoned me to uncertainty and grief. I was alone in the world.

That night I slept in fits, unable to separate dreaming from waking. I imagined my father's voice crying in his death throes. In my mind, a train of ghostlike figures flitted in the corridors of Elsinore, followed by the figure of Claudius, cruelly bent upon his evil course. I heard footsteps approach and pause outside my door. The iron latch rattled and the hinges creaked. I leaped up with a scream, threw myself against the door, and the heavy footsteps retreated.

When I opened the door the hall was black and seemed empty, but a familiar sour smell of onions and ale hung in the air. It had been no dream. I had been visited by the drunken Edmund. But why? Was his old grudge now grown into a jealous passion that he would satisfy? Or had Claudius dispatched him to do me harm? Surely Edmund had seen me flee the king's chamber on the night my father was killed. He would have told Claudius, who would then know that I was present when my father found the poison vial. Did he think that I now had the vial?

I knew that I was in grave danger. Shivering and sweating at once, I struggled to control the fearful frenzy rising in me. I wished that I were not alone, without a father or husband to help me. I wanted to flee, but knew not where to go. I wished that I were anyone but Ophelia, victim of mischance and evil.

Chapter 25

I have seen a hunted deer run from the open field and take cover in a shadowed bower, panting among the tangled bushes and brambles that she prays will keep her unseen. I knew I must likewise hide myself and deceive the hunter. I searched within my trunk for something to conceal me. I pulled out kirtles, caps and bodices, the gilded prayer book and a cracked looking glass Gertrude had given me. There was my father's cloak that he had thrown over me on the night he was killed. Within its folds I kept the miniature of my mother and the Janus-faced token Hamlet gave me that night we met in the maze. It was all I had left of my husband. Finally my trunk held two books I had rescued from the queen's hand and my book of herbal lore. My possessions were scant indeed.

I held up the cracked glass and considered my distorted image. I almost did not recognise myself. My face was gaunt, with deep and dark shadows beneath my eyes. My hair was dull, unwashed and tangled. I sniffed my skin and my smock and wrinkled my nose. I smelled like a creature unfit for the company of men. *What has become of me?* I wondered with growing alarm. I dropped the mirror and it broke in two pieces. *I am no longer my-self. Who am I?* asked the desperate voice within me.

I held up the rustic gown in which I was married to Hamlet, but laid it aside. I would never wear it again! Instead I took my best skirt, the one embroidered at the hem with intricate gold threads. I would have no further need of such proud finery. A plan was beginning to take shape in my mind. With some effort, using my hands and teeth, I tore the rich skirt to rough tatters. I donned this ruined garment and a bodice and took up my willow basket. I would test whether I might slip away from Elsinore under the guise of a poor woman, a mere herb-gatherer. Leaving off my shoes, I emerged from my chamber.

When she saw me, Cristiana cried out, "Look what she has done to her best skirt! Surely she has gone mad!"

Her reaction startled me. *Am I mad?* I wondered. "I have every reason to be so," I said as I passed by her.

Elnora stood up, peered at me, then gasped.

"Where do you think you are going, Ophelia?"

"Denmark's diseased," I said. "Let us find a cure."

They did not stop me as I descended the stairway and left the castle, but they followed at a distance.

The late September air only hinted at the coming cold. I wandered along the highway leading to the village and paused at the edges of fields, filling my basket with herbs and flowers. I watched as the men gathered wheat into sheaves and the women, with bent backs, gleaned the shorn fields. The only sounds were the swish of scythes, the shouts of men, and the cries of birds fighting for bits of grain. I took a dim, remembered pleasure in

being out of doors on so lovely a day, though it was clouded by my recent anguish.

My steps were slow, my way meandering. I noticed that Elnora looked pained and leaned heavily on Cristiana, who pleaded with her to return to the castle. I had not rubbed liniment into her joints for many days, and I felt a pang of guilt. Remembering Cristiana's horror at my appearance, I thought that the guise of madness might serve me well. So I danced a few steps, conversed with myself, and laughed at nothing. I pretended not to see them watching me. I hoped they would think that I had lost my wits through grief.

After a time, I noticed they no longer followed me. Pricked by a sudden fear in finding myself alone, I hastily returned to the castle by the main road where many people travelled. The late afternoon sun beat upon me. I thirsted, like the wilted flowers in my basket. My feet were bruised and bled from many small cuts. The dry grass of the fields had scratched my legs. I felt a perverse pleasure in these pains, for they distracted me from my misery.

But that night I permitted Elnora to rub the juice of violets and pansies on to my inflamed cuts to relieve the pain. I lay back limply, enjoying the touch of her fingers, and let myself be cared for. She fretted over me, saying, "Ophelia, I fear your brain is overheated and the vapours have made you ill. Do you know me?"

"I do; a dear motherlike creature you are. But I do not know myself."

The next day I prepared to go out again. I wanted to be seen and to test the limits of my prison. Moreover, I did not feel safe in my room at Elsinore, alone.

"Must we follow her again?" I heard Cristiana complain to Elnora.

"No, the poor girl is no danger to herself or others. And I fear my feet will not hold me up today. Let her go. Perhaps nature will help to cure her grief," replied Elnora sadly.

At Elnora's insistence, I wore a coif to keep the sun from my head and a large kerchief to cover my shoulders. I also put on shoes to protect my sore feet. I was not mad, for I had the sense to care for myself. I carried some bread in my basket. Avoiding the solitary paths, I gathered berries and ate them slowly so my stomach would not rebel. My garments trailed through brambles, and my feet stirred up dust that settled over me and parched my throat with every breath. Melancholy thoughts drifted through my mind. *What is man but dust? What is woman but a clay vessel, easily broken?*

In the afternoon, I haunted the busy outer courtyard of the castle. There I discovered that I could be visible to the world, yet unseen. I swept the ground idly with a bundle of rushes. I wove garlands of fragrant gillyflowers and fading hedge roses, draping them about me. I hummed ditties and murmured to myself and pretended to weep. These were the actions I expected a simple woman distracted by grief might display. I had never observed such a creature, for, whether from shame or fear, I had ignored the madmen and the poor who lived among us. So, too, was I overlooked. Those who passed by gave me a wide berth. I drew some brief and pitying looks, but no one spoke to me. Some boys threw rotten apples at me. They struck the pavement, releasing their cidery scent.

Then I saw Claudius enter the courtyard with some of his

councillors and guards. I froze in fear, like the deer when she smells the dogs. Claudius looked around him, frowning with suspicion, as if he sensed an assassin lurking. I dared not even lift my hand to draw my coif over my forehead. Claudius passed near enough to me that I could have flung my basket at his head, but he took no notice of me at all. Giddy with relief, I felt myself to be invisible. Boldly I called out to old men who resembled my father, but they hurried away from me, crossing themselves as if to ward off something evil. I felt dazed and weak but had no desire for food.

Young men in their stylish doublets and fine hose all reminded me of Hamlet. Strutting without care and bowing to the ladies, they sent my thoughts flowing to tunes of false love.

> *"Young men will do't, if they come to't;*
> *By Cock, they are to blame.*
> *Quoth she, 'Before you tumbled me,*
> *You promised me to wed.'"*

I found myself singing aloud this song that filled my head like the buzz of a trapped fly. But no one heeded me. The tune would not go away, even when I struck at the air with my hand. Was I mad? If so, how could I recall the words so clearly? I altered my voice and sang the man's part:

> *"So would I have done, by yonder sun,*
> *If thou hadst not come to my bed."*

I found myself weeping true tears, not feigned ones. Regret and remorse welled up within me. Why had I ever believed

Hamlet's false promises of love? I was a stupid girl, as my father said I was. I remembered him saying once, "Only a foolish man will wed her who comes easily to his bed."

"You were wrong, Father. Hamlet did marry me.... *Then he was a fool.*... I'll give *you* a fool!"

I found that I had spoken this conversation aloud and a man had stopped to take notice of my words. He carried a cloak and bundle like a traveller. It was Horatio. I saw by the look of surprise and dismay on his face that he recognised me. He began to approach me, but at that moment a crowd of people passed between us. Among them was Gertrude, attended by an aged gentleman and a young lady I did not know. At once I was angry that Gertrude should flourish while I was neglected and miserable! I longed to confront her.

"Where is the beauteous majesty of Denmark?" I found myself crying in a loud voice. The queen stopped, as if obeying my call, and the lady and gentleman with her. Boldly I drew nearer, but I did not look in her eyes. I gazed just beyond her, as Hamlet had once looked beyond me into the vacant air.

Gertrude stepped back and took the gentleman's arm.

"I will not speak with her," she said, turning from me.

"Her speech is nothing. She is a harmless creature," said the white-haired gentleman in a reassuring tone. The young lady-in-waiting looked on in horror. Was this the new favourite of whom Cristiana spoke?

"Do not fear to look on me, lady. All will be well with you," I said to the girl. No doubt the words frightened her even more than my wild looks.

Meanwhile Horatio had come forward and was speaking

quietly in Gertrude's ear. She nodded, and her expression softened somewhat. She greeted me, though with hesitation.

"How now, Ophelia?"

To that I replied with a song, to remind her of my dead father.

"He is dead and gone, lady,
He is dead and gone.
At his head a grass green turf,
At his heels a stone."

I wished to torment her, I admit. The look of alarm on her face pleased me. When she reached out, I retreated, spurning her tentative touch. I felt no shame to see her face cloud over with tears as she went on her way.

"Goodnight, sweet ladies, goodnight! Come, my coach!" I called as if I were Gertrude with all the court at my command. How grand it was to disdain the queen herself without fear of consequence! I waved away Horatio, who was about to speak to me. I decided I would not be ruled by anyone, neither a husband nor a father nor reason itself.

Absorbed in my rebellious thoughts, I did not mark where my wandering steps took me and found myself in the foyer where I had lately suffered Hamlet's rejection. I leaned against a column and let the stone chill my burning cheek. The wave of my defiance began to ebb.

"Cold, cold comfort!" I sobbed, feeling all my losses anew.

The sound of footsteps startled me from my sad reverie. The image of Edmund's scarred face flashed in my mind, and like an

animal, I was suddenly alert to danger. But I had no weapon, only my hands and my swift feet. Should I fight or should I flee? Before I could do either, I was seized from behind and I screamed. A firm hand was clapped over my mouth, and I fainted.

Chapter 26

When I opened my eyes, I found myself in a dusty, unused room that proved to be a large wardrobe. I was seated on a pile of old linens and Horatio's arm supported me. His face hovered over mine as he dabbed my cheeks and forehead with a cloth. I sat up and drew away from him, suddenly conscious of my dirty hair, soiled hands and torn clothing.

"What happened to me?" I asked, confused.

"Forgive me," Horatio begged with a look of distress. "I am sorry to frighten you. I needed to restrain you, for I did not relish a fight." Though he smiled, it did not erase the worry that creased his brow. "Are you hurt?"

I shook my head and smiled to show my relief.

"I am glad to see you, Horatio. I thought it was my enemy attacking me."

Horatio looked at me questioningly, but I felt too weak to begin to explain Edmund's menacing ways.

"My lady Ophelia, I grieve to see you so changed. I have been away, seeking news of Hamlet, or I would have . . ." His words trailed off.

"Good Horatio," I said hastily. "I am not as I seem. I wear this guise of madness for a purpose. I may put it on and take it off at will."

"So said Hamlet, but his deeds have made me doubt that." He looked at me warily. "What is the meaning in *your* madness?"

"Ah, I prove the common belief that a woman, being weaker in body and mind than a man, will easily run mad when stricken by grief."

"Your mind is as strong as any man's. Why seek to prove what is not true?" Horatio demanded.

"It is a useful lie. For you see that I, a poor, simple creature without reason, am harmless and hence safe from harm," I explained. It seemed clear to me, but Horatio was doubtful.

"From the scene I just witnessed, your madness makes you feared by Denmark's powers."

"What is there to fear from me?" I shrugged. "Denmark will shun me, and I will be alone as I wish."

Horatio would not let me win the argument.

"Learn from Hamlet's example that madness, like a lodestone, draws danger to itself!" he said as loudly as he dared in our secret room. "You deceive yourself. You are not safe."

I began to see the reason in Horatio's words, which gave me pause for a moment.

"Then I will leave Elsinore, with its dangers and deceptions, and live a humble life," I said. "I will find some obscure village or cottage in the woods."

"Claudius would not leave you be," Horatio said, shaking his

head. "For you are Hamlet's wife."

"He does not know we are married. Or does he?" I asked, suddenly fearful.

"I have said nothing. But it may be that Hamlet let it slip before he was sent away. We have seen how indiscreet his madness makes him. And Claudius has spies everywhere."

"There is no proof of our wedding. Words were spoken. That is all. And words vanish on the wind," I said bitterly.

"Still, you are a threat to Claudius; you will be found by him."

"Bah! He did not recognise me today though he passed within a stone's throw. That tyrant should not flatter himself that I would take his life, for I do not value it at a pin's worth." My words were sharp with scorn.

"I also have no care for Claudius's life, but I fear for yours," said Horatio.

"Look at me. I am nothing," I said, suddenly despairing again. "From nothing can nothing be taken away."

"You are wrong, Ophelia. But I am in no mood for scholarly disputation."

"My father was killed as if he were a rat. My life, too, is worth no more than a beast's."

"God knows, it is natural to mourn your father, but do not let your grief destroy your reason," pleaded Horatio, taking my hand in his.

"It is not my father's death that grieves me most, but the coldness of my husband." I cried, unable to stop my tears. My only comfort was a small one, the pressure of Horatio's hand upon mine.

"No one saw, as I did, the private hell Hamlet endured, know-

ing that he had killed, unwittingly, the father of his new bride," Horatio said, his intense brown eyes focused on me. "I know he went to you to beg your mercy."

I remembered Elnora's report of the desperate Hamlet at my door.

"He came to beg my mercy only? Or my love as well?" I asked, hope battling with fear.

"Would you have granted both?" Horatio's gaze was direct. I owed him the truth, though I did not wish to face it myself.

"I could forgive a man who killed my father by mistake, but love him as a husband? By God, Horatio, I do not know!" I cried, flinging up my hands. "I will go and live a solitary life; disappear and be Hamlet's wife — no more!" The final words broke from me like a sob and I rose to my feet, meaning to exit the scene.

Horatio blocked my way and would not let me leave.

"Ophelia, such a course would be vain and dangerous. Claudius is more canny that you know. For proof, I have important news from Hamlet."

News! This would stay me. Horatio reached into his doublet and produced a letter. He spoke with great urgency.

"Read here how Claudius sent Hamlet to England, not for his safety, but to his death! Rosencrantz and Guildenstern were dispatched as well, carrying letters to seal his doom. But he has escaped and foiled their foul plans. He writes that I should join him with as much speed as I would flee death."

Here indeed was a new twist. I scanned the letter, written in Hamlet's familiar hand. It brought me awake like cold water splashed on my face. Claudius's purpose was darker than I had imagined; he had ordered the death of Hamlet, his nephew and

son. I knew he had poisoned a king. He may have had my father killed. Why should he spare me? A foolish beast I was, to think that madness would shelter me. I was only making myself easier prey for the wolf.

"We were right, Ophelia, to fear the consequences of Hamlet's play. You and I are in danger if we stay at Elsinore. Escape with me and we will join Hamlet," Horatio pleaded.

"How will you reach him? He sails with a crew of pirates somewhere on the wide sea," I said, pointing to the letter.

"The messenger who delivered the letter will take us to him."

"Hamlet has spurned my love and hates me," I said. "That is the plain truth." I held up my hand to stop Horatio from denying this while I read the letter again. "He does not ask you to help me escape. Why would you take the risk?"

Horatio appeared to be struggling with himself.

"My loyalty to Hamlet binds me to protect you, his wife. Come with me, and I will take you to him," he urged.

Because Hamlet's letter made no mention of me, I would not consider this offer. I felt, like a stabbing in my bones, the pain of deciding to break from my husband.

"I cannot be such a dutiful wife as you are a friend. I will not go to Hamlet."

Horatio looked stunned. A long and burdened moment passed before he spoke again.

"You cannot stay here," he insisted. "You have dangerous knowledge. It is only a matter of time before Claudius takes aim at your life."

"You are right, Horatio. But how can I leave? How can you leave? Claudius's spies would pursue us."

Horatio sighed and ran his hands through his reddish curls.

"I have cast my lot with my friend, and I will contrive some way to go to him. But your safety is the matter now at hand." His eyes were dark beads almost hidden beneath his furrowed brow.

My fingers played among the herbs in my basket: rosemary, rue, the root of wild ginger and creeping thyme. Their mingled scents drifted in the air, rousing all my senses and sharpening my mind. Reason told me I could not keep up my ruse of madness for long. I resolved upon a different course.

"I will leave Elsinore, Horatio."

He sighed, relieved.

"But I will take my own way, alone."

"How?" he asked, looking doubtful.

"By a seeming death. A careful poison, my means —"

Horatio interrupted me.

"No, Ophelia! You must not despair and harm yourself!"

"Good Horatio, hear me out. I mean to escape with my life, though all will think me dead. I have a plan, but it needs your help."

"I do not understand, but I put myself at your service. I pledge my life to preserve you from harm," he said with the fervour of a new-made knight being sent upon a quest.

"I thank you, kind Horatio. I will trust you. For if I do not, I will surely die."

Chapter 27

In the dusty wardrobe where I plotted my escape, the shaft of light admitted by the narrow window shone like the bright beam of reason in a chaotic world. I bade Horatio memorise every detail of my plan, silencing his doubts and urging his faith instead. Soon he knew his role, my cues, and the place of our meeting at the end. There was no need to swear secrecy, for our trust was already deep. When we parted, he gave me his dagger and made me promise to keep it always on my person.

Though I trusted Horatio with my life, I did not tell him that I might be with child. I wanted to bleed, that my body might disprove this suspicion. Alone in my chamber, I slid Horatio's dagger from its sheath and fingered the sharp point. A crimson bead of my blood swelled suddenly and flowed on to the blade. I blotted the drops with a feeling of panic. With one stroke of such a knife my life would stream away — an undoing worse than the mere loss of maidenhood. And if I were with child, it would also be lost.

I had no inkling of what it meant to bear a child. I knew only that I would grow heavy with the burden, and one day deathlike pains would grip me until the creature sprang from my loins and cried to be cared for. What would I do then? I had not even the instincts of a mother cat. I wanted to flee both Elsinore and the unknown fate of motherhood, though such escape seemed impossible, except by my death.

The fear of death constantly tempted me to turn aside from my course that day. With each new hour I started up to find Horatio and tell him I would go to Hamlet. Then questions stalled my steps. Even if I were to regain Hamlet's love, what safety would I find with him, as long as he sought Claudius's life, and Claudius his? It would be better for me to stand on a hilltop while lightning bolts contended in the sky.

Then I lay on my bed and thought it would be more prudent to delay my plan, and meanwhile hold off danger with my dagger. After all, it was I who had counselled Hamlet against rash action. But this passive course held other dangers. If I were carrying a child, it would soon become evident, and Claudius might suspect Hamlet to be the father. Like the wicked King Herod, he would seek the innocent babe's destruction. For the child, if a boy, would be Hamlet's heir and a threat to Claudius as long as he lived. I could not wait and hope, praying that my grief-stricken body would resume its natural courses. I determined to waste no more time pursuing vain paths of possibility. I would act at once.

That night, I only pretended to sleep. Near the midnight hour, I arose, piled all my clothing on my bed, and covered it with a blanket. If Elnora should look in, she would believe that I slept. Wearing my father's cloak and carrying my basket, I crept from my room with silent and wary steps. In less guarded times, the darkened halls and galleries of Elsinore had stirred with furtive lovers and winking sentinels who let them pass. Now no one dared leave their quarters at night, and King Claudius's men watched like hawks, when they were not drinking or sleeping. I descended the tower stairs to the kitchen, where I put two half-eaten venison shanks in my basket. Unbolting a door near the pantry, I slipped out of the castle.

I emerged into the garden, where the dying stalks of vegetable plants leaned against one another and rustled like thin, dry bones. Scudding clouds raced across the moon and threw shadows in unpredictable patterns. I circled the castle mews and followed the hedgerows past the fields and beyond the village. From time to time I paused and crouched in the shadow of a wall or a tree to be certain that I was not being followed. Through the dark woods, I made my way by a little-used path until I came to the cottage of the wise woman Mechtild. I prayed she would be asleep, for I had no wish to confront her.

There was no light in the cottage. Even the moon had disappeared. Then from out of the darkness, I heard the deep growling of some beast. A ghostly white mastiff lunged at me, its huge jaws wet with foam. With a swift motion, I threw the venison to the ground and the dog fell upon the meat. As I expected, Mechtild now kept a vicious dog to guard against robbers.

In the garden, by the moon's light, I soon found the plant I sought. Its fetid dark green leaves spread like a canopy over the ground and its fruit, like a small apple newly ripened, lurked beneath. Wasting not a minute, I broke apart the earth with Horatio's dagger. I uncovered the thick, whitish root, forked like a man's legs. It was the mandrake, which fools say expels demons and makes women fruitful, but screams when pulled from the earth. I knew this to be an old wives' tale, a myth. The truth was that mandragora, made from the juice of the mandrake, brought a profound sleep. And I knew where Elnora kept the key to the castle apothecary, which held the other ingredients and tools I would need to make the deathlike potion.

Still, as I scraped the earth, I recalled the legends. I feared to hear a cry from the ground that would strike me dead. A cry that might awaken Mechtild. But I dared not delay, lest the mastiff finish eating the venison bones and start to bark. So I jerked the fearsome root from the earth. The only sound was that of a screech owl, near enough to startle me. In haste I covered the hole with dirt and put the root, leaves, and fruit of the plant all in my basket. I hurried back to the castle, thankful that the black curtain of night concealed me.

The darkness covered fouler intentions than my own. When I opened the door to my chamber, I saw that my blanket was slashed and torn, and the clothes I had mounded beneath it were thrown about the room. My trunk was broken open and the contents scattered. I was certain that my visitor had been the villainous Edmund, and I shuddered to think of his fury when he found me absent.

What I stole that night was my very life.

Chapter 28

The certainty that Edmund meant to kill me and the fear that Claudius was behind it made me constantly watchful. I did not stay in my room but begged Elnora to let me sleep with her, saying that I was troubled by dark dreams. Kind woman that she was, she agreed to let me share her bed. That night, I saw how laboured her every movement had grown, and I asked about her pains.

"All the woes at Elsinore of late have left their marks upon my weary bones. I feel as old as the mountains," she groaned, lowering herself on to the bed. "And you, Ophelia, have caused me naught but worry," she scolded, though gently. "I pray this grief of yours will soon abate and that you will return to your usual self."

I wanted to reassure her, but dared not reveal my plan. So I said, "Do not worry about me, good Elnora. My troubles here will soon end." She regarded me grimly, and I feared my words only increased her worries.

"Tomorrow I will tend to your aching bones. I have a notion for a new medicine, made from mallow roots that grow in the marshes," I said.

Thus satisfied, with a sigh Elnora gave herself up to sleep. While she snored like a giant, I sorted through her keys until I found the one that unlocked the apothecary. Covering my lamp, I made my way in darkness to the closet near the kitchen where medicines were prepared. I secured the door behind me and closed the gap beneath it with my cloak so that no glimmer of light would give me away.

With equal measures of excitement and fear, I turned to my work. I cut the mandrake root to pieces and put them in a flask of sweet wine to steep. How much juice did I need to procure a deathlike sleep? Too much poison would be deadly, but too little would also undo my plan. Uncertainty tormented me. I scanned the *Herball* and my other books, but their instructions being general, I was forced to guess. I worked in silence but for the crying of owls, the scrabbling of mice, and the knocking of my heart against my ribs. Sitting with my back against the door, I seized some moments of sleep while the mandrake oozed its essence into the wine.

When I judged that several hours had passed, I fished the mandrake pieces from the flask. With shaking fingers, I pressed the last drop of liquid from the root and poured it back into the wine. I added some crushed berries for good measure, and then I heated the mixture over a candle flame, reducing it to a thick, heavy syrup. By the first light of dawn, I poured the stream of black liquid into a small bottle and stopped it with a ball of wax. When I returned Elnora's key, she stirred but did not awaken.

Then I left the castle, intending to seek the mallow root I had promised for Elnora's medicine. What I found instead was a ready opportunity to enact my plan. On everyone's lips was the news

that Norway's Prince Fortinbras was marching towards Denmark, bent on revenging his father's defeat. Claudius would send his ambassadors off with a public speech that very afternoon. It was his habit on such occasions to walk among the people, with Gertrude at his side, to win their regard or quiet their fears. In this setting I would confront them and play my final part at Elsinore, with Horatio's help. It seemed that Fortune, by offering this occasion, showed she favoured me.

Moved with a strange excitement, I hurried back to my chamber and dressed in my costume of a poor madwoman. As a final touch, I wove flowers into my tangled hair. When I arrived in the courtyard, a large and varied crowd of gentlefolk, servants and shopkeepers was already waiting for the king. People sought out the patches of sunshine or huddled together, cloaked against the early October chill. I wished that I had worn shoes, for my feet were growing numb from the cold ground. I sat down and rubbed them with my hands. A stage hung with the blue livery of Claudius had been erected for the day's events. Despite the gay banners that flapped in the breeze, a sombre mood prevailed, for everyone was aware of the unwelcome prospect of war.

My basket was filled with garlands and herbs I had chosen with care for the king and queen. I had quit my search for the mallow root in my haste to return to the castle, and I tried to ignore the pricking of guilt, trusting that Elnora would forgive my broken promise. Shivering, I wrapped my mantle more firmly around my shoulders. From time to time, I reached into the pocket of my skirt, where I fingered the small bottle of potion.

With nervous, darting looks, I scanned the courtyard. I sighed with relief to see Horatio but shook my head as he began to

approach me. Still, he pushed through the crowd until he stood beside me.

"If you go now, you may slip away unseen," he whispered urgently.

"No, I cannot leave until I have acted my scene. Do you not remember our plan and your part in it?"

"I do, but I doubt that it will work. You will draw attention to yourself, which will increase the danger."

Annoyed that Horatio should remonstrate with me, I spoke sharply.

"The crowd will shield me. I must go forward. Trust me, and do your part!"

He relented with a sigh.

"I will keep my promise. May God go with you," he said, moving away with reluctant steps.

My own farewell, more gentle than my rebuke, was lost in the noise of a loud fanfare that signalled the king's coming. The councillors and politicians began their procession from the castle, followed by guards surrounding the king and queen. Claudius and Gertrude nodded to acknowledge their subjects, though few cheers greeted them and fewer smiles.

As they approached the stage, a sudden commotion broke out near the courtyard gate. Hearing shouts and loud cries, the crowd shifted its gaze away from the stage and began to surge towards the gate. Climbing atop a wooden crate, someone's abandoned seat, I saw the source of the tumult. It was Laertes, arriving at Elsinore.

A wave of happiness surged in me. Hope, so long crushed, rose up in my breast. My brother had come and would protect me.

From my perch I cried, "Laertes! Laertes!" but my words were like water thrown into the wind. Then my shouts died on my lips, for I saw my brother waving a sword. Behind him came a motley rabble of about thirty men armed with sticks and rocks.

"Laertes shall be king!" they called, and shouted that Claudius was a tyrant and a pig. At once the king's soldiers fell upon them, their swords smashing the men's wooden staves like twigs. Some in the crowd cheered, while others took cover as if they were afraid of being beaten, too.

"Who killed my father? Claudius? Tell me! I swear I'll be revenged for his death," howled Laertes.

Three guards seized my brother, who writhed, cursed and spat upon them. His ragtag followers scattered like seeds on the wind.

Sadly I realised Laertes, too, was mad, sick with the contagion of revenge! Rebellious and full of rage, he could offer me no safety, only greater danger. I had no choice but to continue with my plan and face its unknown perils.

I saw Claudius and Gertrude arrive on the stage. Immediately they were circled by guards who swept them towards the safety of the castle. My opportunity would soon be lost! I stumbled off the crate and pushed through the crowd with all my strength.

"Move! Away! Let me by!" I shouted in my haste to catch the king and queen. The guards followed behind them with Laertes in their custody.

The king's ministers, with confused and pitying looks, let me pass. Nor did the guards hinder me as I caught up with them. I flung myself against the door and slipped in before it slammed shut.

Startled by the crash of the heavy wooden bolt behind me, I whirled around. The guard who had thrown the lock wore a helmet that shadowed his eyes. A scar clung to the side of his face like a giant worm, and a cruel smile twisted his mouth. I felt like a deer that has just stepped into the hunter's well-laid trap.

Chapter 29

Inside the great hall there was only dim light, as in a theatre darkened for a play. Behind me was the malign Edmund, before me an angry Claudius deep in private conversation with Laertes. Gertrude stood a short distance away, her back turned to them. My brother's whole body trembled with agitation. I had hoped to confront the king and queen in the safety of a larger crowd. Now I had no choice but to play out my scene here.

Neither Claudius nor Laertes had seen me yet. The king gripped my brother by the shoulders and spoke intently. I heard him murmur, "I am guiltless of your father's death." It sounded like a lie to me, but I saw my brother yield his stiff and rebellious stance and hang his head in submission. The memory of him as a chastened boy stirred my affection and I let a little cry escape me. Gertrude heard it and turned, then seeing me, she gasped and drew Claudius apart from Laertes. They withdrew to witness our sad reunion.

My brother turned. As recognition slowly came to him, his face took on an expression of great sadness.

"Oh rose of May, dear maid, kind sister, sweet Ophelia."

Never had Laertes spoken so lovingly to me. His gentle words nearly overcame my hard purpose. I would have thrown myself into his arms, but caution prevailed in me.

"Can a young maid's wits be as mortal as an old man's life?" cried Laertes. In his voice I heard the suffering and loss that matched my own. I could not speak for the pain in my chest. So I began to sing in a thin and faltering voice. Laertes grasped my hands and looked me up and down. "If you had wits and could persuade me, it would not move me to revenge as much as the sight of you!" He clenched his teeth as anger flooded his being again.

In my brother's eyes I saw violent desire that dims the light of reason. I feared for him, and I knew I could not trust him. Alas, I must act as if I did not know my own brother. Sorting through the contents of my basket, I drew out some wilted stems.

"Here's rosemary; that's for remembrance," I said, tucking a sprig into his doublet, which had been ripped and smeared with dirt in the fray with the guards. I wished for him to remember me as I used to be, to remember how we used to study and play together. "And here's pansies. You know, that's French for thoughts."

Laertes cupped the delicate purple and white flowers in his palm and sobbed.

I turned to Gertrude. She looked away but let me approach her. Around her neck I placed a garland of aromatic fennel stalks, their flat golden blooms woven with drooping columbines. I did not expect her to know that the flowers were symbols of faithlessness, and that with my gift I rebuked her for being disloyal.

My heart pounding, I stepped up to Claudius. My entrance had undone his work of appeasing Laertes, and his face twitched with the effort of repressing his anger. From my basket I drew out a handful of leaves, which I crushed in my fist to release their strong odour. I reached for the king's hand, which he granted unwillingly, and I pressed them into the flesh of his hot, moist palm.

"There's rue for you — it is called the herb of grace," I said, meaning that he should repent his evil deeds. He could not know that the juice of rue healed the ache of the ear or that it was an antidote to the bite of venomous snakes. Thus shielded by madness and metaphor, I boldly told him that I knew of his crime: pouring poison into King Hamlet's ears. With my gift I accused him of being the serpent in the garden of Denmark. His face showed no comprehension of this, only hatred.

"And there's a daisy," I said, throwing a circlet of the white flowers with their sunlike centres. It caught on a point of his crown and hung there. With their bright innocence I mocked his evil and called him usurper. I knew that the daisy, a remedy for every ache, pain and wound of the body, was powerless to cure the disease of his rank soul.

Claudius's eyes blazed with angry humiliation. Gertrude put a hand on his arm to calm and restrain him. Laertes, too, protected me by his presence, for Claudius dared not seize me or abuse me, and thus inflame my brother more. His sudden return had been providential after all.

Judging my play to be at its end, I withdrew. Stretching out my arms in farewell, I sang,

"No, no, he is dead,
 Go to thy death-bed,
 He never will come again."

Laertes ground his fists into his forehead, shaking with grief, while Gertrude made an effort to console him. Only Claudius watched me. His pitiless and hate-filled eyes locked with mine as he threw the daisy garland to the floor and crushed it with his foot.

As I approached the door, which I knew to be locked and guarded by Edmund, I feared that the castle would remain my prison for ever. But to my surprise, the latch of the vast door lifted to release me.

Then I saw Claudius shift his gaze, nod deliberately to Edmund, and jerk his head sideways. *Follow her!* the gesture said.

I had tempted my good fortune too far.

Chapter 30

I left the great and gloomy hall of Elsinore for the last time. Though danger dogged my heels, urging me to hurry, a greater sadness slowed my steps. In the sunlit courtyard, people talked in scattered groups, perhaps weighing the moves of Fortinbras against the king's defence. The sudden tumult of the uprising had passed like a summer storm. But the storm still raged within Elsinore's walls, as Laertes' hot anger confronted the cold might of Claudius. Tears pooled in my eyes and blurred the world about me like rain.

My sadness gave way to colder fear. Had my play, like Hamlet's that touched on the king's murder, been a dangerous folly? Perhaps, but the scene had served as my small act of revenge. Though I could not deliver justice for the crimes of Claudius, nor rebuke Gertrude for being fickle, I did strike at their consciences. I played my scene of madness to its end so that my seeming death would not be doubted.

I crossed the busy courtyard towards the open gates of Elsinore. No one regarded me as I went, yet I felt that I was being followed. Was it Edmund? I dared not look, but I hoped that

Horatio attended close behind. I prayed that Death would not outpace my trusty friend.

I walked on, passing through the gates and on to the highway. A young boy chasing an escaped guinea fowl bumped into me, but he did not ask my pardon. A cart loaded with grain rumbled down the centre of the road, and I jumped aside to avoid being struck by it. I did not look behind me at the castle where I had been brought up to be a lady, favoured by a queen, courted by a prince, and then betrayed by him. When I felt the sun on my back, I knew that I was beyond the cold shadow of Elsinore's walls.

When I reached the crest of the hill, I left the highway and descended through the meadows to where the river flowed. Small creatures fled and flew before my step. Never again, I thought, would I pass this way with the anticipation of delight in Hamlet's company. With my hands I parted the rustling grasses and cupped the dying flowers' heads gently, saying farewell to all that I touched.

I followed the curve of the bank where Hamlet had watched me swimming when I was still a child. I reached the willow tree, the very picture of Nature weeping. Its branches grew upward in a graceful arc, then flowed to earth and trailed their ends in the water. I watched falling leaves skitter over the watery surface, which gurgled as it tumbled over the rocks. The river was swollen and wide from recent rain. I knew the water would be cold. Ducks bobbed among the cattails at the water's edge, and a king-fisher hidden in the bushes clattered its call.

My solitude seemed complete and the familiar natural sights brought me peace. I took the garlands I had made and hung them

about my neck, enjoying their sweet but fading scents. Though I knew that my enemy breathed at my back, waiting to strike, I trusted Horatio to protect me. I had not even brought my dagger, fearing to lose it in the water. I wanted to lie for a short while on the sun-warmed bank and revisit some sweeter memories before undertaking the journey to my unknown future. But prudence warned me neither to waste the time nor weaken my resolve by too much thought. So I reached into my pocket and drew forth the small vial. My fingers trembled as I uncapped it and poured the contents into my mouth. The dark, syrupy mandragora, sweet and strong, slipped down into my belly. I licked the last drops from the mouth of the vial and dropped it into the water, where it sank from sight.

I had only minutes, perhaps less time than that. I did not know how soon the mandragora would take effect. Waiting in utter stillness, I tried to feel the potion working. Nothing happened yet. I sought some pleasant sensation, a comforting memory, but felt only growing panic. Suddenly I feared the coming oblivion, and a desperate desire to stay awake seized me. What if these moments were indeed the last ones of my life? Should I confess my sins and pray, in case the potion proved too strong? My breath grew short as terror rose in me. I pushed against the earth, trying to stand, and found my fingers tangled among the cool, waxy leaves of the mallow plant that clung to the marshy verges of the river. Remembering my unkept promise, I pried its roots from the earth with desperate fingers and filled my basket, hoping that Elnora would somehow find them there. The effort made me weak, and I felt myself grow light-headed. Leaving my basket at the base of the willow tree, I climbed on to a strong limb that grew aslant the brook. Deep, dark water flowed beneath me, its rushing sound filled my ears. My head began to spin and black flecks like ashes scattered across my sight. Then it seemed the world was turning upside down, and the sky and water reversed their places, again and yet again. I clung to the willow branch but the mandragora that now filled my veins had stolen my strength. My eyes drooped, and I felt sleep take hold of me. Against my will to live, my limbs longed for oblivion.

The branch bent under my weight as if delivering me to the deep, and I murmured, "I come to you, waters of death and life. Take me from this world of madness and strife."

I heard a voice cry out "Ophelia!" at the moment that my numbed limbs released their hold and I fell into the water, blackness engulfing me.

Chapter 31

I struggled to open my eyes against the heavy weight of sleep. Dimly I saw a hearth fire casting its feeble light upon the uneven plaster walls of a small cottage. I was lying on a rough bed. I tried to sit up and found that my arms and legs would not obey my will. I did not know where I was. I saw bunches of drying plants hanging from the ceiling, and their scents mingled in the warm air. This was not the crumbling hermitage where Hamlet and I used to meet. Slowly the awareness came to me that I was in Mechtild's cottage.

I was not alone there. Someone was slumped upon a bench in the shadowy corner. My efforts to stir myself roused him instead. To my relief, I saw that it was Horatio. He came and knelt by my side, weary anxiety written in the lines of his face.

"I see that I live yet," I said. My voice sounded strange and distant. "But why am I here?" I had expected to awaken in the cottage in the woods, with everything ready for my journey. "Horatio, what has gone amiss?"

"Have no fear; you are safe. Once I freed you from the earth, I had need of Mechtild's skill."

"How did you know about this place? I have always hid my path hither."

Horatio smiled. "The wise woman and her love potions are not so secret as some ladies believe. Courtiers, too, have resorted to her remedies and advice."

A shuffling step announced the old woman herself, who entered the room with the white mastiff like a sentinel at her side. She regarded me with eyes that were sharp yet kind, set deep in her wizened face.

"The mandragora brought a sleep so deep, even I doubted you were alive," she said. "I administered an antidote but hours ago. Do not try to rise yet."

She went to stir a pot on the hearth, and the dog lay down near the doorway, obeying the command of her hand.

"I told her that desperation led you to seek death. I do not think she believes me. She knows that you stole the mandrake, but she bears you no ill will," Horatio whispered.

I was ashamed that I had wronged Mechtild. But my curiosity was greater than my guilt. Like someone who has fallen asleep during an exciting tale, I longed to hear the story's end.

"Tell me, Horatio; tell me everything that happened, for the potion has wiped clean the table of my memory."

So Horatio related how he followed me to the brook where he watched me drink the potion and climb the willow tree. He told how he raised the alarm when I fell from the branch, then ran downstream, plunging into the water to intercept my floating body.

"It was cold and the current ran swiftly. Your sodden garments enwrapped you and bore you under. I lost my footing and

came near to drowning myself. If not for the guard who heeded my cries, we would both have been lost. He lent his strength to pull your lifeless body from the brook. Together we bore you back to court."

"Oh, Horatio!" I cried, raising myself to my elbows. "That guard was close at hand to take my life. I did barely beat him to the prize." I explained that it was Edmund, my childhood tormentor, and described his menacing ways.

Horatio grew mortified to learn that he had been followed without his knowledge and by such a knave.

"Do not dwell on that," I said. "Think instead that had you not been near, he surely would have killed me. Now continue your story."

Horatio settled himself on a stool near my pallet, resting his elbows upon the thighs of his bent legs.

"The burial service followed swiftly, for many suspected you sought your death, and hence your soul was cursed."

"A quick service, that is well and good. A long and formal one would not have gone well for me, had I awakened too soon," I said with a smile. "But what matters is only that Claudius believes me to be truly dead. Does he?"

Horatio lifted his arms in a gesture of uncertainty.

"You know, Ophelia, that nothing is as it seems at Elsinore. Gertrude wept as the rites were read, and I believe her grief was real, but Claudius betrayed neither satisfaction nor sorrow." Horatio thought for a moment, then shook his head firmly. "There is no reason for him to think that you live. He saw your body white from the water's chill, and he witnessed your burial."

"How did Elnora take the news?" I asked. She was the only

person I regretted deceiving with my feigned death.

"The woman was most distraught. She anointed and wrapped your body, while weeping copious tears. She did not suspect that you only slept."

As the potion loosed its hold on my senses, it also released my emotions. At the thought of Elnora grieving for me, I gave way to tears. I knew she had washed my hair in rosemary, for the scent still clung to me. She had dressed me in my favourite gown of yellow damask over a petticoat embroidered in her own hand, her final gift of kindness to me. How her bones must have ached with the effort! As I wept, Horatio rose and stood apart from me, near the fire.

"Did you return my basket to her?" I asked. "I left it by the willow tree."

"No, I did not see it. Had you told me of it?"

I shook my head, for I had not.

"No, I am at fault. Horatio, I have thought only of myself."

"It is no sin to desire to live, no cause for tears."

"It is a most strange feeling, to be alive yet dead to everyone who has known me — save you, Horatio," I said, feeling loneliness well up in me. I tried again and succeeded in sitting up. Determined to shake my dismal thoughts, I wiped my tears with a corner of the soiled linen sheet that clung to me. It had been my winding cloth. I tore off a piece to carry with me, thinking it would make a good swaddling cloth for a baby.

Mechtild brought me a bowl of steaming broth and stood by while I sipped it.

"This will revive your limbs," she promised. "Mixed with saffron, to shake off lethargy and quicken the senses." Even as she

spoke, I felt new strength flow into my legs and feet. "I will see to Elnora's pains. Horatio shall deliver some medicine today," she said.

I marvelled at her wisdom. How had she read my mind and known my guilt? I thanked her and held the warm bowl in my hands.

"Go on, Horatio," I said, nodding for him to continue his tale. Mechtild would have to be trusted, for it would be useless to try and conceal anything from her.

"You were put into the ground late in the day, and I returned just as night fell to dig away the still-loose earth. I dreaded that the grave robbers would arrive first, for they do not respect those that are self-murdered."

I gasped, for I had not considered that I might be stolen from the earth and my body opened by robbers. I crossed my arms and shivered at the memory of Hamlet's book, with its drawings of the corpse laid open, the vital parts within revealed like a pirate's booty in a torn sack.

"Fortunately," Horatio went on, "no one was about then. But I could not rouse you from this deathlike slumber. I feared you were lost . . ." His voice faltered, and he took a deep breath before speaking again. "I brought you with all haste to Mechtild's cottage, and with the aid of a glass, we determined that you still breathed."

I felt my throat grow tight, hearing that I had indeed almost died. Oh, brave Horatio, who took such risks to save me from the water and from the earth! How can I ever repay your devotion?

"Were you seen in the graveyard?" was all I said.

"Indeed, I do not know." He rubbed his temples in consterna-

tion. "There may have been waiting thieves or a guard who saw me as I bore you away. Concern for your life overrode my caution. I am sorry."

"You have no cause," I said. "It is I who am sorry to involve you, an honest man, in deceit."

"Can this deceit be wrong, if it preserves what is virtuous?" asked Horatio.

"I am in no mood for philosophy, and I am sick of reason!" I cried, discontent rising within me. "I have betrayed Elnora's friendship. I have wronged you and Mechtild. I must leave here before you are discovered and come to harm because of me." I stood up and found that my weak legs supported me well enough. "I doubt that my life has been worth the danger you have endûred, Horatio. Leave me now and hide until you deem yourself safe."

Horatio laid a hand on my arm to still me.

"No. Wait," he said, "I have more to tell. Hamlet has returned to Elsinore."

Chapter 32

Horatio's words almost knocked me from my feet. My mind struggled to understand him.

"What do you mean?" I whispered.

"While I was in the graveyard, watching the sextons dig your grave, Hamlet appeared. Indeed, I was greatly surprised."

"You saw his ghost?"

"No, it was Hamlet, in the flesh and blood," Horatio said, defying my disbelief. "We embraced, then conversed. He was no ghost."

Why would Hamlet return to Denmark, I wondered, and put himself within the reach of the murderous Claudius? It was still more foolish to come without an army if he meant to challenge the usurper.

"His return can mean only one thing," I said. "He means to kill Claudius! Will he do it this time, think you? How did he seem?"

Horatio considered my questions before replying.

"He was both merry and sober. His thoughts ran upon the topic of death. Picking up a skull thrown out by the grave diggers, he said it was that of his father's jester, old Yorick. He mocked the mighty as nothing but dust. But he did not appear desperate, only somewhat melancholy."

"This coming is most unexpected! What happened next?"

"As Hamlet and I spoke, your funeral procession passed by with Claudius and some lords who were your father's friends. Gertrude strewed flowers. Laertes wept loudly over your sheeted body and rebuked the priest for his paltry prayers."

"When Hamlet learned of my death . . . how . . . did he . . . ?" I could not finish my question.

Horatio shook his head, and distress showed in his eyes. I steeled myself to hear that Hamlet jested about my death, or that he showed no care at all.

"Do not stint on the truth now, Horatio. Though it be painful, I will not hold it against you," I said.

Thus I heard, to my horror, how Hamlet, losing his composure, leaped into my grave to challenge my brother, who held my lifeless form. Then, like enemies, they fought with their hands at each other's throats.

"He grew quite mad. I had to break them apart, and it took much to calm Hamlet again," said Horatio, and he sighed heavily.

"Hamlet and my brother, who used to spar as playfellows! They traded mortal blows over my lifeless body?" Disbelief and anger warred within me. "They should have been as brothers, both fatherless and sharing their sorrows. Why must they rage, both of them, like madmen? There is no sense in it!"

"I do have this comfort to offer, my lady," said Horatio. "Hamlet cried out to the ears of everyone present that he loved you."

"But did he claim me as his wife?" I demanded.

"No, not in those words. But he said his love was more than that of forty thousand brothers."

"That is no comfort to me!" I said bitterly. "Let him measure his affection in numbers. What he calls love deserves not the name!" Thus I raged, but inwardly I hoped that Hamlet meant his words of love, and I wished that I had heard him speak them. My anger spent, I asked, "Does Hamlet know that I live?"

"No, he does not," Horatio admitted. "Seeing him so intemperate, I knew you would not wish it. And I would not break my promise to you."

"So you deceived your life's friend, for my sake?"

"It weighs upon me," he said simply.

"You have not done wrong," I said. "Hamlet does not want a wife, for I only hinder his revenge."

This truth hung in the air, and Horatio did not contradict it.

"I once hoped for Hamlet's return, but it comes too late," I said sadly. "I have already exited the stage. Now you must bear this news to him. Tell him that I had knowledge that could have aided his revenge, had he come sooner on the scene."

"What do you mean?" asked Horatio, bewildered.

"Fortune has been my fickle friend, Horatio. On the night Hamlet killed my father, she showed me proof of Claudius's guilt —"

"What was it?" He leaped to his feet. "Where is it?"

"— but she would not let me keep it." I held up my hand to stay Horatio. "Mechtild, was a vial of poison not stolen from you this April, before King Hamlet's death?"

Mechtild, who was following our conversation with keen interest, nodded.

"What substance was it?" I asked.

"Juice of henbane, black and deadly," she said. "Makes the blood thicken in the veins."

Horatio's eyes grew wide in wonder as he remarked, "Henbane! Hamlet told me his father's ghost did name that killing poison poured into his ear!"

"Indeed, Mechtild's word confirms that of the ghost," I said with certainty. "Now listen, Horatio. After Hamlet's play I followed my father to Claudius's bedchamber, where I found a hidden vial of poison. I held it in my hand and saw the drops of black juice that remained. Surely it was the poison that murdered the king! We contended for it, and the vial was dashed from my hand. Hours later, my father was dead, his secrets sealed for ever. It was no benevolent divinity who oversaw that night's black deeds," I said bitterly.

"And you could not tell Hamlet of your discovery, for he was immediately sent away," said Horatio, grasping the situation at once. "Yet had he known of it, he could have wrought a just and swift revenge. Alas, Fortune truly is a false dame!" He thought for a moment, then added, "But why was your father in Claudius's chamber?"

"He said that Claudius had sent him there. He must have known that Claudius poisoned King Hamlet. So to prevent my father from betraying him, Claudius set him up for his death at Hamlet's hand. This I cannot prove, though I am certain of it, for my father's death gave the king reason to send Hamlet away — to his own death."

Horatio seized his head in his hands, making his red curls wild and unruly.

"Oh, what a dense and knotty path evil treads, full of twists and turns! Yet what you say is most likely. Your father played a dangerous game and diced away his very life. And Claudius is a tyrant, whose each crime compels the next one, until he bathes and feeds himself with others' blood."

"You agree, then, that all these events are linked to one another?" I said, relieved that Horatio did not think me mad.

"Like pieces of an iron chain," he said grimly. "If only we could bind Claudius with it! Meanwhile, Ophelia, you are in greater danger than I imagined."

"Yes, and being powerless to bring him to justice, I had no choice but to flee Elsinore myself."

"Take heart, brave Ophelia, for you and Hamlet alike can boast that you have cheated Claudius of your deaths," said Horatio with spirit.

"Ah, but the game is far from decided in our favour," I said. "And my brother still plays, unwary of his foe. Laertes is vengeful and rebellious. You saw him threaten the king. I fear he may be the next victim."

I had dwelt so long upon Claudius's evil that I believed I knew what his next step would be. I took Horatio by the shoulders and spoke in a low and intense voice.

"Listen, Horatio! Hamlet slipped the first trap laid by Claudius, who even now lays another. I saw the king trying to win my brother to his side and persuade him that he was guiltless in our father's death. You saw Hamlet and Laertes fight in my grave." My voice rose with growing agitation. "Claudius is stirring my brother against Hamlet, to provoke him in turn. He stokes the fires of their rivalry, these two who threaten his rule and his life.

To keep his own hands unsullied, he will have Hamlet and Laertes destroy each other! Only you, Horatio, can stop them."

Horatio's eyes grew wide with understanding and his brow creased with firm intent.

"I will make it my duty to preserve Hamlet and your brother," he pledged. "But tell me, Ophelia, how is it that you, a lady of great virtue, understand Claudius's wicked heart?"

"I do not know. Perhaps by reading so much of greed and passion," I said, thinking of all the stories and tales I had savoured while disbelieving the wickedness in them.

At that moment, the old woman's mastiff rose from its sleep and growled, a sound like the rumble of thunder. The door to the cottage swung inwards with a creak of its hinges. A shaft of sunlight spilled into the dim room, and the cool morning breeze stirred the dust motes into life.

Outlined against the bright daylight stood the figure of Gertrude.

Chapter 33

The queen stepped into Mechtild's cottage, her leather-shod feet soundless on the earthen floor, the gold strands of her gown reflecting the light. I withered in her presence, like a flower that blooms too early and is frozen by a sudden wintry blast.

"I am undone! Horatio, we are betrayed," I cried, sinking to the pallet.

Mechtild fell to her knees with an agility that belied her age. Horatio stepped protectively in front of me. He bowed to the queen, but his hand touched his sword hilt as he made ready to spring at any sound or movement outside the cottage.

Gertrude dismissed Mechtild with a nod, and the old woman and her skulking dog disappeared. Then she addressed Horatio.

"I have come alone," she said. Horatio's tense body loosened, and he stepped aside, leaving me to face Gertrude.

"I am glad to see you alive, Ophelia," she said. I could not fathom what feeling lay behind her words.

"How . . . did you know . . . ? Why have you come here?" I whispered, confusion and fear tying my tongue.

Gertrude seated herself on a stool near me, erect as though she inhabited her throne, and began her tale.

"On the day that Laertes returned, vowing mayhem and revenge, the sight of you would have moved a stone to pity. You looked the very picture of ruined Nature, so wild and desperate that I feared you might harm yourself. I tried to follow you when you left Elsinore, but Claudius restrained me. Instead he sent a guard to watch you."

Did Gertrude know that Edmund meant to harm me? I watched her closely for some clue in her look or speech.

"He soon returned with Horatio, who carried you in his arms. A crowd followed, some in tears, others merely curious. The guard reported he had seen you take poison and cast yourself into the water. He testified with a certain satisfaction that you had 'done the job doubly', as he said."

"How did the king react?" I asked, unable to restrain myself from the interruption.

"Unperturbed, with no show of grief, for so a king ought to take news of a subject's death," she replied with the merest hint of bitterness. "He made a show of chastising the guard for not keeping you safe. Still, the unworthy sot remains in his service."

"I should have dispatched the villain myself!" Horatio muttered to himself. I wondered what reward Edmund had reaped by my death. But I would not waste my thoughts on him.

"How did you suspect that I still lived?" I asked the queen. I recalled how often she had observed me when I thought she paid me no heed. Had I underestimated her perception yet again?

"Horatio, I bid you leave us for a time," the queen said.

He bowed and left the cottage. Gertrude and I were now alone.

"Earlier, when you sang in the courtyard and would not meet my eye, I believed you were touched by madness. But when you bestowed the rosemary, fennel and rue, I saw that your actions were intentional. I understood you," continued Gertrude, "even if Claudius did not. I know you deem him guilty of many sins and that you accuse my failings, too."

Gertrude, then, had seen through my guise of madness. I was ashamed that I had charged the queen, my mistress, with so many faults. But I was also afraid. What had she told Claudius of me? I longed to know, but I could not speak.

"When I heard that you drank poison, I suspected you had procured a potion or brewed it yourself. Of course I knew where you and Elnora obtained your medicines and rare tonics. I used to visit the wise woman myself, before Elnora grew skilled with herbs." She paused, and I heard her skirts rustle as she adjusted her position on the stool.

"I coaxed you into ladyhood, Ophelia. I taught you the ways of the court, and watched you grow into a clever and learned woman." The queen turned her sharp gaze on me. "I did not believe you would destroy yourself from grief or rejected love. Thus I supposed that you only feigned your death," she said, with the satisfaction of someone solving a puzzle.

"It has been done in books," I whispered, thinking of the stories we read together.

"What was most natural and unfeigned, however," Gertrude went on, "was Horatio's look of desperate grief when he bore your limp, wet body, and his tears when the physician pronounced you dead. He is no actor who can dissemble his feelings."

She gave me a knowing, sideways look.

Despite myself, my cheeks grew warm. "You do not understand —" I began.

"Ah, but I do," she interrupted. "More than you realise. How is it that you do not recognise the signs of love? I know. Now your heart is shrouded, like a valley hidden in fog, but when sun returns and your sadness lifts, you will see clearly again."

Gertrude's own face clouded over and her eyes grew misty as she spoke.

"Although many thought you unworthy, I confess that I wished for you to wed Hamlet and become my daughter," she said, her voice barely audible.

Her words bathed my ears like a soothing balm. Had I not longed for years to embrace Gertrude as my mother? To have her approve my love for her son? I was sorely tempted to cry out the truth, to confess that Hamlet was my husband. But prudence and mistrust held me back. A long silence grew between us that I did not dare to break. The only sound was the popping of embers that glowed in the hearth. Gertrude seemed lost in memory. Finally she looked up again.

"So, to make my tale brief, my instinct led me here, to Mechtild's cottage. I hoped to discover the truth but, I admit, I did not expect to find you here. Now I will behold the resolution of this plot of yours and take my role in it."

My mind raced. Was she toying with me like a cat does a trapped mouse? Would she now betray me to Claudius, as a loyal queen and dutiful wife must do?

"As I came nigh to the cottage door, I heard your accusations of the king." Gertrude paused, and I held my breath. "I admit that I am frail in my flesh. I, too, fear Claudius." A deep, shuddering

sigh escaped her. "And I can do nothing to save Hamlet. He is lost to me, as well as to you."

She spoke as if she knew of our love. So I dared to admit it.

"I did love your son, most dearly."

"And he loved you. Like me, he found you witty as well as beautiful." She raised her eyebrows at me. "And ambitious, to set your sights on a prince."

"I have lacked humility, that is true. But it was you who taught me to reach so high," I said in my defence.

Gertrude only smiled slightly and shook her head.

"I do not have your courage, Ophelia, though I am a queen." She looked with moist eyes into the fire, which burned feebly.

"No, I only have it from you," I whispered. I knew I should not contradict the queen, but how else should she know I was grateful for the virtues she had taught me?

After a moment, Gertrude reached into the folds of her skirt and drew forth a leather purse, which she placed in my lap. It weighted my skirt like a heavy rock. Confusion rendered me speechless.

"I have loved you, Ophelia, though I treated you badly by deserting you in your time of need. Forgive me."

"I do. But you owe me nothing," I protested.

"I had hoped to spend this upon your wedding gown and feast. Take the gold now and begin a new life."

"But how can I ever find safety, if Claudius knows I am alive?"

Gertrude's grey eyes were wide with surprise and hurt.

"I promise that the king does not know that you live, nor will he ever learn it from my lips," she said, pausing to give weight to her vow. "To my regret, I have overlooked his crimes. But I will

abet his evil no more. I will not be accountable for your destruction, Ophelia. Perhaps that will atone . . ."

Her voice trailed away. For what wrong would she atone? I would never know.

"Go, but do not tell me your destination," she said. "I must remain ignorant of your whereabouts."

Filled with gratitude and relief, I seized the hem of her skirt, dusty though it was, and buried my face in its folds, crying like a sorry child that I had ever mistrusted her. She rose from her stool and lifted me to my feet, embracing me with a surprising strength. I inhaled deeply the scent of rosewater and lavender hyssop that for years hence would bring her image to my mind.

"I commend you to Horatio. He will be faithful and care for you," she whispered.

I did not try to explain that I would depart alone. I longed to speak, but could summon only words of paltry thanks and pale affection, so I left them unsaid.

"I find that my feelings . . . lie too deep for words, only . . . God be with you," I stammered, weeping now for the loss of a second mother.

"May God go with you, too, my would-be daughter, and may you soon have cause again for laughter," murmured Gertrude, while her tears fell upon my head.

Then, with the same regal bearing with which she entered Mechtild's cottage, she departed, closing the door behind her and leaving in the gloom her lingering scent and the echo of her rustling gown.

Chapter 34

Horatio found me in a daze, weighing Gertrude's purse in my hand. I told him of the queen's vow to keep my escape a secret. Together we counted the gold, which amounted to little less than a princess's dowry. I would have preferred a mother's love and a queen's protection, but since Gertrude could give me neither, her gold must suffice.

"Truly, she is a worthy queen," Horatio said, admiration in his voice.

"Yes," I agreed, tying up the purse firmly. "This heavy sum will ease my travel. Now I must make haste, for to delay any longer is to invite discovery."

"Everything is ready, stowed here since last night," said Horatio, dragging several bundles from Mechtild's cupboard and woodbox. "Though I wondered at some of your instructions."

Inside the bundles I found Gertrude's prayer book and the likeness of my mother, both wrapped in my father's cloak. I fingered Hamlet's token, his first gift to me, which I had sewn into an inner pocket. Horatio had also obtained some small valuables of my father's. I had planned to sell these to fund my journey.

"I thank you, kind Horatio. Let me repay your troubles," I said, reaching for my purse, but he stopped my hand.

"It was nothing. Your chamber was unattended, and your father's goods were unsecured, for Laertes was expected to return and claim them. Only your brother's mare, tethered nearby, may soon be missed. I shall attend to her now," he said with a polite bow and departed.

Digging further, I found what I needed first, the dagger and a looking glass. I set the glass on a bench and knelt so that the sunlight entering the small window shone on my head. Then without hesitating, I cut off my hair, watching with regret the long flaxen curls fall to the ground. At least the dagger was sharp and easy to use. Soon the hair on my head was no more than a finger's length all over. Next I slipped out of my damask gown and wrapped my shorn hair and my clothes in a tight bundle for Horatio to destroy. I tore a strip of my winding sheet and wrapped it around my bosom to flatten my breasts. From the sack of clothing Horatio brought, I pulled on an embroidered shirt that belonged to my father and a pair of worn breeches whose loose fit would hide the roundness of my hips. I donned a leather jerkin and laced it up. I fastened the stockings and admired the fine, double-soled shoes and their good fit. There was also a short taffeta cloak, somewhat shabby, and a simple, flat-crowned hat.

As I fitted the hat over my short hair, Mechtild entered the cottage again. She bade me join her at her cupboard, where her busy fingers darted through small drawers, poured powders into folded papers, and filled several small jars with essences and

extracts. I watched, wondering what her purpose was. Finally, she spoke, summing up her work.

"Chamomile and ginger tea for sickness in the stomach. A tea of raspberry leaf and motherwort to tone and strengthen the womb. And for when your time comes to be delivered —"

"Wait. How do you know I need these things?" I asked, amazed. "For I am not certain myself." I smoothed the cloth of my breeches over my belly, which was still as flat as any boy's.

"There are signs on the body long before the belly grows. Trust me." She put the herbs into a small cloth bag, one by one. "Fenugreek, with the cloverlike leaves, and tansy and goldenseal promote easy labour. Parsley and false unicorn root will bring away the afterbirth. And fennel or dill with chamomile will increase the milk."

I did not doubt Mechtild's wisdom, but I struggled to take for truth what I had hitherto only suspected. Then a sudden fear seized me.

"The mandragora —" I murmured, thinking of its deadly powers.

"You did not sleep too long. The child will be well. You are young and strong." She handed me the bag and left me alone, while surprise, relief and dismay stirred inside me like the ingredients of some strange, unsettling elixir.

I was still standing there, clutching the bag to my breast, when Horatio returned. Seeming confused, he looked around the small cottage, where there was no place for a person to hide.

"I know I left a lady here. What have you done with her, you false Jack?"

So rarely did Horatio jest that I laughed with delight.

"Go to, Horatio. You are not fooled!"

"Ah, you *are* Ophelia!" he laughed, pretending surprise. I watched him take in my shorn head and stare at my breeched legs. "You look like a man in all points. It is an excellent disguise."

"Indeed, I feel like some strange, newly made creature," I said, striding about the cottage with long steps, marvelling at how easily I could move without a petticoat, a kirtle and a gown clinging to my legs. "How delightful it is to be a man and free!" I said, tossing my head, which felt light without its heavy crown of hair. "But alas! I am every inch a woman, still!" I cried in a woeful voice, thinking of the life within my woman's body.

Horatio smiled uncertainly and held up a glass.

"Look at yourself," he urged me. I steadied the glass by putting my hands over his and peered closer.

"Why, I look like a brother to myself and Laertes!" I mused in wonder, turning my face from side to side. I had never realised that we resembled each other.

"Here is the final piece of your new self," said Horatio, producing a set of papers, a pen and a map. I studied them as I would a scroll that told my future. After I made a few small alterations, my passport seemed authentic.

"Now I am no longer Ophelia. I am Philippe L'oeil, bound for France under the protection of King Claudius," I remarked wryly.

"Where in France do you go? Please tell me, as your friend," said Horatio with a gently pleading tone.

I hesitated. I would be truly safe only if no one could find me.

"You must trust me; have I not held your life most dearly of late?" Horatio's voice held a hint of rebuke.

Truly, he had. I knew Horatio to be steadfast and incorruptible, the unmoving centre of a world that turned unpredictably. So I relented.

"The convent of St Emilion is my destination," I said, "because it is convenient for a traveller disembarking at Calais, and but a short distance from Amiens. Laertes told me he once travelled nearby and thought to find some sport there, but was denied. So it will suit my purpose, for it is remote and not a worldly place."

With this admission, the wilderness that would swallow me for ever became no longer impassable. I felt less alone, but little comforted, for an unknown and solitary journey lay before me still.

"I vow to hold your secret close, Ophelia."

"And do not forget your promise to keep Hamlet and my brother from destroying each other."

"I will work without rest to make them friends again."

"Remember, Horatio, that I am dead. Never speak of me as though I live." My voice began to break at the finality of my farewell.

"I promise." Horatio's voice was itself a harsh whisper.

"For if you ever break your vow, I will haunt you most terribly, being even now a ghost," I said, forcing a smile. The thought of Hamlet, made desperate by his father's ghost, passed over us as a hawk's shadow flies darkly over an open field.

"Is there no hope for Hamlet then?" asked Horatio, sounding despairing.

I pondered his question, which was edged with double meaning.

"May he hope I will rejoin him someday? May we hope he will return to himself?" I shook my head. "I tried and failed to

change his bloody course. There can be no peace or good in being yoked to a husband who is intent upon revenge. Therefore I go."

I stepped into the bright sunlight and tied Gertrude's purse securely about my waist so that it was hidden beneath my jerkin. I tucked Mechtild's bag of herbs into my pack, which I fixed behind the mare's saddle. With Horatio's aid, I mounted the horse and sat astride her, not sideways like a woman. My legs gripped her flanks securely and she started briefly. A sudden impulse moved me, too, and I reached behind me and pulled my cloak from my pack. I fumbled with it until I had torn open the hidden pocket. I took out the Janus-faced token, gazed at it one final time, and handed it to Horatio.

"Return this gift to Hamlet. Tell him you found it on my body."

Horatio regarded the painted image.

"How like my lord's own changeable moods these two faces are, one that laughs and one that weeps," he mused. "How like life itself. Why do you not keep it?"

"It might tempt me to look back," I said, fighting my tears.

"Then go now . . . . No, stay," he pleaded.

"I must go. You, Horatio, are Hamlet's sole hope now. Go to him. He may yet heed you, whom he trusts more than anyone living."

Horatio gripped the bridle to still my restless horse.

"You know the saying, Horatio, that the friend in need is a friend indeed. Be Hamlet's friend. And always be wary of Claudius. Your good heart is but a slight shield against his great wickedness." Then I laughed at myself. "I will be silent now, for I begin to sound like my father."

A brief smile played over Horatio's features. The sleek brown mare shook her mane and snorted, stamping a hoof as if impatient to depart. Still Horatio held on.

"May I go?" I said quietly.

"What if you lose your way?" Horatio asked.

"I will find the route, for I have a map."

"Let me come with you and see you to safety." Horatio reached up to grasp my hand.

I pressed his hand in return and pulled my fingers free. With the reins I turned my horse's head towards the wooded path.

"No, dear friend; this journey belongs to me. One who dies must cross the river Lethe alone. And though I live still, from this world I must be gone."

With those heavy words, I bade farewell to Horatio, to the country of my birth, and lately the place of love and its companion, loss.

Chapter 35

My journey from Denmark to the convent of St Emilion in France should have been the stuff of an adventurous tale such as Gertrude and I had often relished. It featured a heroine in disguise, a perilous sea voyage, rogues and brigands, and deep forests in which to become lost, perhaps for ever. Living such dangers, however, proved quite different than reading about them. In truth, the journey was not romantic but filled with misery. The *Seahawk* was a creaky, leaky vessel that I feared would sink beneath the waves at any moment. The brazen rats that ran throughout the ship would often wake me with their scrabbling and squealing. Being a cargo vessel, the *Seahawk* carried few passengers. Fearing to be recognised, I kept apart from them and from the ship's crew. Day and night, the wind whistling through the rigging and the mournful cries of gulls gave voice to my loneliness.

Most unbearable was the constant tossing of the ship, for it made me green with sickness. I chewed the leaves Mechtild gave me to soothe my stomach, but they were soon gone. Day after day, the sea battered the ship and my frail-ribbed body with a force that seemed intent on our destruction. Then she would relent for a time and push us with the gentle hand of a mother rocking a cradle, and, exhausted, I would sleep.

When the sea was calm I would venture above deck to consider the blue expanse of sky and the distant horizon, beyond which lay my future. It seemed on such a ship that I could go anywhere in the world. With Gertrude's money, I could marry a nobleman or buy a merchant's wares and set up my own shop. But I was already married and my husband yet lived, though he had abandoned me and I him. And I was with child, if Mechtild's eyes did not deceive her. I would continue my course for St Emilion as I had planned, a convent being the only refuge for a woman in my condition.

Upon landing in Calais, I walked like a drunken man on weakened legs unused to land. My mouth fell open and my eyes grew wide to see so many unfamiliar sights at once. Nothing in all my books about foreign places had described a scene like this before me. The noise of rumbling carts laden with creaking cages and barrels of goods, the smells of raw fish and flesh, and the cries of sailors and merchants overwhelmed me. I would not have been any more amazed to see many-headed animals, tall Ethiops as black as night, or mermaids thrown upon the sands by the tides.

I felt safe among the jostling crowds, but soon my fears returned. Claudius would surely learn of my escape and take it as proof of some guilt. Was the dock hand, whom I had paid to return the mare to Laertes before I sailed, a spy of Claudius? What if Horatio had been seen with me and forced to reveal my whereabouts? Or, refusing to do so, had been imprisoned at Elsinore, or worse, killed? What if Claudius discovered the missing gold?

If Elnora found my belongings to be missing, or Laertes reported that our father's goods had been taken, would my death be doubted and my plot discovered? I feared that every Danish ship that entered port carried the minions who would seize me. My worries tormented me like bad dreams, making life on land more perilous than on the sea.

So I determined to waste no time in leaving the city. But again I discovered that travellers' preparations are more easily accomplished in books than in life itself. Wandering through winding streets, I rued my lack of experience and the customs that kept women from the byways of commerce and public life. I did not know how to conduct any business at all. My courage failed me at the sight of a countinghouse or shop crowded with men, bartering and contending loudly with one another. Finally I came upon a nearly deserted shop where, despite being tongue-tied at first, I succeeded in pawning a cup that belonged to my father. The owner knew me for a Dane, but as I spoke French, I believe his attempt to cheat me failed somewhat. This merchant directed me to a dealer who sold me a serviceable horse. I paid his price too readily, but I was anxious to be on my way.

Leaving Calais, I kept to the well-trodden roads. Merchants and tradesmen with business in Paris passed me, galloping on much finer mounts. I often found myself among pilgrims, men and women both rich and humble, speaking many languages like the builders of Babel. In this company no one marked my own strange speech. My plain, mannish appearance also let me pass unnoticed. It gave me the liberty of looking at everyone about me, a freedom not allowed to courtly women. On the road and at the inns, I marvelled at the diversity of mankind, the people with their strange manners and outlandish clothing more varied than the bright array of flowers in all of Denmark's fields. I felt myself a small creature in a vast tapestry of nature. Soon I began to lose my fear of being apprehended.

I went on my way unmolested, even in the inns and alehouses, where, thanks to my disguise, I escaped the lewd attentions of men. Like all who travel, though, I watched for thieves. At an inn one night, I suspected a skulking, one-eyed man of having designs upon my purse. I did not relish using my dagger, so I befriended a jolly friar large enough to be of some protection. It was customary for several travellers to crowd under a single cover, but when the friar offered to share his bed with me, I let out a horrified cry that almost unmasked me. So I passed a sleepless night on the floor, thinking that the evening had provided good matter for the kind of ribald tale that delighted Gertrude.

I had not considered that travel would have so many discomforts. My legs and back ached, for I was unused to riding for hours. The days and nights were growing colder and in the mornings my clothes were touched with frost and my feet were numb. I did not know how to start a blaze without glowing coals, so I relied on kindly pilgrims to let me warm myself at their fires. I was soaked by rain and shivered until my clothes dried. Mud spattered my horse and stiffened my shoes. I could not undress to swim in a river or even wash my shirt without fearing that my true sex would be discovered. Once I paid dearly for a basin of water and a tiny solitary room in an inn so that I could wipe the dust from the road off my body.

Desperate and dirty though I was, the faint promise of happiness glimmered before me like sunlight through the ceiling of the

forest. There on the road, I felt the babe within me move for the first time. Mechtild had not been mistaken. Hope stirred in me, and I believed that Horatio would succeed in calming Hamlet's madness and reconcile him and my brother. Hamlet would bring Claudius to justice in a court of the lords. Then he would restore virtuous rule in Denmark as its legitimate and well-loved king. Gertrude would be released from her fear of Claudius and reconciled to her son.

So while I trod the dirty road, alone among strangers, my thoughts pursued a primrose-strewn path. I imagined that Hamlet, restored to himself, would learn from Horatio that I lived. He would seek me out and woo me again, begging for my love. Would I forgive him? What task would I set for him to perform? Once he had proven his worthiness, I would present the child to him and behold his joy. I would return to Denmark as its queen, beloved of Hamlet and the people. Despite my misery and the uncertainty of what lay ahead, the hope in my breast fashioned a life as heroic and happy as the tales I had read in books.

Passing through Amiens, I turned from the highway and travelled alone for two days. Or was it longer? A fever possessed me suddenly, and I felt cold and hot at the same time. My mind grew dazed and my senses dimmed; my thoughts scattered like dry leaves. My horse wandered from the road, and I could not lead him back. Then, searching for my map, I discovered that I had lost it. I cried out in despair, but the sound fell upon the mossy earth, unheard. Making a bed of dry leaves, I buried myself and slept there until unquiet dreams roused me again. I mounted my horse, determined to seek the path again. How had Laertes even found the convent? It seemed to have disappeared into the woods like an enchantment. I rode downhill, hoping to come upon a river that would lead me to a village where I could ask the way. But delirium came over me again. My hopes and my health both failing, I tore a page from my prayer book and wrote in French, with a trembling hand: *As you are a Christian, please help this burdened traveller to his intended refuge, the convent at St Emilion, and let the contents herein be pledged in return for sanctuary.* I signed the note "Philippe L'oeil" and thrust it into my purse, praying that it would be discovered and sting the conscience of my would-be robbers.

Though I had lost the path to St Emilion and was barely conscious, still I clung to my horse until he found the convent and stopped at its brass gates like an obedient beast led by an invisible master.

Chapter 36

When I awoke from my fever, I found myself wearing a clean linen shift and lying on a hard, narrow bed. It took up most of the tiny cell, far smaller than my chamber at Elsinore. At the foot of the bed, beneath a crucifix, was a rough kneeler, and by it I knew that I had reached my destination. On the kneeler rested my Book of Hours, the gift from Gertrude. I knew that I should rise and pray in thanksgiving for my deliverance, but I felt too weak to move.

My door creaked open to reveal a young nun with a round and honest face.

"Philippe L'oeil, indeed!" she said, seeing that I was awake. Her smile was playful, like a young girl's. She commenced talking at once, not waiting for an invitation.

"Your coming has caused a stir such as we have never known! A young man, looking like death, slumped over his starving horse! At first Sister Marguerite would not open the gate. But Mother Ermentrude, our prioress, insisted that we must aid the poor fellow. Sister Angelina, who once had a husband, was charged with undressing and cleaning him. Her. You, that is." She laughed.

"Angelina cried out and nearly fainted upon discovering your true sex. We were all most astonished." She put her hand to her face and raised her eyebrows, delighting in her tale.

"Your purse and the note within aroused still greater interest. We all talk of it in chapter, where we meet and study, and everyone has a different explanation," she said. She sat on the edge of my bed and leaned close, her brown eyes bright with curiosity. "Who are you, and why have you come here?"

I decided to say little until I knew for certain that I was safe.

"I do not understand everything. I am still unwell," I said, hearing the contrast between my rough, foreign accent and her lilting, native one. I closed my eyes to make my point.

She sprang away and began to apologise.

"I am sorry! I was so pleased to find you awake at last. I will go now, but you must drink this water and eat some bread. Shall I bring meat?" She gestured to the tray.

I nodded, for my hunger had returned. She smiled and turned to go, but just before she disappeared, she gave a little laugh, pointed to herself, and said she was called Sister Isabel.

Every day, Isabel came, bright with expectation. Though I smiled to see her and ate the food she brought, I did not satisfy her desire for conversation, so she soon left again. I spent days lost in my thoughts. It had been barely three months since Hamlet and I exchanged our vows in the wood, but it felt like years had passed. Outside the narrow window of my convent cell, leaves of linden and oak turned gold and brown and red and fell to the ground with every gust of wind. Soon the trees would be left naked, their branches like skeletons revealed against the sky.

I felt a oneness with the trees that changed their leafy vestments with the seasons. I asked myself Isabel's constant question: *Who are you?* I had been my father's rowdy daughter, then the queen's favoured lady-in-waiting. Later, a shepherd girl in a homespun frock, weaving garlands for her lover. Then a secret wife. Too soon a grieving one, wearing rags like a madwoman. For a time, a free young man striding in breeches and travelling alone. These were but roles I acted. Who was the true Ophelia?

I had wanted to be the author of my tale, not merely a player in Hamlet's drama or a pawn in Claudius's deadly game. But what had I gained in devising my own death and escaping from Elsinore? An unfamiliar life, hemmed about with secrets. A doubtful future, containing only one certainty: that I would become a mother, a role for which I had no earthly preparation. What would become of us — my little girl or boy and its ignorant mother? What if I did not love the child who would remind me of my greatest grief, the loss of its father's love?

I did not want to face these questions that thrust themselves on me. Instead, I dwelled in the happier days of my past. When I heard footsteps in the hall or a knock at my door, I remembered Hamlet coming into my room, his blue eyes flashing with wit, mischief, or desire. When the sun spilled through my window, its weak warmth made me think of the sunny gardens where, hidden behind the tall foxgloves, Hamlet and I had embraced as lovers not yet troubled or torn apart by madness.

One evening as I stoked this memory like a fire against November's chill, a knock sounded at my door. I opened it to admit Isabel. Her eyes shone and her step was quick and stealthy. In her hand she carried a letter.

"A white-haired man came to the gate bearing this letter, as he said, 'for the young traveller who had sought aid at the convent.' I knew at once whom he meant, and I accepted the letter on Mother's behalf. But may the saints forgive me, and I believe they will," she said, crossing herself, "for I did not take it to her, but brought it here directly." She held out the letter, as if offering a key that might unlock my silence. "The messenger would not stay for a reply, but disappeared into the night," she added.

My habit of suspicion made me hesitate. Was this a trick? A mistake? Who would have written to me? My heart contracted with fear as I considered that Claudius had discovered my hiding place and now would toy with me, as a cat does a mouse. But hope and courage moved me to take the letter from Isabel's hand. Turning it over, I saw that it bore the name "Philippe L'oeil". The seal was unbroken. It must be from Horatio! My heart leaped at the longing so soon fulfilled by mere wishing. With impatient, shaking hands I broke the seal in order to devour the good tidings I had waited to hear.

The letter bore, alas, Horatio's news of the death of Hamlet and the ruin of all Denmark. *The final fruits of evil have spilled their deadly seeds . . . It was the sight of his dying mother that spurred Hamlet's revenge at last . . . Laertes and Prince Hamlet have slain each other . . . I have failed in the task you set me . . . Forgive Hamlet . . . he loved you deeply.* Horatio's words filled my veins with sorrow and touched my heart like the quickest poison, bringing blackness like the oblivion of death.

Part Three

St Emilion, France
1601-1602

Chapter 37

Outside, the wind whips the bare-branched trees; it whistles through the cracks in the stone walls, chills my body, and reaches all my bones and inner parts. My heart is cracked; no, it is broken in pieces, like an earthen bowl dropped from a great height. Hamlet is dead. Gertrude and Laertes are slain. I have no husband, mother, brother or father in the world. I have no home, for I am cut off from Denmark for ever. I am like a severed branch flung by a storm from the trunk of a great, dying tree. That Claudius is also dead gives me little comfort now.

At night, frightful dreams awaken me. In my mind I see the face of Hamlet, his blue eyes reflecting my image like a watery glass. Then his body folds over a sharp blade in the hands of my brother. In their eyes, blood pools. I see myself lying in a tomb beside my father's sheeted body where the worms feed. Then I dream that I am falling into deep water, and I cannot swim but awaken gasping for air. Like an uneasy ghost, I rise from my pallet and pace up and down the corridor to shake the fearsome visions. And like the spirits who roam the night, I return before the dawn.

When sleep finally overcomes me, the morning light creeps through my narrow window and forces my weary eyes open again. The sun's faint warmth restores my hope, assures me that I am safe now. In its light, the tragedy at Elsinore seems only an invention of my grief-oppressed brain. Then I remember reading Horatio's letter, and despair, like a cold wind, dispels the momentary peace. But I cannot find the letter, though I turn every stone, every page, every fold of cloth in my tiny cell. I must have destroyed it so that no one would learn what I wish to keep hidden.

Every day, closeted in my stone cell, I write. A sister named Marguerite, who is as beautiful as the golden-faced flower for which she is named, has brought me pen and ink.

"To pen a letter if you desire. And to please our Lord and Mother Ermentrude by recording your daily devotions," she says, and leaves.

I write neither devotions nor letters. To whom would I address them? Rather, I write of my life, beginning with my earliest memories and including all events leading to my late woes. I secrete the pages in my mattress. One day I will give them to my child. I discover that writing is like applying leeches to my mind, curing its grief and drawing out humours that cloud my understanding.

The chapel bell rings throughout the day and night, calling the nuns to constant prayer. I sigh, put down my pen, and let the clamour drive away my thoughts. I will at least observe the rules of this place. As there is nothing else to read, I take up my book of prayers, the gift from Gertrude. I read: *Out of the depths I cry to you, O Lord. Bring my soul out of prison, that I may praise your name.* Hamlet once said that Denmark was a prison. Now he is free of the world's prison. My prison is my own mind, where dark thoughts and sorrows shackle my soul. Praise is beyond me. For what is left to worship that is not destroyed? I once praised my lord Hamlet, turning his name on my tongue like the bread of life itself. Was that a sin? And was Hamlet's death my punishment?

I fall asleep in the midst of these vain prayers, and when I awaken, my knees ache from the cold stone floor and my hands are numb. What has stirred me? I start up, sensing a presence at my door. It is only Marguerite, a cool Madonna with her ivory face framed by its white veil. Her hand resting on the latch, she regards me with suspicion. Have I cried out in my sleep? Did I, unaware, name Hamlet or the king?

"Mother Ermentrude asks that you mark this receipt for the gold in your purse, which she has put into safekeeping," she says, holding out a document and a pen. "As her secretary, I make this request."

I hesitate, suspecting a ruse to get me to sign my name and reveal myself. Then I take the document and sign *Philippe L'oeil*, the name I travelled under. When Marguerite takes the paper from me, she does not study my signature.

"I saw that the coins bore the seal of Denmark's king," she says. Her gaze probes me.

I had not considered how easily my connection to Elsinore might be uncovered. But I return Marguerite's gaze without flinching.

"I pray you, do not accuse me of dishonesty," I say, disguising my fear with careful words. I wonder if my speech also bears a Danish stamp.

Marguerite draws her full lips into a thin, tight line.

"The Lord protects the innocent," she says, then leaves as silently as she came.

The scene unsettles me. What did Marguerite mean? I am suddenly afraid, though Claudius can no longer touch me. Alas, the habit of fear dies hard, and perhaps I will never trust anyone again. With these distressing thoughts, I toss upon my bed until I fall asleep.

Into my restless sleep a figure in white intrudes. It comes to me like a soul freed from the bonds of flesh. But it touches me and calls me lady. I open my eyes, and Isabel stands before me.

"Good evening, lady. Will you eat?"

"I will not." Since the news came from Horatio, food turns to ashes in my mouth.

Isabel sets the food down despite my refusal. She waits. The scent of fresh hot bread stirs my hunger. So I take a bite, and another, and soon I have eaten it all and drunk the soup, too. I am compelled to live almost against my will.

"Shall you speak to me today? Are you well enough?" Her brown eyes in her round face are full of compassion. "Please tell me your name, that I may call you by it," she pleads.

"Please, do not ask, for I fear . . ." I shake my head, and the tears gather in my eyes.

Isabel, her brow knit in concern, strokes my hair. It is still short and unevenly shorn, a reminder of my recent trials. Only a nun would crop her hair so close to her head. Or a young woman who wants to be taken for a man. But Isabel does not demand to know why I have done this. Her touch is gentle, softening my hardness. I realise that I long to be spoken to by my name. Surely to say it would not reveal my secrets.

"I am Ophelia."

"O-phel-i-a. The sound of it is sweet," Isabel says, caressing with her voice the unfamiliar syllables of my name. "Philippe L'oeil! Now I understand! How clever you are to disguise your name so." She thinks for a moment. "*Ophelos* is Greek for 'help,' for which you have come here. And *phil* is a word meaning 'loving'; you are loved by God," she says, pleased by this interpretation.

"You are learned, Isabel."

"I have a little learning," she admits. "And you understand French perfectly, do you not?"

I nod, unable to deceive her in this. But she does not press me further.

"I do not like to study," she says, shaking her head, "but Mother Ermentrude is a great patron of learning. Our library has many treasures. One day I will show you."

"I would be grateful," I say, unable to hide my eagerness.

Isabel bids me goodnight, and I am alone again. When she comes the next day, she brings clean bedding and clothing. I bury my face in their folds, inhaling the crisp scent of outdoors.

"Thank you," I murmur.

"That is the work of Therese, who is most diligent in the laundry," she says.

From my window I have watched a girl with halting steps spread the wet linens on shrubs, rocks and fences. She works, not knowing my misery, and I watch, not knowing hers.

"Tell me, how did she become crippled?" I ask, thinking of the childhood wounds on my own legs. Though long healed, the smooth, whitish scars still ache with the cold.

"She has been lame since her birth. Her father, being a poor man, sent her to work for us, for he knew that with such a defect, she would never marry," says Isabel, as if beginning a story.

"She works, while you pray?"

"She is only a servant who earns her bread and board here, yet she prays with more fervour than any nun."

"Alas, I am of no use. I neither pray nor work," I say, not able to disguise my bitterness. I rise and look out from the window, where I see Therese struggling to carry a heavy basket.

"Do not say such things," Isabel says gently. "You are our guest. By the rule of our order, we give aid to those in need. Soon, you will be well again."

I watch Therese in silence. Her breath crystallises in the cold air. Suddenly she drops the basket and falls to her knees, her face to the ground. Her body shakes.

"Look, she is hurt!" I cry.

"She is not," says Isabel calmly. "Most likely she is having a vision of the Lord. They come upon her and sometimes she loses her senses. She will recover without our aid."

"I, too, suffer unwanted dreams," I murmur, feeling a thread of sympathy draw me to the suffering girl.

"Yes, I know."

Startled, I look up at Isabel.

"I have heard you cry out in your sleep," she explains. "A dream can be a fearful thing, but a vision of our Lord is what every sister desires for herself. So many envy Therese while others doubt that she sees Christ and deny that the blood on her hands is his."

"Blood on her hands?" I echo, wondering what evil Therese has committed.

"Yes. It may be the blood of Christ's wounds, or it may be the effect of the hard work she does."

"What do you think?"

"I do not know. It is not for me to judge such matters," says Isabel, but I sense disapproval in her tone.

Bloody hands. A sign of the Lord's favour — and a mark of guilt. I look at my hands; they are white. My conscience protests that the deaths were not my fault. My love for Hamlet was no sin. Our promises were holy, spoken before heaven. But Hamlet said the same of his revenge! Alas, I do not wish to entertain these unwelcome thoughts now, so I push them from my mind.

"How did you come to St Emilion?" I ask Isabel.

"You will not answer my questions, yet I should answer you?" she chides, but with a smile, revealing a gap in her front teeth.

"My father is a duke, and my mother was a servant, a wet nurse to his children. She died of smallpox when I was an infant. The duke presented me to the nuns as an oblate, with a purse that would have been my dowry. He did so to atone for his sins. I have never spoken to him."

"I am sorry," I say, feeling tears spring to my eyes. Isabel, like me, is motherless.

"Be not sad for me! I am at peace. I took my vows two years ago. Now I know I shall die in this place," she says. Her cherub-like face shines with joy.

I do not have Isabel's faith that welcomes everything, even Death, with joy. I have fought Death, and illness and despair have sapped all my strength. Yet I feel my desire for life like a rope knotted and coiled within me. Now Isabel has taken hold of its end in her small, strong and patient hands.

Chapter 38

I look forward to Isabel's visits as I once looked forward to reading with Gertrude in her chamber. She brings me books from the convent library: a history of the wars in France, and a volume of the English poet Chaucer, containing *The Legend of Good Women* and *The Tale of Troilus and Criseyde,* translated into French. I put these aside for when I am alone.

Isabel loves to talk, perhaps more than she loves to pray. Her bright voice fills my room like the music of a lute, and she is like a troubadour with her tales, though none are bawdy or bad. Sometimes her stories are interrupted by calls to prayer or work, but the next day she easily picks up the thread again.

"Do you not think that Mother Ermentrude is beautiful?" she asks, eager to begin a story.

"Yes," I say, for I have seen, even from a distance, that her nose is fine and her skin like whitest alabaster. "Why did she never marry?"

"Ah," Isabel begins, as if sounding a note on her instrument. "She was the youngest of five daughters of a wealthy baron and his wife. All his wealth was spent on dowries for her sisters. He could not make a good marriage for her, so he gave her up to the convent when she was a young girl."

"But did her mother agree to the baron's decision? Did she not fight to keep her daughter?" I ask.

"Perhaps, but what can a mother do? A daughter is her father's property," Isabel says without bitterness.

I do not say what I feel — that no mother, while she lived, would willingly part from her daughter.

"Now she has lived here some thirty years, and she has been prioress for ten years," Isabel continues. "The baron's influence helped her to the position. But her father is now dead and her brother is an enemy of Count Durufle, our convent's patron. She is mother to us all, by the grace of God." Here Isabel crosses herself, then adds, "And the goodwill of the count, and the dispensation of the bishop. We pray for her always."

I sigh to think of the insecure state of women, who must always abide the earthly authority of men.

"An even better story is that of Sister Marie. Her father betrothed her to an elderly merchant, but her mother defied her husband and used her own dowry to bring Marie to this convent."

"So the mother did defend her daughter," I remark.

"Yes, her husband abused her cruelly, for she would not say where she had taken Marie. He was also a drunkard. One day, he stumbled into a puddle and drowned! She sold his chandlery and with the money she returned here and begged to be taken as an oblate."

"Why should she beg?"

"She was not a noblewoman. Her husband made candles and

her father was only a poor blacksmith. But her purse was fat, and that settled it!"

"Is Marie still among you?"

"No, for she fell ill one winter and died before she was twenty." Isabel dabs her eye with her fingertip, moved by the sad thought.

Alas, I think, even a mother's courage cannot keep her child from all danger.

"What became of her mother?" I ask.

"Why, she is Sister Angelina, our dear cook! She rails against men, but we pay her no mind, for she is an angel in the kitchen. She feeds our bodies, while Mother Ermentrude feeds our souls."

I think about Angelina's sacrifice for her daughter, its ending in loss, her grief. Before sunset, I walk in the small graveyard that nestles against the chapel's north face. On the gate I read words from a psalm: *My flesh also shall rest in hope.* I find the stone marking Marie's grave. A rosebush grows there, its leaves withered by frost. The sight does not sadden me, for I know the bush will bloom again next year. At this hour, in this grey month, Nature utters no sound, and in this resting place my own heart is also silent.

The next day when Isabel comes, I am curious for another story.

"Tell me about Sister Marguerite, whose beauty is like the golden flower she is named for."

Isabel frowns and lifts her shoulders in a shrug.

"I know little of Marguerite. She is the secretary of Mother Ermentrude and privy to all her business. She is most secret, and excels in piety among us," she says. "Though you see how proud

is her manner." Then she leans forward and speaks in confidence, "I confess I do not love her as I ought in charity!"

"I understand," I say, thinking of Cristiana.

"But enough; it is wrong for me to speak ill of her." She shakes her head and continues in a sprightly tone, "We cannot sit here chattering, for Mother Ermentrude has requested that you be brought to her today."

The announcement fills me with dread.

"I am not ready to meet her. Tell her that I am fevered again," I plead. "Or tell her that melancholy afflicts me still."

"You are much better; anyone can see that," she says, rebuking me lightly. She takes my arm. "Do not fear, for she is kind."

Isabel leads me through the hallways and down the stairs. I take small, slow steps, for I am unwilling to obey this summons. Mother Ermentrude is no queen whom I have pledged to serve. Sensing my hesitation, Isabel urges me gently through the alleys of the cloisters. Their rounded arches frame a square courtyard and a garden that is brown and shrivelled by frost. The November air bites my skin.

We enter the chapter house. With its oiled wood panels on the walls, it reminds me of the chamber at Elsinore where the king received his visitors. A hallway leads to Mother Ermentrude's quarters. Marguerite waits there, a silent sentinel. Isabel presses my hand and departs.

Without speaking, Marguerite ushers me into the room and withdraws when Mother Ermentrude nods her head. I make myself small within my linen robe. I kneel before the prioress of St Emilion so that I see only the broad swath of her simple habit, edged in green velvet. Crossing my arms over my chest, I avoid her gaze.

"Ophelia, my child, you have come to us for aid. What is the trouble?" she asks.

So Isabel has told Mother Ermentrude my name. It is good that I have been sparing in my speech with her. No one must learn my secrets yet.

"I have been afraid for my life, Your Grace. More I cannot say now."

"You grieve beyond what is natural, and your body does weaken and waste away," she says gently. "Our duty, and Isabel's particular care, is to restore you to soundness of body and soul."

"I have suffered a great loss. I am most grateful for your aid," I say, fixing my eyes on the simple cross on her breast. It has a single bright jewel at the centre, yellow, the colour of hope.

"What is it you desire?" she asks.

"I desire solitude and prayer." This is not all the truth, but it must suffice, for words cannot draw the vast map of my longing.

"Your generous purse and the circumstances of your arrival suggest to me that you are a gentlewoman of means. Do you flee a cruel father or a forced marriage?"

"No." I strive to keep my voice even and my tears in check.

"Do you wish to pursue the cloistered life and take vows of poverty, chastity and obedience?"

I am already poor, having lost everything I treasure, and no longer pure. I was never obedient. But I do not say this.

"I do not know," I say truthfully.

"Have you committed some wrong for which you repent?"

"Yes . . . No! Please, in due time I will reveal all. Do not cast me out!" I plead, bowing almost to the floor. I see only the hem of her garment now and her leather-shod feet. I would kiss them if

doing so would persuade her to let me stay.

"You may remain here," she says. "But you must work and pray with us and study God's purpose for you. Sister Isabel will be your guide."

Like an angel of the annunciation, Mother Ermentrude spreads her arms and folds her hands over my head. "Now rise, and go in the peace of Christ."

Deep within, I feel something like the touch of a finger's tip against my soul, rekindling hope there.

Chapter 39

The whiteness of winter surrounds me. The nuns await the day of Christ's birth, only weeks away. Bells call them to vespers, to matins, to noonday prayer. In their white habits, the sisters tread in each other's snowy tracks on their way to chapel. Their breath, expelled in small clouds, vanishes like smoke from a chimney. Do their prayers also vanish on the wind, or do they pierce the dome of heaven and reach God's ear?

Under the frozen earth, curled in darkness, all life waits. I also wait through the long Advent nights that are lit by a feeble white moon. Though I dress in white like a nun, I feel the stain of sin, of mortality, around me like a bright girdle.

My body grows round again with recovered health, and my belly swells more than the rest of me. I am still able to hide it beneath my loose-fitting dress. Only I see the growing mound when I bathe myself. Only I feel it when the child moves while I am reciting prayers with the sisters, *"Pray for us, O holy mother of God, that we may be made worthy of the promises of Christ."* I hope these promises of Christ are more certain than those of men.

Often my mind wanders during prayers. I find myself remembering Gertrude's kindness as I gaze upon Mother Ermentrude, whose humility contrasts with my queen's grandeur. Sister Angelina, with her rough but loving manner, reminds me of dear Elnora. Isabel, who shows her gap-toothed smile even when she prays, makes me wish that I had known such a cheerful friend at Elsinore. Sister Marguerite is proud, like Cristiana, and seems to harbour some secret ambition, which rouses my curiosity.

"You pray with growing devotion, I see," says Isabel, mistaking my dreaminess for piety.

"No, in truth, I am thinking how much this convent is like a prince's court," I say, then hasten to add, "A place I have read about in books."

"What do you mean?" she asks.

"Your prioress is like a queen, the fountain of all goodness. All the sisters are her ladies-in-waiting, happy to live under her benevolent rule. There is a hierarchy, with servants in the lowest place." I pause, considering the comparison. "But I see one vital difference. Here there are no men to vie for your love. You worship only Christ, and he bestows his love equally. At a prince's court, no woman would share her lover, nor would a man share his mistress."

Isabel understands quickly.

"Yes, for if a lady is desired by more than one man, it brings about jealousy and much strife. I also read those books, long ago," she says, lowering her voice, though there is no one to overhear us. The nuns have all left the chapel. "But do not deceive yourself that St Emilion is a perfect place. We have our faults, such as envy, if one of us has a finer voice or is more favoured by Mother. We are vain, too. I have seen Marguerite hold up her graceful hands and gaze on them in admiration. Once I was punished by Mother for keeping a small bit of lace beneath my pillow."

"Such poverty would sit hard with a queen and her ladies," I admit. "Still this place seems to me a peaceful realm where no tyrannical king can oppress you."

Isabel's usually cheery face grows clouded.

"There is no king at St Emilion, as you say, but man's power still holds sway here. Mother Ermentrude is bound to obey Bishop Garamond, as he is God's deputy on earth," she explains. "But this bishop serves Count Durufle, who is our convent's chief patron and a morally scrupulous man." She shows me a stone monument, like a proud claim staked upon the humble chapel. "Durufle erected this to honour himself though it was his ancestors who gave this land to found our convent some two hundred years ago. For this past generosity, he thinks himself God's favourite and the bishop's equal!" she says, indignant. "He sorely tests my charity!"

"How like a royal court," I muse, "where powerful lords and councillors direct the king's course."

"At least Durufle and the bishop are seldom seen among us. But the count has appointed his nephew, a surly and discourteous youth, to be our steward. He oversees the servants and the convent's business, though he has no ability for the work. Last week Marguerite called him a fool to his face!" Isabel laughs at the thought, then rolls her eyes. "You begin to see why I am grateful to be a nun. I could be married to such a one. Or, God forbid, to a man as old as Father Alphonse, who trembles as he says the Mass and is almost completely deaf. I have to shout to make him hear me, and then my sisters overhear my sins!" Isabel says with some distress. "So I confess only that I have neglected my prayers, which is a fault most common with us."

"Your only fault, Isabel, is too much kindness to the undeserving," I murmur, thinking of her goodness to me.

"No; I am more unkind than you know. I am jealous of Marguerite's beauty and her favour with Mother. I boil with impatience at Angelina's slowness and I blame her when we must fast and eat nothing but stale bread. Sometimes I steal sugar from the larder!"

I smile at her offences, for they fall far short of deceit and murder and revenge, the crimes that went unconfessed at Elsinore.

But Isabel takes my hand and says in earnest, "Ophelia, you shall be my priest, for you are as secret as an effigy on a tomb."

"Confess, then, and I will absolve you," I say, trying to sound like Father Alphonse, and we both laugh. Yet how her trust tempts me! I long to share my stories with her, but discretion holds my tongue and silence feeds my loneliness.

I often lament that I have no place at St Emilion. At Elsinore I knew my role as one of the queen's ladies. Here I am neither a servant nor a nun. I may not sit with the nuns in the sanctuary of the chapel, but I pray their prayers. I may not share their table, yet I eat the same food. Like a departed spirit not yet at rest, I travel between worlds. I am free to leave the convent grounds if I wish. Instead, I spend hours in the library, often losing myself in *The Consolation of Philosophy* by Boethius the Roman. I also translate prayers into French for the nuns who do not read Latin.

One day Mother Ermentrude, seeing me studying intently, asks me to help tutor the girls of the convent school. I agree, for I wish to be useful here. But pity overwhelms me at the sight of these small, sad-eyed children taken from the arms of their parents and given to a God whose embrace they cannot feel. One girl, the picture of despair, leans her cheek in her hands, her too-short skirt revealing bare legs above her shoes. I remember wearing such ill-fitting dresses and wish I had some stockings to give her. I long to put my arms around the child, but I am afraid of her large, frightened eyes. Instead I give her something paltry and useless: a verb to conjugate. While the girls bend over their books, I draw from my pocket the miniature painting of my mother that I carry always. In her face is my exact likeness; I see my own hair, cheeks, and nose, all mirrored in miniature. I dig in the deepest recesses of my mind for a memory of her touch.

"Oh, teach me how to be a mother, and give me courage!" I whisper, willing the image itself to speak to me. "What will we do, my babe and I? Where shall we make our home? Tell me!" I feel like a child, abandoned in the dark woods; not even my mother's image comforts me.

Then I see that Marguerite has come into the library. How long has she been standing there? The girls have finished their exercise and are whispering and giggling among themselves. Marguerite regards me with her cool, unsmiling gaze. I feel like a book laid wide open, where my story is written in plain words for her to read.

"It seems that teaching does not suit you. I will inform Mother Ermentrude," she says. Her voice is without pity or judgement.

I am unable to reply, so full am I with longing for the mother I never knew.

Chapter 40

December holds us all in its thrall; not even the fires in the stoves and grates can loosen its icy grip. I rub my hands together for the feeble warmth as I pass by the door of the refectory, where the nuns eat in silence, their heads bent in a row over their food. Spoons scrape dully on the wooden trenchers. Steam rises from a pot of soup. The voice of Mother Ermentrude rises and falls as she reads aloud.

"Let us partake with temperance and sober piety and due thanksgiving, only food that is proper and nourishing. Remember that Christ's body was broken and that bread and water are here broken to be taken into our bodies. So in the Eucharist does Christ's body nourish us."

I wonder what Hamlet, the philosopher and man of reason, would have made of the nuns' simple faith that they consume Christ's true body. The bread served at meals and the bread served at Mass look and taste the same to me. I find it strange that the sisters' eating is governed by silence and strict rules. I think of the feasts at Elsinore, loud with laughter and the cracking of bones and sucking of marrow, with dogs growling and fighting over food thrown to the floor. Wine flowed from hogsheads like water from a fountain, and at each meal fish, fowl and a joint of beef were served.

With the thought of such plenty, my appetite grows. The babe within me makes me long for cider and sweetmeats, roast meat, rich milk and apricots. But the nuns are fasting now, eating only bread with salt and water. So I eat in the kitchen with the scullery maid and steward so that I may have meat and fruit. They are quiet in my presence, for I am still considered a mystery at St Emilion. A poor farmer who tills the nuns' field, his three hollow-eyed children, and a guest, a travelling scholar, round out the company.

Therese, being a servant, should also eat in the kitchen. But she does not appear for meals. When I ask about her, the steward, his mouth full of bread, merely shrugs.

"Indeed, milady, she doesn't eat that I know of," offers the maid.

"Who would not eat when hunger bids them?" I ask. "I will take her this portion of meat and some cakes."

"She won't eat it, I say. I've never seen her touch meat."

Against this warning, I take the food to Therese's room, a damp cell even narrower than my own. The door opens at my touch, and a wall covered with crucifixes greets my sight. I count at least a dozen. All are crudely made and painted with an image of the Lord in agony. Beneath the crosses, Therese kneels on the hard floor, rocking back and forth. She does not acknowledge my presence; indeed she seems not to hear or see me. Her eyes are lifted up and fixed upon the air. Ashamed of my intrusion in the closet of her soul, I leave the food upon her bed and silently depart. But the image of the laundress, dazed with prayer, will not leave me. Later I return to see if she has eaten. The plate of bread sits on the floor outside her door, untouched except by the mouse that nibbles the bread and scurries away at my approach.

I wonder why Therese abstains from food, though she is not bound by the nun's vows. I decide to observe her more closely. Like a spy, I pretend to read a book while walking in the corridor near the kitchen. Therese wears a veil that she wraps around her head when she works, making her look like a Turk. Her sleeves are rolled up to her shoulders, and I see that her flesh barely covers her bones. She moves slowly, pausing often as she carries a bucket of hot water.

I cannot bear to see her struggle with simple tasks, so I set my book down and offer to help her. To my surprise, she accepts with a look of gratitude. I had imagined her to be proud in her isolation from the sisters, but she seems glad of my company. Now Therese drops the soiled garments in soapy water with fingers that are long and tapered, like a lady's, but red and rough, like a servant's. I beat and stir the clothes with wooden paddles. It surprises me how much strength the task requires, and soon my face is damp with sweat, despite the cold.

"God grants you health again, I see. We are joyful to see you well," says Therese. Her words surprise me, for I did not think she noticed me or knew of my illness.

"I cannot rejoice in my strength while yours weakens," I reply.

"The Lord upholds the weak," she says in quick reply, as if she is used to defending herself.

"Your spirit indeed is strong, but your body wastes away. Why do you not eat?"

"I need nothing but the Lord who nourishes my soul in the bread of the Eucharist," she says. Her eyes are bright, though her cheeks are sunken, making her look no longer young.

"He also gives us daily bread to nourish our bodies, that we may have strength for our work in the world," I say, feeling a contentious spirit rise in me.

"I care nothing for the world, which has shown little favour to me," she replies. Her voice is calm, without bitterness. "I was always shunned for my twisted leg, and my parents were ashamed of me. My only desire has been to become a nun. But the bishop has told Mother Ermentrude that my visions are improper and he forbids my admission as a postulant. So I find my own pathway to God."

"Does God ask you to suffer for him?"

Therese draws back from me with an air of injured dignity.

"He bids me praise him daily, and so I do."

Desperate for her to understand my good intentions, I lay my hand on her arm, stilling it in the water. Her forearm, like a child's, fits within the circle of my thumb and finger.

"Therese, you must eat daily, or you will die!"

She does not even flinch at my words. I realise that perhaps she wants to die.

"When I do not eat, the Christ child himself comes to me and nurses at my breast, which swells with rich milk," she says with perfect calm. "I taste honey and sweetness in my mouth. No mortal mother feels such joy."

Is this the conviction of faith or evidence of madness? I think of the ghostly visions that stirred Hamlet to revenge, while Therese's fill her with joy. Both are beyond all reason. Who can judge whether they are true?

I take her hands in mine. The palms and wrists are scarred.

"My hands bleed sometimes, as Christ's wounds bled," she says, a look of bliss on her face.

"It is no wonder; your skin is so dry. Let me make a liniment that will soften it and ease the pain." I know I can help her overcome this undeserved suffering.

Therese shakes her head vigorously and withdraws her hands as if I am offering to take away a precious gift. She turns from me and will not speak again.

I fear that Therese's mind is made feeble by her suffering. I do not want her to die, for I have seen enough of madness and death.

Chapter 41

It is the new year, and like the two-faced god Janus, I look forward and backwards at once. Looking behind me, I remember Hamlet giving me the token, the pressure of his fingers on my palm, our brief joy and the long despair that followed it. Looking ahead, I see only a blank page on which I know not what to write.

I sit beside Isabel in the chapter house, listening to the daily reading of the monastic rule.

"Obey the Lord and his laws, and the prioress and her rule, and your every need will be fulfilled, your every fear assuaged," Mother Ermentrude's voice intones. "With obedience comes perfect freedom."

Isabel nods, a blissful look on her face. But for some reason the lesson vexes me. So I slip away and, despite the cold, make my way to the cemetery, where I know I will be alone with my thoughts. As the damp night descends, I consider how I disobeyed and deceived my father. "Is this my punishment?" I whisper, touching my belly. The babe has been more than five months in my womb, and the burden grows each day. My secrets, too, oppress me. Grief for my losses fills my heart, and I fear being alone. "Is this the bitter fruit of my disobedience?" I cry out, and a flock of startled blackbirds lifts from the snowy ground to merge with the black sky.

Feeling the cold grip my bones, I continue walking, disputing with myself this question of disobedience and punishment. I discover that my wandering thoughts and steps have brought me to Mother Ermentrude's lodgings. Isabel tells me her ear is always open to our needs. So I knock and Mother Ermentrude herself opens the door, showing no surprise to see me, though the hour is late. I hold my cloak fast around me, hiding my belly.

"I am sorry to disturb you at this late hour, Mother Ermentrude, but I am troubled and in need of your wisdom."

She opens the door, and I start to kneel before her, but she motions for me to be seated instead. Then she sits beside me, as if we are equals.

"I have been meditating upon today's lesson of obedience," I say. "Help me to understand: what is the virtue in denying one's own desires to satisfy another's will?"

Mother Ermentrude breathes deeply while she fashions her reply.

"You have seen a vine, how the gardener tames it and makes it cling to a branch or post. It obeys his hand that it may grow upwards towards the sun. In the same way, obedience to God's will frees the soul to reach heaven."

This comparison does not satisfy me, for my father was not God. But had I been more obedient, would I in time have become upright and virtuous? I think of Hamlet, who disobeyed the command of his father's ghost. Had he obeyed at once, perhaps only

Claudius would have been slain and Hamlet and I would still be together. But would heaven have been pleased with Hamlet's deed? Or would hell have rejoiced?

"What if the gardener's intention is good, but his hand harms the plant he nurtures?" I ask, thinking of my father, who in seeking my safety would have sacrificed my happiness. "Or what if the gardener's will is evil?" I consider how I resisted Hamlet's revenge, repelled by the violent act he had vowed to commit.

Mother Ermentrude does not try to probe the deeper meaning of my questions. There is no guile in her replies, only sincerity and truth.

"Every deed and intention calls for careful discernment. An evil will can never be God's will," she says simply. "One must resist it."

My mind seizes on her words like a prisoner grasping for pardon. I was not wrong to condemn Hamlet's vengeance, for murder is no godly deed. Nor was I wrong to defy my father when he wished me to betray my queen. My will was just and right, I decide.

As if she reads my thoughts, Mother Ermentrude continues her lesson, saying, "Our wills, however, are corrupt and often lead us astray. But a will that is holy is a joy to submit to."

With these words I am plunged into doubt again. I had my will in marrying Hamlet, but it brought me only brief joys and long sorrows. I must have sinned and hence brought the grief upon myself. Could I atone and be rid of my suffering?

"Please, teach me to submit and find this joy you speak of. I will obey you!" I am on the verge of confessing everything, laying all my deeds before her to be judged. I fold my hands together and pinch my lips between my fingers to restrain my words.

"Then go, return to your cell and read the Psalms. Let them do the work of searching your heart, scaling its mountains and descending its dark valleys. Commit them to your memory."

Inwardly I groan. What painful, time-wasting study is this? How will it help me? But if I desire contentment, I suppose I must learn to obey. So I read the Psalms, especially the despairing ones, until their words become fixed in my mind, but no peace settles there. A week later I visit Mother Ermentrude again.

"I have studied the Psalms as you bid me, yet I have questions still. How may I believe, as David tells us, that the Lord opens his hand and satisfies all our desires, when everything has been taken from me?"

Mother is not disturbed by the challenge in my voice. She fingers the cross around her neck as if it is a token from a lover.

"You have God's love always."

"I do not feel it," I say doubtfully. "Rather, I feel like Job railing against God for taking everything from him. I am not sinless like Job. Yet I do not understand my sin!" I cry in confusion. *How could there be sin in loving Hamlet in truth and faith?*

"In the end, God restored everything to his servant Job."

"It is too late," I say bitterly, "unless he will raise the dead who are lost to me."

"Do not despair, Ophelia. God's ways are a mystery," she says, "and our sufferings often blind us to joy."

Indeed, I am stumbling blindly along winding paths of loss and sorrow. Hamlet's love led me into this maze, where he abandoned me. Is there no path that will lead me from this dark tangle?

Despite my mind's desolation, reason's light still flickers there.

It comes to me that I might, as the nuns do, put Christ in the place of a husband, and thus exit this labyrinth of worldly love. Christ would not die or abandon me or be untrue. He would forgive my disobedience, and in submitting to him, I might find joy. I begin to see the painful remedy. Once I have given birth, I will give my child to some gentlewoman more fit and more deserving to be a mother than I am. That hard sacrifice will wipe out my sin. Then I will take a new path, join the convent as a nun, and become pure again. But before I reveal my plight to Mother Ermentrude I must receive her assurance. The very picture of humility, I appeal to her on my knees.

"I believe that Christ alone can rescue me from despair and cleanse me from sin," I say, tears spilling from my eyes, though I try to stop them. "Please allow me to join this holy sisterhood. Let me begin now to prepare to take my vows. I will obey you in everything."

It is not easy, I have heard, to gain entrance to the convent. The Rule calls the nuns to test the supplicant's spirit, to see if it comes from God. Let them question or reprove me. I will knock without relenting, for the Bible says that the door shall not remain closed to those who persevere. Moreover, I believe that Mother Ermentrude favours me and has been praying for me to make this bid.

The prioress bids me rise and searches my face. I dare to meet her eyes. Why is she not smiling?

"I do not doubt your earnest desire to love God, Ophelia. But you come here not in freedom, but bound in spirit."

"Obedience will grant me freedom; therefore let me vow it. I will reveal my life's story and confess my sins if you let me stay among you always!"

Mother Ermentrude shakes her head slowly.

"I will not bargain with you. Nor will God. You must run to him freely, looking forward, not encumbered by your past griefs."

"Does it matter how one finds God?" I ask, trying to sound meek while my frustration grows. "Are you not glad to receive me?"

"There are many paths to God," concedes Mother Ermentrude. Then she fixes me with her calm and knowing gaze, saying softly, "I do not believe God calls you to this life."

"I believe I know my will and my way!" I am surprised and shamed that she should reject me. Nothing in this scene is unfolding as I had planned.

"You are young. Too often the young would rather bend the world to their will than listen and wait to be called."

"I cannot wait," I wail, thinking of how soon my babe will arrive. I must have her promise of protection. "Why may I not do as I will? I am not as young as you think." My voice breaks with desperation. "I am free to make this choice, to take Christ as my true love!"

"Let God's will, not mine or thine, be done," says Mother calmly.

"God's will! How do you know God's will? Does he speak to *you* about me, and not deign to answer *my* prayers?"

I am ashamed by my lack of control, but Mother lets me rage. She remains unmoved, like a rock splashed by mere drops of rain.

"What is God's will for his servant Therese?" I demand, my mind suddenly leaping from one passion to another. "That she, too, suffer? Do you observe her? She grows weaker each day, doing God's will. I do not believe that God wants her to die!"

"Nor do I," Mother admits, sadness on her face. "But our wills are free even to frustrate God's intentions."

"I cannot stand idly by while she suffers. I have some skill with plants and potions. Let me administer a medicine that might restore balance to her mind," I plead.

"It is God who heals and afflicts," she says, neither refusing nor accepting my offer.

"Yes, but you say that God gives us freedom. Does he not also give us in nature the means to make ourselves well or ill?"

"Studying has made you wise, Ophelia." Mother smiles faintly, as if pleased.

A sudden image comes to my mind of the garden near the cloisters, blasted by winter's wrath. I see it turning green again in the spring. What plants are there, buried in the earth? Is there the purgative rhubarb or thyme that cures the long lethargy? In the woods around the convent must be all manner of roots and wild berries and plants unknown in Denmark. No, the dark and tiny cloister garden will not suffice. There must be a field where the sun can shine unhindered. Why have I not considered this before? Was my mind so dulled with grief?

I choose my words with care to express the idea that is but a germ unfolding in my mind. I go to the arched windows of Mother Ermentrude's chamber and peer out into the night. There, wooded hills, lit by the moon, slope gently beyond the convent walls. Surely there is land among them suitable for a garden.

"Is it not true," I say, "that the nuns are loath to allow the village doctor to examine them when they are ill?"

"Yes." She sighs. "Some of the nuns fear that the touch of any man compromises their chastity. Thus Angelina suffers greatly

from a boil, for she refuses treatment. And any complaints of the womb go sadly untended."

"I am no man, but a woman like them," I say. I will build this house with care, stone by stone.

"Indeed, your quiet presence has gained their trust," she admits.

"For years I have studied the qualities of all manner of plants and herbs. Books and experience have been my teachers. I have helped in healing many and easing their pains. Let me put my knowledge to use here, and serve you with my skill." I realise that for the first time since I have come to St Emilion, I am not dwelling in the past but anticipating, without dread, the future. I have put my pen to the blank page before me.

Mother Ermentrude smiles and lifts up her hands, their palms facing heaven.

"Ophelia, my dear, you are hearing God's call."

Chapter 42

Thus did Mother Ermentrude in her wisdom deter me from my desperate course and guide me to a new path. In my new profession I am like a confessor, for I listen as the nuns reveal their ailments, and I prescribe balms, tonics and poultices. These they take away and apply with devotion, like a healing penance from a priest. But Sister Lucia, an elderly, corpulent nun, is less trusting than the others.

"I am troubled with dire thoughts, and then my heart beats too fast. You must bleed these ill humours from me, as the village doctor used to do," she demands.

"I do not favour leeches, Sister, for bleeding drains vital spirits along with bad humours, making the patient weaker," I explain in a soothing voice. "I recommend an infusion of mint leaves and chamomile to calm you." She purses her lips, dissatisfied. I wish that I had spoken more firmly. After a moment, however, she relents.

"All right, for the sight of my blood does make me swoon. But surely you will look at my water."

I duly inspect Sister Lucia's urine, though little knowledge can be gained from it, and pronounce her fit.

My healing methods are simple, the tools of my new profession few. I use wine to cleanse cuts from a kitchen knife. A bit of aqua vitae relieves tooth pains. The store of herbs that Mechtild gave me remedies disorders of the womb, which are common even among nuns. Salts, dissolved in hot water, draw the suppurations from boils. While I examine my patients, I teach them Nature's laws regarding disease.

"In the body, the hot and dry humours that make one mad contend with cold and moist humours that cause lethargy. To heal the body is to temper its elements, for Nature herself always seeks a balance." My prescriptions are simple and usually painless. "Eat foods that are green and wholesome, dress against the cold and damp, and walk every day to aid digestion and stir your blood," I tell them. My herb and mustard poultices are favoured, but my most effective treatment is the firm touch of my hand. I probe sore flesh and rub scented balms into stiff joints. The nuns sigh with contentment as they do when their bellies are full of wholesome food and their souls sated with prayer.

Therese is my only unwilling patient. She will let me talk with her and assist her work, but she turns to stone when I ply her with food. Daily she grows more infirm, eating only enough to keep her soul from fleeing in the night. Now she suffers from headaches. The pain, which is written on her face, would fell the stoutest soldier, but she does not complain. Every day she is more of an outcast within St Emilion. I believe I am her only friend.

Today as we labour in the cold sunshine, Therese pulls her

threadbare cloak tight about her thin body. She shivers from excitement as she tells her latest dream.

"Last night a great wind blew, and I awoke to see a seraph above me," she says, looking towards heaven at the memory. "The angel touched a burning coal to my forehead, bringing a sharp and blissful sorrow, and I saw before me the shining face of my dear Saviour."

I see that her eyes are mere slits and that her brow is contracted with pain.

"I cannot look upon the whiteness of the linen," she says, covering her face with her hands.

I know how sunlight can sharpen pains in the head, so I tell her she must go inside. When she obeys, I am surprised. Her pain must be terrible. I collect the frozen garments and carry the bulky pile to the bakery, where the warmth of the ovens will thaw and dry them.

I believe that once her pain diminishes, she will desire to eat again and then recover her strength. But I also know that Therese treasures her weakness and cares nothing for the simple pleasure of being without pain. What can I do to cure her malady? I will be the proverbial parent who deceives the child by offering medicine laced with sweet syrup.

"A tincture of bayberry juice and oil of roses may relieve the pain, so that the sensation of Christ's sweetness becomes even greater," I say. This promise appeals to her.

"Then give me some of this divine medicine, and pray do not tell anyone. I am hated already. Marguerite says that my visions are evil and shuns me as if I am a demon," she says.

I wonder if Marguerite's pride makes her despise the lowly

Therese, or if she is jealous of her visions.

"Perhaps you should be more secret and guard your Lord from shame," I say, for I am learning to speak her pious language. "Do not expose him to the mockery of those who do not believe."

"Yes, you are right," she says, her voice growing desperate with fear and longing. "Count Durufle has a horror of witchcraft. If he hears that my visions do not abate, he may appeal to Bishop Garamond, who will force me to leave, if he does not put me to trial. I have nowhere to go. These visions I share with you – I beg you to be silent about them!"

I consider that Therese may be deluded, for who would accuse her of such an evil as witchcraft? Perhaps her fears as well as her faith are a sign of madness. But I, too, am afraid of the power others hold over me. If we are mad, then we are safe, but if our fears prove true, we are both lost.

"I promise to tell no one about your visions," I say to calm her.

In the warm bakery, steam rises from the laundry, and sleeves and skirt folds that were stiff with frost now hang limp. I decide to infuse the headache potion with a poppy seed extract to calm Therese and bring her rest. My aim is to reduce her visions, not to make them more intense. I do not tell Therese, but reveal my treatment and its purpose to Mother Ermentrude.

May God forgive me for these deceits.

Chapter 43

There are no idle hours at St Emilion. No one, from the youngest novice to the prioress, is excused from kitchen work. According to the rule, all are called to serve each other. Yesterday Mother Ermentrude herself cleaned and dried all the trenchers and spoons. I have even seen her on her knees, scrubbing the floor with rags.

A tower of strength, she is firm and does not yield, except in loving. When the sisters say the prayer of the Virgin, *I am the mother of beautiful love, and of fear, and of greatness, and of holy hope,* I picture Mother Ermentrude. Her convent is a place of chaste simplicity, with none of the luxuries whispered of in some nunneries: eating from gold plates, drinking wine, entertaining men, and neglecting the hours for prayer. Mother is not only virtuous and thrifty, but wise. I marvel how she led me to understand that it was not marriage to Christ that I desired, but sisterhood. My work now ties me to the nuns more firmly than a pledge to share their poverty. I am glad to do Mother's will without a formal vow of obedience. She asks nothing beyond what is just and reasonable, and she waits with patience for me to reveal my secrets.

My thoughts this wintry day are hopeful ones, as Angelina, Isabel, Marguerite and I prepare a broth together. The kitchen is a warm refuge from the cold, and here the air is sharp with the yeasty smell of bread. Holding a knife, I contemplate a rabbit carcass slung over a hook on the wall, waiting to be cut open and skinned for the stew. I wait to ask for advice, while Angelina relates some new transgression of Durufle's lazy steward and Isabel chatters about the icy weather. It still surprises me how much the sisters love to talk. If their prayer is like plainsong, chanted in unison, their work is like harmony, a bright medley of voices.

Marguerite, more comfortable behind Mother Ermentrude's desk than in a messy kitchen, waits to be given a task. I see her take a ripe pear from a bowl and hide it within her habit. No doubt she will savour it later, when she is alone. Watching her, I wonder if she, too, is guarding some greater secret. She looks at me sharply, daring me to reveal her small theft. Her brows arch over pale green eyes. Surely her hair beneath her wimple is as yellow as the marguerite's petals. But her beauty often seems at odds with her piety. It is her habit, like a self-anointed preacher, to choose a moral tale from her memory and tell it to those nearby, whether or not they wish to hear it. I have heard Isabel say she is more strict than Count Durufle himself.

"Today is the feast of Agnes," Marguerite begins when Angelina finishes her complaints against the steward. "Which reminds me of poor Agnes of Lille, who once lived among us."

"Do not remind us," says Angelina, wiping her brow. "We know the story well. See to the parsnips now." I see Isabel lift her eyebrows and look upwards as if praying for patience, and I almost laugh, for I did the same when my father lectured me.

"But Ophelia does not know of Agnes," says Marguerite, turning to me with a pretended graciousness, as if she would introduce me to a friend.

"Oh, please spare us!" begs Isabel, unable to find the patience to keep silent. But Marguerite will not be deterred. Does she think herself a princess who can disregard the will of others?

"Agnes took her vows at Pentecost, and seemed a veritable angel as she sang in the choir. But she deceived us. By the Feast of All Saints, she was heavy with child."

"The parsnips!" Angelina interrupts, impatient. Marguerite pauses long enough to fetch them. I concentrate on the rabbit, having decided to cut it open myself. Blood from its inner parts oozes between my fingers.

"Mother Ermentrude did not even consult the bishop, but wasted no time in expelling her from our midst," she goes on. "The girl married a blacksmith from the village, but it was said the child's father was her confessor, a monk."

Though I feel Marguerite's eyes on me, I do not look up. Is she trying to draw out my secrets? Does she somehow know of my condition and judge me a sinner? Perhaps I was wrong not to confide in Mother Ermentrude. I must go to her at once and confess the truth. I will pray that she believes me and does not cast me out like Agnes.

"It was the only time such shame fell upon St Emilion," Marguerite says to conclude the tale. Then she crosses herself and delivers the moral that all such tales carry: "We ought to thank God for our vocation. What a blessing it is not to be a creature of passion like poor Agnes."

My bloody hands shake with the effort, but I cannot stop my

282

angry words from spilling out.

"And what of the monk? Did he offer to share her guilt?"

Marguerite looks confused by my question.

"Are not men also creatures of passion?" I demand. "Do they not beg, force and sometimes deceive women into yielding their virtue? Women do not sin this way alone, you know."

Marguerite falls back as if I have struck her. She is speechless and her pale skin is as white as the flesh of the raw-cut parsnip. Is my anger so terrible? Or have I touched some deep fear within her, some wound or scar?

It is Isabel who speaks, seeking peace.

"All of us are sinners. It is not the purity of the body, but the integrity of the mind, that best pleases our Lord," she says.

"And if the dear Lord can forgive me for all the times I wished my husband dead," said Angelina, crossing herself, "surely he has forgiven poor Agnes her sin."

Seeing by my trembling hands that I am in danger of cutting myself, Isabel takes the rabbit and the knife from me. With five swift strokes, she cuts it into pieces and adds them to the steaming broth.

"But our Saviour is much more pleased with a bride whose virgin seal is unbroken by man," Marguerite persists. "Is he not?" Her voice rises, sounding uncertain.

"You forget, Marguerite, that most women do bring children into the world. You and I were born of women," Isabel says gently. "Indeed, what would befall mankind if all young girls were to join our ranks?"

"There would be no more virgins born!" Angelina offers, with a hearty burst of laughter.

Smiling, Isabel spreads her hands to emphasise the point. Marguerite, defeated, presses her lips together and says no more.

I realise then that I love Isabel, my champion. She has been my steady friend, like Horatio to his Hamlet. How can I continue to deceive her when she loyally defends me? I will confide in her at once and ask her advice about approaching Mother Ermentrude with my secret, lest Marguerite expose it first.

That very night I seek her out and find her kneeling in her cell, praying before a simple icon. I change my mind and begin to withdraw.

"Ophelia, come back. I will leave off my prayers at once. See, I lay down my book. Now tell me, what troubles you?"

Without any preamble, my words come in a torrent.

"Isabel, my friend, I know that I can trust you as I have never trusted anyone." I sink to my knees beside her, while she leans back on her heels in surprise. "Hear me now, for I can no longer keep my story a secret." I grasp Isabel's hand, and her eyes grow wide with expectation. "I loved a man who was forbidden to me. I enjoyed his caresses, then married him in secret. He renounced me and now he is dead. All of my family is dead." My voice caught on these words, but I went on. "I am without a home, for ever alienated. Though I am not a nun like you, I also died to the world in coming here."

Speaking these long-held secrets brings intense relief, like the shedding of a heavy cloak in summer.

"There is no shame in being a widow," Isabel says. "Why have you concealed the fact that you had a husband?"

"Because I cannot name him, therefore all would think me a liar, a sinner trying to hide her shame," I explain. "But my story is

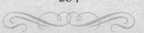

still more complex. I have taken part in such a drama as would only be believed on a stage, a tragedy ending in the death of kings and princes."

"I know some of this," says Isabel slowly.

A cry of surprise escapes me. "How?"

"I read the letter that came to you from the man named Horatio, after you fell senseless and it dropped from your hand," she confesses. "I knew you wanted to disguise yourself, so to help you stay unknown, I hid it."

I am both amazed and relieved at this news. I watch Isabel go to her cot and reach deep within the mattress to produce Horatio's letter. She hands it to me, and meeting her eyes, I know the knowledge is locked within her, that she has not told anyone.

"So you know how I have suffered in love, and that all is lost to me." Still I dare not name Hamlet, though Isabel must know of him.

"Yes. Considering your terrible grief, I also took away your dagger, fearing you might harm yourself with it." She shrugs and smiles faintly. "Not knowing where to put it, I buried it in the cemetery. Will you forgive me?"

"There is no need for me to forgive you, for you are an angel," I say. "But now I must tell you how I have been punished for my rash loving."

Isabel hushes me and puts her arms around me. Tears burst from me, for I have not touched anyone so nearly since I bade farewell to Gertrude. I do not want to let Isabel go. But soon she draws away, and her hand caresses briefly the small, firm mound of my belly. As her eyes meet mine, I see complete understanding there.

"This is no punishment, Ophelia, but a blessing," she says, touching my belly again. Her eyes shine with joy.

"Yes, I am to bear a child!" I cry. "I confess it was conceived in delight, and I grieve to think that it will be born into misery!" I think of Agnes's misfortune, Marguerite's seeming malice, and the certainty of Mother Ermentrude's justice. What will befall me, now that my long-held secret has been brought from the darkness into the plain, full light of day?

Chapter 44

Buried beneath winter's white blanket, tiny snowdrops unfold their hardy green leaves. In patches where the snow has melted, they thrust their bell-shaped blooms to the sun. Soon the pointed shoots of the playful daffadowndillies will break the frozen ground. At Easter time, their frilled yellow trumpets will proclaim spring's annual triumph over winter.

Wrapped in my father's cloak and warmed from within by the babe's heat, I do not feel the cold. Despite my heavy belly, my steps are light, lifted with new hopes. All the nuns now know my secret. Voting in chapter, they have decided that I may remain among them. Now there is no reason to hide my awkward shape.

Mother Ermentrude summons me and in brief terms informs me of the decision.

"Your confinement draws near, and your need is great, thus we will aid you. Isabel did testify to your virtue, though whether you are married or not is no matter now."

Her tone lacks its usual warmth. She does not invite me to confide in her.

"I can only humbly thank you, and beg your pardon that I have not been truthful. One day you will know why."

"What is truth, Ophelia?" I only lift my shoulders, not knowing what she wishes me to say. "The truth is what will free you," she replies in answer to her own question. Then she nods, ending our strained meeting.

I feel keenly her disappointment in me. When I ask Isabel whether Mother Ermentrude believes me a sinner, she gives an indirect reply.

"Perhaps you should have revealed your secret earlier and trusted to her mercy."

I know Isabel is right, and so her words pain me all the more. Then Angelina asks me why I look so downcast.

"Mother Ermentrude is angry that I deceived her. I fear she does not want me here," I say, fighting back tears.

"Ah, pregnant women are often moody for no cause but that they are pregnant! I know, for I have been one," she says, patting my hand. Then she adds, more briskly, "Be sensible, Ophelia. Mother Ermentrude would not send you away, for then who would tend to our aches and illnesses?"

Her words comfort me, as do the sisters who smile kindly and bless me in passing. Only Marguerite avoids me. She will not meet my eyes but crosses herself when we pass, as if to protect herself from a contagion. Isabel attends to me like a sister who expects to become an aunt. When no one is about, she puts her hands on my belly and laughs with delight when she feels the child move.

We never talk about what will happen after it is born.

While I am still able, I go about the business of healing, crushing leaves of rue to rub on aching joints and applying poultices to

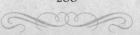

clear the lungs. By my work, I will regain Mother Ermentrude's trust.

"Praise God and thank you, Ophelia!" Angelina exults one day. "My boils are healed. But now that it is Lent, I must find some new suffering to endure." She tweaks my cheek and goes on her way.

Lent is the season of penitence, the time of grief one must undergo before the joy of Easter comes. Though I follow the rules and routines of convent life, Angelina will not allow me to abstain from meat, as the sisters do. She insists I need the nourishment. So I eat gladly and do not hunger. Yet I feel guilt at being full, for Therese again refuses to take food. She has become too weak to work in the laundry. Now I am the one who heats and carries the heavy buckets of water, stirs the soapy brew, lifts the sodden clothes to be rinsed, and spreads them to dry. Therese folds linens, pausing often to rest her weak arms.

"Why am I no longer favoured with Jesus's blood?" she says, regarding her open palms with despair. The hands that once bled from the harsh work have healed.

I say nothing, for I have no words that will comfort her.

In the next day's laundry I see Therese's night shift, stained with blood. I bring her a clean one and help her change. On her back I see abrasions and bloody welts. As I suspected, she has lashed herself with a rope, trying to purge herself of sin. Mother Ermentrude frowns on this ancient penance, though some of the older nuns still practise it. I wonder where Therese finds the strength to whip herself. Pity and anger stir in me.

"Why do you harm yourself in this way?" I ask her, trying not to recoil from the torn and oozing flesh.

"If I mortify my body, then I become one with Christ, who in his suffering and dying became one with mankind," she says.

"I do not think that God wishes his creatures to suffer." I try to argue with Therese, but her faith will not be persuaded by my reason.

With her back flayed and blistered, she falls asleep on her knees, her face on her cot. Then I treat her torn flesh with oil. I summon Angelina and Mother Ermentrude to help lift her wasted body, and while they hold her head, I pour a trickle of broth down her throat.

"She wants to die. What madness holds her in its thrall? What grief moves her to want to end her life?" I entreat Mother Ermentrude. I think of Hamlet's despair, which was beyond my remedy. I must not let Therese destroy her life as well. "I try to cure her, and constantly she resists me!"

"Be still, Ophelia. We must pray for her return to health," says Mother Ermentrude, a look of sorrow on her face.

At the weekly Mass, the priest raises a thin wedge of bread and says the words "This is the body of Christ". I think of Therese, light as the unleavened bread, and I look at my own body, heavy with two lives. I am afraid of pain, of being tormented, even unto death, in giving birth. This is why I go to the chapel. This is why I take Communion. Even though she knows my doubts, Mother Ermentrude permits it. My belly is large and I mount the steps to the railing with care. When Father Alphonse sees me, he reddens to the very roots of his sparse tonsure. I extend my cupped hands, but he will not give me the bread. I wait and will not leave.

"When Elizabeth was with child, she visited her kinswoman Mary, who carried Christ in her womb. And she was not turned

away from the Lord," I say in a low and modest voice. Isabel read me this gospel story just yesterday.

"Verily, you are not Saint Elizabeth. And most certainly you are not the Blessed Virgin!" the priest whispers, and the hissing of his voice carries throughout the chapel.

"God is merciful, if you are not," I say, looking directly into his rheumy eyes. "Who are you to deny me his grace?" I surprise even myself, that I would dare to dispute with a priest during the Mass. Five months of convent life have, in their way, furthered my education, if not my humility.

The priest is too stunned to answer me. He looks away, places the bread in my hand, and draws back as if he has touched fire. I frighten him, as a madwoman frightens those who believe themselves sane.

After the service, I put myself in the path of Father Alphonse as he hastens from the chapel.

"Please, I pray you take the Communion to our servant Therese. She is fevered and too weak to come to chapel."

"I must be on my way," he says, unwilling to be stopped.

"Your way must be to bring Christ to her," I say, my voice rising with indignation. Unable to dispute that point, he follows me to Therese's room. I watch as he puts the thin wafer between her dry lips and administers the cup, murmuring in Latin. I marvel how the scrap of bread on her tongue fills Therese with a visible joy. The drops of blood red wine in her mouth invigorate her frail body, seeming to ease her pain. Her forehead is cool to my touch and her breathing easy. I have hope that she may yet recover.

I begin sitting for many hours each day with Therese, for my own burden grows too big to carry with ease. When she is awake

I read to her; when she sleeps I rest as well. On this wintry morning, a rumour flies through the convent. As a frightened bird caught inside a house startles one person after another, the news stirs up the servants and nuns alike. It is carried in whispers by those who hurry to the chapel, and it passes with the bread and cheese shared at the midday meal.

The meeting in the chapter house that night confirms it. Mother informs us that Count Durufle is en route to the convent. He has learned that one of the members is with child. Was it the steward or the priest who carried the news? Was it Marguerite? No, even she looks pale and fearful. Durufle is said to be outraged, for the convent's reputation is at stake. He threatens to withdraw his patronage and force its doors to close.

Worse news yet is that he is not alone. Traveling with him is Bishop Garamond, who has the authority to enforce whatever Durufle wills.

Chapter 45

No words of comfort or assurance can be spoken, for Mother Ermentrude has ordered silence and solitary prayer. *Deliver me from evil, now and at the hour of my death.* Constantly my mind utters this plea, as if it could prevent the count and his bishop from coming. When I fall asleep, my dreaming is a medley of all my fears. Edmund pursues me, a dagger in his hand. I feel his hot breath on my neck and his hands on my breasts, but my feet are chained to heavy stones and I cannot move. A glass vial shatters on the floor, spilling thick blood that forms the shape of a grinning death's head. An arras hanging on a wall billows, as if stirred by a strong wind, and from behind it scurries a creature with the face of my father. The voice of Hamlet shouts, "What is this, a rat?" and his laughter echoes in a vast chamber. Then the chapel bells awaken me, but I feel no relief to find myself at St Emilion. This place of refuge has suddenly become a prison where I await the trial that might condemn not only me, but Mother Ermentrude and all the sisters.

When the pale but striving sun has lifted the grey morning

mist, Count Durufle and the bishop arrive. I hear the clatter of horses' hooves, but I have not the strength nor will to look out of my window. There will not be the usual ceremonies of an episcopal visit, for this is no occasion of celebration. A heavy silence, more fearful than pious, engulfs the convent.

It grieves me to think that I have brought shame to the place that has sheltered me, that by my unwitting deeds, St Emilion might be ruined. I will throw myself at the bishop's mercy and insist that I am sinless in this matter. But will they force me to disclose my history? Where would I go if the bishop orders Mother Ermentrude to send me away? In my condition and in such cold, death would be my certain end. The violent knife, the drowning waters, poison, and fever — I defied them all in my escape from Elsinore. Will vengeful Death now seize my life and my child's, too?

Interrupting these black thoughts, Isabel comes to escort me to the chapter house, where the bishop will question me. I am filled with regret at the thought of losing this friend.

"Dearest Isabel, I am sorry for this whole affair. I will try —"

"Hush! Do not fear. The bishop is a good man; just be humble before him. But beware of Durufle, for he is the powerful one. And remember the words of the psalm: *Our Lord lifteth up the bruised . . . Strangers, the fatherless and the widow he will receive.* What more certain promise could there be?" she says, gripping my hand, desperate to comfort me.

Even Marguerite has the grace to show some pity with a tilt of her head as I pass into the chamber where Mother Ermentrude conducts the convent's business from a table piled with books and papers in neat bundles. The panelling that surrounds me is carved with figures of angels and the apostles. If only these wooden figures could spring to life and intercede for me!

Marguerite follows me into the room and takes a seat at a slanted lectern near the window. Of course, because she is the secretary, she must make a record of the proceedings. How I wish that she were not a witness to my shame.

In an oaken chair with arms like a throne sits the bishop. Mother Ermentrude stands at his left hand, Count Durufle at his right. The count has a sharp-featured face with a nose like a hawk's beak. His black eyes accost me as if I am the devil made flesh. He wears a severe black satin doublet and hose. The plume in his hat is the only thing about him that is not stiff. It quivers with his every movement. With short, bowed legs, he is not much taller than I am.

Mother Ermentrude's hands are folded and her face does not reveal her thoughts. Will she remain my mentor in this matter, or will duty and obedience put her on the bishop's side? I resolve to hold my tongue rather than to speak untruth.

I steal a glance at Bishop Garamond. He holds his miter on his lap, exposing a head of fine silvery hair. His crozier rests against the armchair. He wears a scarlet cope with sleeves lined in fur. Remembering myself, I kneel and kiss the heavy jewelled ring that squeezes his wide finger. I do not dare to look at his face.

"What is your name, child?"

"I am known as Ophelia."

"You see by her garb that she has not professed any vows," Mother notes. By touching my head, she indicates my simple coif. The nuns wear longer veils.

But Bishop Garamond is not looking at my face.

"I see by her shape that indeed her confinement is imminent," he says, frowning thoughtfully. "When did she arrive here?"

I know what he is thinking: that there are convents where men — even monks and priests — are admitted as guests, and the nuns are unchaste.

Without hesitating, Mother Ermentrude replies, "Late October. On the feast day of Saints Simon and Jude." Do I hear in her voice a hint of indignation?

We are in the final days of March. The bishop must know, then, that my child's conception could not have occurred at St Emilion.

"She has been among the sisters for months, displaying the evidence of her vile harlotry!" Durufle says, his disgust evident.

My face burns with suppressed fury. I cannot be silent, despite my resolution.

"I am no harlot, Your Grace, but an honest woman. My husband is dead."

I glance at Mother Ermentrude, to see if she believes me. But she only frowns slightly as if in warning, for she knows my tendency to speak passionately. I will not disappoint her again.

"Hah! What else should she say?" barks Durufle in mocking disbelief. "Then who was your husband, girl?"

I would not tell the story of my love to this hard-hearted fiend should he press my thumbs and threaten to pull my limbs apart on a great wheel!

"I will not say."

"See! She lies, without a doubt," Durufle cries.

Mother Ermentrude glares at the count with evident dislike, and Bishop Garamond holds up his hand to silence him.

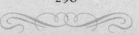

"Has she confessed her sins and repented of them?" he asks.

"That, Your Excellency, is a matter for her conscience," replies Mother.

I have not confessed my sins to Father Alphonse, and Mother knows this. She knows my heart and its struggles. Not the priest, but Mother, should be my confessor. Why did I not tell her all, when I had her open and forgiving ear?

The bishop regards me, tapping his cheek with a finger.

"What is her habit of life here?" he asks.

"Ophelia prays and communes with us, and abides by the rules of community life. She displays charity to all, humility and a love of work," says Mother.

"How can we be sure she does not deceive you?" Durufle interjects. His harsh expression matches his unyielding figure. "Surely she has run away from another convent. That is why she will not tell you where she is from or how she came to be in this state. Or the name of her *pretended husband*." He spits out the words mockingly.

"She came to us weak and sick in body and mind. She asked for our protection. She brought a generous purse with her. Now she works among us as our physician and healer," says Mother, like one who patiently repeats a message for a child.

"Witchery, you can be sure. She and that servant — that base laundry maid — are surely conspiring in some evil," growls Durufle.

Again, I must speak, though my words might endanger me.

"Therese loves our Lord with all her heart. She is, however, afflicted with a wasting disease which I treat with plants provided by our Maker. To call this witchcraft is an affront to the Lord," I say, trembling all over with the effort of speaking. Mother

Ermentrude presses my shoulder, either to calm me or to bid me be silent.

"I see she has a passionate nature. No doubt she continues to lie," insists Durufle. "She should be expelled, like the wicked woman she most certainly is."

"The law of Christ and the rule of Benedict alike require us to give her shelter," says Bishop Garamond. "But they do not allow us to condone immorality —"

"Rather you must condemn it, Your Excellency," Durufle interrupts. The plume on his hat quivers with his rage. "Evil is a contagion that spreads with contact. Root it out here, at its source!" He stamps his foot for emphasis, then adds in a low and oily voice, "This foul business impugns my family's good name. I tell you, it bodes ill for this convent."

Bishop Garamond is silent, perhaps considering this threat. I dare to look at his face, even into his eyes. They are grey and troubled, like a dark-clouded sky, but there is no unkindness there. In the silence, I hear the scratching of Marguerite's pen.

"Tell me whence you come and the identity of your child's father," he commands me, though gently. All wait for my reply. The sound of Marguerite's pen ceases; she, too, waits.

Isabel has told me the bishop is a good man. When she took her vows, he presided over the ceremony and, like a tender father, gave her in marriage to Christ. If I cannot trust this kindly-seeming bishop, what man can I trust?

"No harm will come to you or to the child. Speak," he urges again.

How can he make such a promise? No one on earth can ensure our safety. Though Claudius can no longer touch me,

Edmund may still live. And King Fortinbras would be no ally to me or my child. Above all, I do not trust the powerful and vengeful Durufle.

I offer the bishop a reply from a psalm I am sure he knows.

"No more will I put my trust in princes," I say.

A strange sensation overcomes me, and the edges of my sight grow dark. I waver on my feet and, against my will, I sink to my knees. Does God strike me for defying his deputy?

Bishop Garamond sighs heavily. Durufle makes a sound like the grinding of teeth. Mother comes to my side, and her strong arms keep me from falling prostrate.

After a moment, Bishop Garamond announces, "She may remain among you until she has delivered the child. Meanwhile we will inquire and discover the truth." He sounds weary.

"Your Grace, I must protest —" hisses Durufle, but the bishop cuts him off by stamping his crozier to signal the finality of his judgement. Once, twice, three times. The sound echoes loudly from the wood-panelled walls. Then I feel the bishop's hand on my head as he murmurs a prayer in Latin. With Mother's help, I rise to leave, but I am seized by a pain that grips my entire belly and I cry out for help.

Chapter 46

Darkness like water swirls about me. Pain seizes my belly, stopping my breath. Its grip loosens and I gulp the air, greedy for life. Then the weight of all my suffering sinks my body again as water closes over my face and seeps into me. I kick feebly against the resisting shroud of my clothing.

Fragments of Psalms float to the surface of my mind. *Save me O God for I have come into deep waters where the floods overflow me.* I am seized again and again with pains that mount like sins and pierce like swords. Oblivion opens before me like a dark chasm, and I am too weak to step back from its edge.

Let not the deep swallow me up nor the pit shut its mouth on me.

I see a glowing fire that heats my flesh. Death and sin must not claim me now! I hold fast to life though my body bends, twists, and arches as if it will break. My blood flows out. Voices cry to me and whisper softly. The dead, in a masquelike procession, beckon to me to join them.

Then strong hands lift me from the water. They raise me from an earthen grave, newborn like Lazarus. They pull from the clutches of my body a slick, wet baby that renounces my darkness for the light.

My flesh also shall rest in hope, for you will not abandon me to the grave.

The ghosts are dispelled. Death is defeated again. The flood-waters recede; it is only salty sweat that trickles down my face and into my mouth. Isabel lays in my arms a tiny boy, gasping his own first breaths with lusty cries. He is swaddled in clean linen and smells of purity itself.

She and Angelina hover over me like angels wreathed in human joy.

"Children are a heritage from the Lord, and the fruit of the womb is a gift," says Angelina. Her red face is bathed in sweat, but her smile tells me that all is well.

I have delivered the babe on a pallet in the bakery, for it is the warmest place in the convent. The fires have been stoked and the ovens left open to disperse the heat.

"Angelina, bring my small cabinet of medicines and the bag of herbs. A hot poultice placed on my belly will help to shrink the womb and parsley will bring away the afterbirth."

"Did I not say she would soon be about her work again?" says Angelina with a laugh as she does my bidding.

Mother Ermentrude comes into the room and kneels by my pallet, a gesture of humility that belies her authority. She looks tired. Marguerite stands behind her.

"We have prayed these two days and now thank God for your safe deliverance," Mother says, taking my hand. She has tears in her eyes. Her touch moves me to speak truth at last.

"I am sorry that I ever deceived you in this matter. I wanted to

tell you, but I was afraid you would send me away. Do you forgive me?"

"Shhh. There is no cause, Ophelia," she says, smoothing my damp hair from my face and touching my baby's forehead.

"I have never known a mother's care," I whisper. "I do not know how to be a mother." Even as I say this, I realise it is no longer true.

"Do not fear," says Mother Ermentrude. "Think of Our Lady, the mother of beautiful love, greatness and holy hope."

"No, I will think of you," I say to this woman who kneels at my bedside as my very own mother would. "You are a kind mother to many daughters. Look how they love you, as I do." At this, Mother Ermentrude smiles so broadly that her eyes almost disappear into the many folds and creases of her face.

I look at the baby cradled in my arms. His mouth is a perfect O, like that of a tiny chorister singing God's praises. I know that I will love him beyond all reason. This must be what Gertrude felt upon seeing the newborn Hamlet, what my own mother felt holding me before she died. The thought comes to me: *This, then, is the fruit of it all. Not the punishment of death, but the gift of life.*

Strength and courage flow into my body like new blood. The heavy burden I have borne so long now lifts from my soul. I am afraid no more as I open my mouth to confess.

"My son's name is Hamlet, as was his father's, and he is a prince of Denmark."

Chapter 47

It is April now, and the rain falls in sweet showers that bathe every root and swelling bud of nature. The yellow daffadown-dillies have burst into bloom, and the tiny cupped flowers of crocuses are spreading their pied blankets of white and purple. My son, Hamlet, is as new and as full of wonders as the spring. Isabel tells me that when they learned his name, the nuns wept with surprise and joy.

"This is no usual babe, but a prince! He will be a bringer of peace!" Sister Lucia even cried out.

Soon Mother will send word of his birth to the bishop, who will rule on our future, but for now my delight in Hamlet overcomes any fear.

Every earthly joy, however, is tempered by sadness. For weeks, Therese has been too sick even to rise from her bed. Tomorrow is the feast of Christ's resurrection, and while the nuns attend the Easter Vigil service in the chapel, I keep my own vigil at Therese's bedside. She is out of her senses and does not recognise me. Now the precise outlines of her skull show through the skin of her face, presaging death. She murmurs incoherent words and plucks at her bedding with bone-thin fingers. Her weakened body rejects even the tiniest crumb of bread and drop of water.

Therese's illness oppresses the convent like a heavy blanket laid over spring's green floor. Those who resented her piety now are ashamed that they turned away from her. In Mother's drawn face, I can see the regret that she did not champion Therese in her desire to become a nun. Though speechless and unaware, the dying woman rebukes us all. That I could not make her eat fills me with sadness, even as I joy to watch my baby grow fat from my milk. I have failed Therese, and she will soon die.

As if in a waking dream, I hear the voices of angels. Have the hosts of heaven come to claim my patient? I open my eyes to see that the candle has expired, and there is no light left to pierce the dark. But Therese still breathes and sleeps.

The singing commences again, and I realise that the Easter matins have begun. I pick up baby Hamlet in his cradle of rushes. The steady chanting draws my wearied steps, which know their way despite the dark, to the chapel. In the nave, scores of country folk stand or sit on mats and benches. They have risen before dawn and walked in the dark to witness this annual drama. In the sanctuary, candles illuminate the solemn faces of the nuns. The crosses are covered in black cloth, signifying the death of Christ. The audience waits, expecting a great drama.

Finally the act begins. Mother Ermentrude, in a gold-edged green cope, sends the three Marys to visit the tomb of Jesus, a large stone that has been hauled into the sanctuary. The women, played by Angelina, Marguerite, and Isabel, lament the death of their Saviour, moving their hands in small and eloquent arcs as they sing. Then they see the angel, played by a farmer's son in a tunic covered with goosefeathers. He carries a jewelled box, and as he opens the lid, he lifts his eyes to signify that the box is empty. Rejoicing that their Lord is risen, they carry the news to the nuns seated in the choir.

Then the village priest enters, dressed in a brown cloak and carrying a shovel like our ancestor Adam. Marguerite, who represents Mary Magdalene, falls to her knees, for she recognises the resurrected Christ. Her clear, sweet voice rises in joy as she sings of her love.

This is a play quite unlike anything I saw acted at the court of Elsinore. Here nothing is feigned, no action is false or pretended. The nuns' upraised hands, their solemn steps and their shining faces convey hope and earnest faith. It is truth they enact, a truth that shames all human falsehoods and deceits.

Now Hamlet begins to cry in my arms and struggles against his swaddling clothes. I put him to my breast and cover him with my cloak. There he sucks contentedly, like a bee deep in a flower.

Singing and bearing candles, the nuns leave the choir and follow the priest to the sepulchre. Sombre chanting rises through the floor. Then I hear a rising cadence of joy that makes the benches, walls, and windows seem to tremble.

"*Christus resurgens,* Christ is risen," the nuns sing, emerging again into the nave with candles. "Christ has conquered darkness and death." The priest holds up a flat round bread on a silver plate, a symbol of Christ's body. At that moment the rising sun's rays reach the rose window above the altar, bathing the sanctuary in blue, red, and gold light. The sun glints on the silver, sending shards of light flashing across our faces. The congregation gasps, as

305

if an unseen bellows were blowing the very breath of life into them. Overcome by the brightness, I bow and clutch Hamlet to me as if he were Christ himself and all my lost loves restored to me.

The drama concluded, the crowd empties from the chapel, and the nuns file out in a silent procession. Not wanting to disturb the sleeping Hamlet, I stay. The changing patterns of light transfix my sight. Then a bone-deep weariness overcomes me, and I fall into a dreamless sleep on the rush-strewn floor of the chapel. When I open my eyes again, Hamlet's solemn little face is before me, and his fingers are tangled in my hair. I am filled with hope and a sureness that Therese will revive. In my mind I see her sitting up and drinking broth, and her eyes are bright again.

Carrying Hamlet in his basket, I hasten to Therese's room, where the three Marys are gathered. Isabel sponges Therese's forehead while Marguerite holds a useless spoon. Angelina prays, sitting on a stool. Beneath the blanket, Therese lies flat, just as when I left her.

"Is she no better?" I ask in dismay.

"I prayed for an Easter miracle," says Isabel. "But God wills otherwise."

"She opens her eyes only to cry out to God, like a lost child. She does not see us here," says Marguerite. Tears well in her green eyes like ice melted by the sun.

I feel betrayed by my new hope. The bitter truth is that Therese will die, perhaps on this Easter day.

"Why will God not save her? He brought his son, who was dead, to life again. Why can he not raise this sick woman from her bed?" I look into the faces of the sisters, not caring to hide my distress from them. They, too, are grieved and have no answers for me. I sink down on the foot of Therese's bed and this time address my complaint to the heavens above. "I have tried to help her, God, but you are not helping *me!*"

Isabel comes to me and rests her hand on my shoulder.

"It is not your fault, Ophelia," she says.

"I wanted to see her grow healthy again. To cure her would have atoned for a broken promise in my past. I let down my dear Elnora, who was like a mother to me." My failures weigh upon me like a yoke across my shoulders. But I must shake the burden off and do what good I can. "Marguerite, find a bolster and blankets to put behind her back. Fetch my medicine box, and bring Mother Ermentrude."

Marguerite lays down the spoon and complies without question. Lately her manner toward me has changed from one of pious disdain to an awed humility. Evidently she is persuaded that I am not a weak and sinful girl, but an honest widow and mother to a prince.

I bend over Therese and examine her eyes and skin, feel her faint pulse.

"Have you thought of a new remedy, some untried cordial?" Angelina asks, her voice inflected with hope.

"No, the time for such treatment is past. I cannot cure her, but I believe we can ease her pain in dying."

Marguerite returns with Mother Ermentrude. She and Isabel lift Therese's frail form into a sitting position and support her with blankets. Therese turns her head weakly from side to side, like a hungry baby or a bird in want of food. Mother Ermentrude begins to pray, fingering her beads.

I do not know what I am doing; I only act as if I have a

purpose. I pour some oil of rosemary steeped in cloves on to a cloth. I have read that its pungence can sometimes restore memory and speech. With the cloth I wipe Therese's face.

Her eyelids flutter open. She sees me and shakes her head slowly.

"Jesus, come to me," she says, her voice weak and plaintive. "Why does my Lord come no more?" Therese spreads her hands on her sunken chest.

"Alas, she no longer has the vision of suckling the Christ child," whispers Angelina. "And now she is in despair."

"I have nothing to give. See how I am withered. Oh, Jesus, have mercy on me."

Without thinking, moved by a will that is not my own, I turn and with one swift motion lift baby Hamlet from his basket and unwrap him. His arms and legs, freed from their swaddling, beat the air. I hold the infant upright before Therese. His eyes open wide in his rosy face and he waves his tiny fists.

When Therese sees the infant, she smiles and her eyes shine like bright lamps revealing her very soul. With sudden strength, she leans forward and takes the baby in her bony arms, cradling him close to her. Tears spring from her dry eyes like water from the rock in the desert.

"It is my salvation!" exclaims Therese. She strokes the baby's smooth, warm flesh. She breathes deeply.

"He smells of honey and roses and milk," she murmurs, a look of ecstasy on her face.

Inspired, Angelina begins to pray the words of the aged Simeon when he saw the child Jesus.

"*Lord now let thy servant depart in peace, according to thy word. For*

mine eyes have seen thy salvation, which you have prepared before the face of all people, to be a light to lighten the nations —"

Before Angelina is finished, Therese has died. Her head nods forward in the pose of a painter's Madonna regarding her child. As I lift my baby from her limp arms, they fall open in her lap, palms facing upwards.

Isabel and Marguerite gasp. Mother Ermentrude crosses herself. I stand unmoving and speechless, while Angelina grabs my arm for support. Our eyes are fixed on the amazing sight. There, at the centre of Therese's hands, spring bright beads of blood.

Chapter 48

In the twilight of the Easter evening, the day's strange events fill my thoughts. Already the nuns are saying that a miracle was manifested in Therese's death. To call it so is beyond my weak belief. Yet I do not understand the appearance of the blood on Therese's palms. Perhaps, I think, her own fingernails pierced the skin. I clench my hands as hard as I can and conclude that this would be impossible, especially considering Therese's weakness. Yet such a flow of blood must be a natural wonder that physicians have surely witnessed and philosophers written of. I will read further, searching until I find an explanation that enlightens me.

I am surprised that grief for Therese does not shake me, though the image of her lifeless body is fresh in my mind. How can I be sad, when she died in great joy? Instead I feel strangely calm. I have come to believe that God takes to himself those who are afflicted with madness. Perhaps he will not condemn them for holding his gift of life so lightly. That may mean my husband,

Hamlet, rests in peace, and so I am comforted. No fears disturb my mind, but a peace envelopes me.

The pressure of a firm hand on my shoulder startles me from this tranquil state. It is Marguerite, who has come in her usual stealthy way into my room. She carries a small writing case.

"I knocked, but you did not hear me. I pray you, forgive me this intrusion. My business cannot wait," she says, her voice both quiet and insistent. In her position, she is used to having her way.

My first thought is that the bishop has already learned of Hamlet's birth and has rendered a decision about my future. I have made no provisions for this day, but I will not be afraid.

"Am I to be turned away from St Emilion? Must I prepare to leave now?" I ask, sitting up and gathering Hamlet into my arms.

"No, that is not the matter."

I am relieved somewhat, but still curious. Marguerite waits to be invited to stay. I nod my head towards the stool, inviting her to use it. When she is settled, she opens her writing box on her lap so that the sun's failing rays fall upon it and takes up her pen.

"It is my duty to record the events of this day and the testimony of eyewitnesses, for a report must be made to the bishop. I must start today, while the scene is still fresh in our memories. But my true aim is to publish Therese's story to the world. This day's wonders shall make our convent famous throughout France and Christendom," she says with a grand sweep of her arm. Her eyes are bright with zeal.

"Ah, a new story for your catalogue of saints and sinners. What will be the moral of this tale?"

"Pray do not mock me, Ophelia," says Marguerite, with a semblance of her former haughty manner towards me. "Today

we witnessed a miracle. For though the dead was not brought to life, a stony heart — my own — was softened and made a welcome bed for God's grace. Perhaps others may be brought to a truer faith by hearing of Therese's godly death."

Her evident sincerity makes me regret my light words.

"There are, indeed, many strange things about this Easter day. But I doubt that I can help you, for I do not understand the meaning of it all."

"What is there to understand? A miracle must always be a mystery," she says simply.

"I do not believe in miracles. But I grant that there are things — events and beings, perhaps — beyond the reach of reason," I say, turning my thoughts into words with difficulty. "Yet though our faculty of reason be weak, it seldom descends into madness." I shake my head, wondering what brought that affliction upon Hamlet and Therese. "Perhaps only some forms of madness spring from a diseased mind, while other types of madness may be divine in origin."

"Must I write that Therese was mad?" Marguerite asks, clearly dismayed.

"No, that is hardly the sum of it." Nor does it sum up Hamlet's case, I think. I rest my chin in my hands, still musing. The silence grows until Marguerite breaks it with impatient words.

"Come now, Ophelia, I cannot tell the story without your help. To begin, I must describe the means you used to treat Therese's illness. Then an account of your friendship will follow. For you alone have treated her with true charity. I regret that I did not," Marguerite says, glancing down and to the side. It is a coy motion I have seen in court ladies, but in her it passes for humility.

"In a moment. But first you must know that I did not act

purely out of charity. I wanted to prove my skill by curing Therese. I wanted to cheat Death of her." It is easy now to admit my wrongs, even to this proud sister, for I no longer fear the consequences of speaking truth. "Marguerite, I have drunk poison and almost drowned and was buried alive before I escaped from Denmark. This is no lie, but truth," I say, seeing her eyes grow wide. "I tell you for this reason: Because I was so desperate to preserve my life, I could not bear to see Therese choosing to die. It was my own will that I tried to force upon her, defying her wishes and perhaps God's as well. I confess that I have a long habit of disobedience," I say with a wry smile. "Surely this is no fit matter for your holy tale."

Marguerite holds her pen still. I am relieved that she has written nothing of what I have said.

"You did no wrong by trying to save her life," she says softly.

"But I failed!" I say, feeling anew the disappointment of being unable to cure Therese. "Indeed, I have not been able to preserve the life of anyone I have loved!" I realise that I have given voice to the essence of my loneliness. Tears spring from my eyes like a sudden shower and fall upon my sleeping child, whom I hold tight to my breast. "Now I would give my very life, to preserve his," I say between sobs.

"But that is it, Ophelia — the miracle of salvation!" Marguerite's eyes shine with excitement.

"What did I say? What do you mean?"

"Christ gave his life to redeem us. Today, on Therese's hands, we saw Christ's blood. It is the sign that you are forgiven; I am forgiven. Now you are willing to give your life for another's. That is the miracle of salvation! This is what I will write." Breathless,

she dips her pen in ink and begins to write rapidly.

I am dazed by her words. The idea, that by Therese's death I am forgiven, comes over me like the tide, lifting me with its gentle force and bearing me towards a solid shore. I see my griefs begin to sink below the waves, and I ride the crest in hope.

The scratching of Marguerite's pen has stopped. I see her gaze fixed on the wall as if on a mirror that will reflect her inner self. I long to know her thoughts, the meaning of her manner towards me. How is it that she, whom I once hated, now listens without judgement to my sins and even persuades me that I have taken part in a miracle?

"You say Therese's death has changed your heart," I begin. "But you were already changed. Before, you disdained me for a sinner. Since Hamlet's birth, you have not been cruel to me, but mild in your manner, even kind. Why?"

Marguerite grips her pen and her eyes meet mine for a moment, revealing anguish, before she looks away. Her ivory brow furrows in delicate lines.

"Must I confess that I have been proud and vain and given to false judgements? God knows this, and so do you," she says.

"No, I am not a priest who wants to hear your sins. It is your story I long to know. Won't you tell it to me?"

Marguerite shakes her head. "My purpose is to write the life of Therese, and you are distracting me from it," she says, sounding officious.

"I will help you with that task. But first, I must have a story, for I am in the mood to hear one," I say with a smile, meaning to coax her tale from her.

"I see your plot," she says with a wary, sideways look. "But I

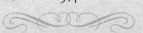

am not accustomed to speak of myself to anyone. Like you, I would conceal my past. Even Mother Ermentrude does not know it all."

"Let us be fair. You know my secrets, now let me know yours. It will lighten the burden to share it." I feel the wall of her self-defence begin to crumble. "You may trust me, I assure you."

Marguerite sighs deeply, and then begins to speak.

"One reason for my pride is that I was born to a prince of Sweden," she says, laying down her pen. "I was called Margrethe. In the king's court I was raised to the brink of womanhood. Then my father died and my mother grew sick with sorrow. It fell to my uncle, the king, to contract a marriage for me. His aim was to enhance Sweden's fortunes, but he also sought a worthy man, for he said he wished me to be happy as well."

The only sound in the room is that of baby Hamlet sucking his fist. The chapel bells ring, calling us to evensong, but neither Marguerite nor I move.

"I had many suitors, all chosen by my uncle. Some did not speak my language. Others were grizzled with age, and I cried to think of myself bound in marriage to an old man. One day there came to our court a prince whose youth and vigour made him a most fair suitor. He was handsome and ambitious, a worthy match for Sweden. I favored him, for he was fair of tongue, and by praising my beauty he persuaded me to grant him certain favours. Having conquered me in part, he pressed for full possession. When I denied him, he grew angry, saying that all my body would soon be his. He said he would not marry me, if I prized my virginity above his lordship. Still I refused him."

Tears spring to Marguerite's eyes at the recollection. She

315

wipes them with a napkin produced from her sleeve. "I believed I loved him, but I began to doubt that he would be a worthy husband. And then — I cannot bear to speak of this," she whispers. "I am afraid."

"Go on. Be bold." I remove her writing box from her lap and take her hand in mine.

"One day he assaulted me as if I were a land to be invaded and seized. I fought to repel him and was nearly overcome, when by fortune a servant heard my cries and discovered us. I denounced this suitor to the king, but the prince denied his crime and instead impugned my virtue. He called me whore and spurned me."

"Fie upon him, wherever he is now!" I cry, remembering Hamlet's similar words. "Why do these proud men cast their sins upon us? Go on." But Marguerite needs no urging, for now she is caught up in telling her story.

"When the prince refused to marry me, the king was angry at the loss of this alliance that he desired. My reputation ruined, I was unfit for marriage with any man of rank. Forgetting his care for my happiness, my uncle sent me to St Emilion, which he chose for its obscurity. He did not even send word of my mother's death until months had passed." She sighs, but she is no longer weeping.

Marguerite's is a story well suited for a book of sad romance, I think, remembering how I used to relish such tales.

"When did these events occur?" I ask.

"Some five years ago I came to this place, pretending to be a devout and willing postulant. And here I have held my maidenly purity to be the greatest virtue, for I preserved it from the

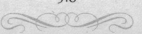

wicked, and it is all I have left." She spreads her empty hands and regards them.

I have one more question to ask, to know the final piece of her life's puzzle.

"Marguerite, who was this vile prince, and what became of him?"

Marguerite looks me in the eye. Her face is open and guileless, her beauty plain. Unblinking, she replies, "He is Fortinbras, Prince of Norway."

My hands fly to my face and a cry escapes me.

"Yes, the same who now rules your Denmark," she says grimly. "When you arrived, I saw the Danish coins in your purse, and I heard in your speech the accents of the Northern tongues. I raised my guard against you, for I did not know your purpose in coming or your allegiance in those kingdoms."

"And why did you tell me the tale of Agnes? Was it to frighten me?"

"I did suspect you carried this babe, for it was rumoured among us. And I was jealous, for the sisters embraced you, while I have been friendless here."

I only shake my head, still overwhelmed by her revelations.

"Please, Ophelia, will you forgive me for being unjust and cruel?" she asks, not pleading but with a noble dignity. "For I see now that virginity is not the highest virtue of a woman."

"Please say no more, for I have forgiven you." I hold up my hand to silence her. I am pondering these strange coincidences: that Marguerite's abuser and the invader of Denmark are the same Fortinbras of Norway, and that she and I should discover each other. Perhaps it is not chance, but the work of some divinity that guides our unknowing steps to their ordained destination.

317

Baby Hamlet now begins to fuss, and I pick him up and rock him back and forth. The movement soothes my roiled spirits, too. Marguerite smiles and reaches out her hand to grasp his tiny fingers. Her face softens with a kindness that enhances her beauty.

"Now I have cause to hope that Fortinbras may someday face justice," she says. "For the Psalmist writes: *Like arrows in the hand of a warrior, are the children of one's youth.* Perhaps it will be your son who brings about his downfall."

"I will never return to Denmark, to live under the yoke of another tyrant who would not hesitate to kill my Hamlet." I lean over my baby, kissing his fat cheek. "You are not ambitious for a crown, are you, my sweet love?" I murmur to him. "No, Marguerite, I embrace this exile, for I wish to live in peace. But will you ever return home?"

"Home? This is my home now. Here I will stay and write of Therese."

Laying Hamlet down again, I pick up her writing box, set it on her lap, and hand her the pen.

"You must also tell your own story, Marguerite; write it, by all means."

Little Hamlet is a sprightly child with his father's dark hair and Gertrude's grey eyes. He loves to dig in the dirt and pick wild-flowers, and I help his chubby fingers weave them together. At three years of age, he prattles like my father did, but I attend to every lisping word he speaks. I search his face for some hint of my own, but he has none of my features. Instead I have given him all of my affection, which springs like water from a deep fountain within me.

My Hamlet is a tiny prince in this realm of women. The old nuns laugh and their eyes dance when they bend down to receive a garland of daisies or cowslips from his hand. Isabel loves the boy almost as much as I do, and he binds us like sisters. As he has no children to play with, he befriends the wild rabbits, offering them food and stroking their fur until he can touch their twitching noses.

Since Hamlet's birth we have lived in a stone cottage near the convent gate. I have taken over the duties of the steward, who was dismissed upon the death of Count Durufle. The puritanical count had been long afflicted with syphilis, it was discovered. With his death, Mother Ermentrude's brother, a virtuous noble-man, found favour with Bishop Garamond. St Emilion is now secure under his patronage, and the convent prospers as a result of my commerce with the local merchants and farmers, so Mother Ermentrude and the bishop are pleased. When Mother tried to return Gertrude's money to me, I made her keep it as payment for my salvation, for it was she who kept my body and my soul together. In turn, she set up the apothecary I now use and fitted it with every tool of science known in France today. I draw some profit from my work, storing this new wealth towards the day when I might leave St Emilion to seek out a different course.

The memory of Therese keeps me from too much pride in my abilities, even as my reputation for healing grows. Not only do I tend to the complaints of the nuns, but country people and villagers pay for my services, and the poorest are granted them. Soon I will need an apprentice and a gardener, too, for my garden flourishes like the first Eden. Replete with common herbs and exotic plants, it is a garden worthy of Mechtild, and every year its dimensions increase.

I often visit Therese's plot in the chapel cemetery. The villagers have made it a shrine, and it is always fragrant with their offerings. I add bouquets of columbine, fennel and daisies from my garden. On her grave I planted a rosemary bush, and it proves as enduring as an evergreen tree.

Despite three years of study in philosophy and medicine, I have not discovered a cause in Nature why Therese's hands bled at her death. It is one of the body's many mysteries, which the study of anatomy seeks to unlock. One day I hope to write a compendium of all my cures, including those Elnora taught me. It will include an essay on how the mind can assist — or resist — the body's health. Like a generous patron, Mother Ermentrude has made every book in the convent's great library open to me. Some days I share a desk with Marguerite, who labours with great devotion on a book she calls *True Lives of Godly Women.* I tell her that if she will not include the story of her own life, then I will write it for her. As I check the progress of her book, Marguerite in turn checks the progress of my infant faith. I tell her that I profess God's goodness and mercy, but what I love most truly is his marvellous creature, my son. She has made peace with her past, as I have with mine.

When Hamlet was born and I revealed his father's name, Bishop Garamond believed my claim that I had fled Denmark for my safety and that of my child. Shortly after the tragedy at Elsinore, news of it had reached France, along with a rumour of a royal heir in hiding. The bishop disbelieved it, for such stories always attend the fall of a kingdom. But Marguerite did vouch for me, Isabel offered witness, and I produced Horatio's letter. The bishop acknowledged me to be a widow and allowed me to remain at the convent. Now he has become the young Hamlet's protector, promising to educate him well. Marguerite warns me that he will one day use my son to fulfill his own political designs, for even churchmen long for empire. I tell her I will trust in his kindness now, for I must dwell in the house of today, where little Hamlet plays in all the innocence of childhood. Someday in that far future, my son must hear of the foul crimes of Denmark, the revenge unleashed there, and its tragic ending. When I tell him of his father's madness, his mother's grief and their unfortunate love, what will he make of this true but unbelievable tale?

I am content for my story to end here. But there are no endings, while we live.

Now is the month of May, which marks the end of spring and promises a full and fruitful summer. I am toiling in my garden after a rain, moving tender seedlings. I am grateful for the clouds that prevent the sun from wilting their leaves before they take root again and resume their growing. My skirts are gathered between my legs and tied like pantaloons so they do not drag in the dirt. I relish the feel of soft, wet earth beneath my bare feet. My hair, long again, is wrapped carelessly in a wimple.

Hamlet is napping within the cottage. I pause and lean on my shovel, calling to mind his sleep-composed face, the eyelashes that brush his fat cheeks, his red mouth that curves like the bow of Cupid. Then a sudden movement catches my eye, breaking my reverie. I see Isabel retreating with quick steps from the far edge of my garden. How unusual that she does not stop to greet me and pass the time in talk. It is not like her to be furtive. I will question her later and tease out her purpose.

Then I see, leaning against a tree near where the poppies display their bright faces, a figure that is somehow familiar. It is not a sister clad in convent linen. What is a man doing within these walls? Tall and somewhat stooped, he steps from the shadows into the light. I glimpse red hair, and I cry out, dropping my shovel.

"Horatio?"

Never was the sight of a man or woman more welcome to me. Forgetting all decorum, I leap through the soft wet soil, careless

of the seedlings underfoot, and rise on my toes to embrace him. I feel his arms around me and relish their strength for a moment before I pull away.

I see tears in his eyes, but when he speaks his words are light.

"When I bade you farewell, Ophelia, you were also dressed in a boyish way," he says, gesturing to my makeshift pants.

Abashed at my appearance, I quickly unbind my skirts so they fold about my legs, hiding my muddy feet. I pull off my dirt-streaked coif, letting my hair fall down my back.

"Now you look like an angel in white, yet by my soul I am glad to behold you alive." His earnest manner has not changed, I see. It makes me smile.

"Dear Horatio, you are a most welcome apparition yourself," I say lightly. "But why have you come?"

"I could not for a day forget you as if you no longer lived."

His plainness astonishes me. He speaks as if there is no time and no need for words that are not direct and true. Though I cannot say in turn that I have thought of him daily, his presence now fills me with an unaccustomed delight.

"To see you again — this is unexpected, to be sure. Like some unasked-for gift. But how did you come here? Who let you in? I usually admit visitors at the gate myself." I am confused, but I begin to suspect Isabel has a role in this.

"I wrote to your prioress, who received me herself, when I arrived. I inquired if you had any needs. She said little but summoned another sister, the one with brown eyes and a round face, who assured her that you would welcome me. She led me to this garden just now, and left me here. They are very protective of you."

Thinking of Horatio being studied and judged by Mother and

Isabel makes me laugh. I spread the cloth from my head on a fallen log, and motion for him to sit with me.

For a long moment there is silence between us. How do we begin, I wonder, to take up the broken thread of our long-ago story?

I tell him about my journey to St Emilion. How the arrival of his letter soon dashed my hopes and brought me to despair. How, when the letter was lost, I wondered if I had merely dreamed its horrors.

"It was the full and terrible truth, alas," Horatio assures me, and I see by his eyes that his own griefs have not died, but only diminished. I look down and see the wild pansies, small purple and white violets, growing at my feet. I pick a handful and open his palm.

"*Pensées.* That's for your thoughts," I whisper. Does he remember this long-ago gesture, how he consoled me when Hamlet disdained my gift? Horatio cups the little flowers with their thin stems and speaks with difficulty.

"I held Hamlet as he took his last breath. He and your brother forgave each other their wrongs. That much I did achieve."

"Thank you," I whisper.

"Hamlet lamented that he left behind a name so wounded, and he bade me tell his story, which I do still."

"Horatio, I am sorry for your burdens. You may lay them down here, for a time, in this peaceful place. Or better still, share them with me."

"I will, but first finish your story."

So I tell him about my life at the convent, its simple routines and pleasures. How much I love Isabel and Marguerite, the sisters who befriended me in my need. How I have found purpose in be-

ing a physician and gained a mother in the prioress Ermentrude. How I tried to save Therese and was forgiven my failure when she died.

"Now you must satisfy my curiosity. Have you news of dear Elnora? And Cristiana and her Rosencrantz, are they married?"

"Rosencrantz and Guildenstern are dead, justly served for their treachery. Hamlet learned of their role in Claudius's plot to kill him, and he sealed their fate first."

"Poor Cristiana, to lose her love, though he was unworthy," I say, surprised that I feel pity for my erstwhile enemy.

"Cristiana's grief was short-lived once she learned of her friends' villainy," says Horatio. "Now she climbs, as nimbly as ever, the ladder of favour in the court of Fortinbras, who has yet to take a bride."

I wish for some way to warn Cristiana of the new king's knavery.

"And Elnora? Does she yet live?" I am afraid that Horatio hides more sad news from me.

"Yes, though the loss of both you and her queen laid her at Death's door for a time. Lord Valdemar retired his post at court, saying he could not serve a foreign king. They settled in a humble cottage in the village, where Elnora, attended by Mechtild, has recovered a measure of her former strength."

Though I am relieved, Horatio is now distressed. His brow furrows as he describes the perilous condition of Denmark and relates how Fortinbras seized control after Claudius was killed.

"With his dying voice, Hamlet said he favoured the Norwegian prince. Hearing this, Fortinbras pressed his claim more boldly. Very soon we felt the heavy arm of his oppression as he

took revenge against Denmark for seizing his father's land. Then the rumour spread among the people that King Hamlet had another heir, that Hamlet his son had a cousin, or even an heir himself." He shook his head. "But it proved a baseless hope."

I search Horatio's face, but as always there is no guile in him. He does not suspect the truth. How shall I tell him?

"Now the Danes seek the overthrow of Fortinbras. Some pin their hopes on me, a mere friend of the prince who should have been their king," he says with some dismay.

"You would have been Hamlet's most trusted adviser, had he become king of Denmark."

"I am not a warrior," he says, shaking his head. "And though I will speak truth to the powerful, I seek no power myself. There are noblemen here in France, however, who may aid the cause of Denmark."

"And this is why you have come to France, to seek their support?"

"No, I come to seek you," he says, startling me with his frank reply.

"Horatio, I am at peace now, though what is past remains always with me —"

I look away, towards the cottage where Hamlet sleeps.

"Do not look back," Horatio says. He brings up his hand to turn my cheek towards him. The pansies scatter in our laps. I see how his eyes, brown like the rain-soaked earth, are gentle, wise and sad. His lean figure inclines towards me on the bench.

"Horatio, my heart leaps with joy that you have come. I have not realised until now how deeply I need you." These words spill from me and my tears spring unbidden. "My life is

in your debt, and as I own nothing, I repay you with this token of love."

I take his fair face in my hands, not minding that they are creased with dirt, and I kiss his lips, inhaling for a moment the scent of him, which is new to me, for I had never touched him so nearly.

His hands in turn become tangled in my hair while he returns my kiss like a hungry boy. Then, abruptly, he pulls away.

"No! I should not have touched you, nor kissed you. God forgive me," he murmurs, his face turning scarlet.

In the distance, thunder sounds, heralding more rain. A few sparrows hop on the ground at our feet. I am confused and hurt by his sudden repentance.

"Why? Are you married?" I ask.

"No, on my honour, or I would not have kissed you."

"And I am a widow. So we do no wrong."

Now he looks at me with genuine dismay and begins to stammer.

"Still, it would…I must not…dishonour you." He gestures towards my linen habit and falls silent.

I suddenly realise the reason for his reluctance, and I laugh with a delight that soon melts into compassionate tears.

"Mother Ermentrude and my friend Isabel did you a great wrong not to tell you more about me, Horatio. But I will not be so cruel, nor sport with you as if we lived still at court."

"Then tell me now, Ophelia, what I must know," says Horatio, still holding himself aloof from me.

"I live like a nun and look like one, but I am not bound by any vows. Horatio, I am free."

Relief and joy show on his face.

"In that case, dear Ophelia, may I kiss you again?"

"I give you leave, kind Horatio," I say, leaning towards him.

Horatio takes my hands and his breath on my cheek makes me shiver.

"Mama! Where are you, Mama?" The childish cry comes, and I spring to my feet.

"Here I am, dearest boy! In the garden!"

Little Hamlet, his thumb between his lips, toddles from the cottage. His cheeks are rosy and his hair tousled from sleep. His chubby legs and bare feet poke from beneath his wrinkled shirt. I hold out my arms and he runs to me, grabs my skirts, and stares from behind them at this stranger.

Horatio, his eyes fixed on the child, rises like a man entranced by some ghost or magical creature. Speechless at first with surprise, he then looks from me to my son until recognition dawns on him.

"I do not dream! I see the face of Lord Hamlet on this youth, overspread with Ophelia's beauty and her truth," he says in a tone of wonder. He steps closer and takes my hand in his. Still holding it, he kneels, putting himself eye to eye with young Hamlet, and bows as if offering allegiance to him.

My trusting boy smiles and reaches out to touch Horatio's red curls.

Defying the storm that threatened, the clouds that curtained the sun now pass, and we three survivors of a long-ago tragedy stand together in silence, beholding one another in the sun's light.

Acknowledgements

I wish to thank Karen, Katie, Amy, Cynthia, Leslie, Teri and Emily for their helpful criticism; Dad and Erin for their encouragement; and my husband, Rob, for his unfailing support. I am grateful to Carolyn for believing in the book and Julie for her wise and cheerful guidance in editing it. Finally I acknowledge with gratitude the students who, over the years, helped feed my imagination as we studied *Hamlet* together.

If writing well is the best revenge, it is because of all of you that Ophelia now has her due.